FICTION

DRY YOUR SMILE
THE MER CHILD
THE HANDMAIDEN OF THE HOLY MAN

NONFICTION

SATURDAY'S CHILD: A MEMOIR
THE WORD OF A WOMAN
A WOMAN'S CREED
THE DEMON LOVER: THE ROOTS OF TERRORISM
THE ANATOMY OF FREEDOM
GOING TOO FAR

POETRY

A HOT JANUARY: POEMS 1996-1999
UPSTAIRS IN THE GARDEN: SELECTED AND NEW POEMS
DEPTH PERCEPTION
DEATH BENEFITS
LADY OF THE BEASTS
MONSTER

ANTHOLOGIES
(COMPILED, EDITED, AND INTRODUCED)

SISTERHOOD IS FOREVER
SISTERHOOD IS GLOBAL
SISTERHOOD IS POWERFUL
THE NEW WOMAN (CO-ED.)

For dear Ellen,
with enduring
affection,

[signature]

R O B I N   M O R G A N

THE BURNING TIME

ROBIN MORGAN
THE BURNING TIME

MELVILLE HOUSE PUBLISHING
HOBOKEN, NEW JERSEY

Cover image: ©Archivo Iconografico, S.A./CORBIS
From *Life of Ludovic of France at the Purgatory of Saint Patrick*,
14th century

Book design: David Konopka

Melville House Publishing
300 Observer Highway
Third Floor
Hoboken, NJ 07030

www.mhpbooks.com

First Edition March 2006
A Paperback Original

ISBN 10: 1-933633-00-x
ISBN 13: 978-1-933633-00-8

A catalog record for this book is available from
the Library of Congress.

Printed in Canada

FOR DEBORAH ANN LIGHT,
FRIEND, PRIESTESS

AND

FOR VERONICA MORGENSTERN,
NIECE, MAIDEN

THE BURNING TIME

ALL HALLOWS' EVE was not when you wanted to be out of doors—bolted doors. Not even in your own yard. Certainly not on the heath or the roads, surely not in the worst storm in memory, and especially not in the deliberate pursuit of witches and demonic spirits.

The commander had only fifty lads, lacking even a full complement, since the Bishop had split up his troops, sending men-at-arms in all four directions to follow every road out of Kilkenny. Worse, His Eminence had personally ordered him and the three sub-commanders to batter down doors along the way, interrogate everyone, and do whatever was necessary to elicit information about any—*any*—passing travelers. A man of discipline, the commander had masked his shame at how much terror he and his men had caused this night. It would be some time before he would be able to erase the memory of such fear, raw on the faces of peasants and innkeepers along the route to Wexford, as they knelt before him and wept, pleading that truly they had seen no one, heard nothing.

Well, His Eminence might not have believed them, but *he* did. The roads were deserted. The sole upright shapes he and his men passed had turned out to be ghostly tree spines bowing in obedience to the storm's wrath.

He spat, craning his neck to peer back at his troops through the sputtering light of the torchbearers' beacons. They, like him, were soaked to the bone with freezing rain. At least he and his two lieutenants sat astride, but the other poor bastards had been trudging through this maelstrom that pelted them with hailstones and sleeted the roads until the troops slipped and fell, cursing, while the horses skidded sideways, shrilling as they scrambled to regain footing on the muddy ice. And now they faced a steep hill road ahead. *Good lads*, the commander thought, grateful the gale's whine buffered him from their grumbling, *but sent on a hopeless search*. No one, certainly no woman, dare move through such a night. Unless witches really could fly.

Dimly, he heard a rhythm, and all his senses sprang alert. Hooves. Distant hooves. The pounding grew louder, more distinct. Then he spied the outline of a lone horse galloping through the fog, down the hill road toward him and his men.

He ordered a halt as the animal's shape drew nearer and pulled up on an outcropping of rock above them. He never took his eyes from it, as gradually his footsoldiers came up behind and clustered around their leader. The torchbearers' spitting brands gleamed yellow through the fog, reflecting on the men's spear-points and swiftly drawn swords. But as the commander and his troops squinted upward, the flares began forming strange fogged aureoles of light. A spectral form emerged from them, floating through the mist.

It sat astride the horse with an air of unchallengeable authority, as if enthroned. A heavy black cape denoting rank and wealth billowed from the shoulders of the Rider. Yet the figure's face was veiled by a curtain of rain, its hair drenched by the storm to the colour of shadow.

But with the next stab of lightning, the commander started in terror, as did his men, many of them dropping their weapons, falling to their knees, and crossing themselves.

The flash imprinted on their gaze a sight they would never be able to forget. The lightning had exposed, like a reflection, the head of the Rider. It glowed in the light, inhumanly large. It was crowned by two sharp, bright, upcurving horns.

The commander's thoughts skittered and spun wildly. *This is a tale to tell for years—if I live to tell it.* He managed to keep his seat and stay his horse from rearing, but his entire body shook as it never had before, even in battle, and he could feel the tremors of the terrified animal beneath him.

Motionless, the apparition shimmered at them, waiting.

The commander knew he must address this creature. He opened his lips. He worked his jaw. But no words came. He felt his voice shrivel into a knot of panic in his throat.

Then it no longer mattered, because all his questions were answered at once.

It spoke.

It called out to them with a ringing voice, in a tone of absolute command. Phrases clipped with contempt came riding over the storm's howl with the majesty of lightning itself.

"Merry Meet, this Samhain Sabbat," It roared, *"You need search for Me no longer. You have met the One you seek."*

TEN MONTHS EARLIER...

I

GOOD INTENTIONS

GREEN, such defiant green! At the bleak heart of winter, this brazen, shameless green! No wonder they call it the Emerald Island, he thought, peering through light fog at the emerging coastline, verdant even in January, though as veined with snow as a gemstone faceted with light.

St. George's Channel had finally calmed, so Richard de Ledrede was now able to hazard a stroll abovedeck, his corpulence bundled in a sable cloak. Rather pleasant, this, to lean at the ship's rail breathing in the salt air and enjoying the vista—better than having to stagger up from his cabin again and again to drape vomitously over the side and retch. It had been tortuous, this journey—intensifying in chill, damp, and discomfort as he'd moved northward, leaving behind the sunny south of France, braving English Channel squalls, riding through sleet on the frozen fields of England, enduring the Bristol Channel's heaves, traversing the neck of Wales to the port of Anerystwyth, and now at last nearing harbor at Wexford—but only after an Irish Sea crossing so choppy

that his normally ruddy complexion had turned its own shade
of pale green. But it was almost over. He had survived again.

Soon he would be back—well, not home, but on terra
firma in Kilkenny Town, answerable only to himself, the Papal
Emissary to Ireland, the supreme authority of the Roman
Catholic Church in his own bishopric of Ossary. Soon he
could relish the comforts of a floor that stayed beneath his
feet, a blazing hearth, decent food and wine—at least as
decent as might be imported into this benighted bog of a
country. Though only for a while. *Sic transit misera.* How long,
he wondered, must he tolerate Ireland this time, before
winning permanent release and restoration to the Papal
Court? *Patientia.* He sighed. Then, distracted by shouts, he
turned to watch the scurry of seamen and cabin boys as they
worked sails and ropes in preparation for dropping anchor.
Across the deck, a slender young man in a black cassock was
pacing slowly, reading his breviary. Glancing up, he saw his
superior gazing at him, and he smiled.

The Bishop did not smile back. Young Father Brendan
Canice had been making himself unbearably useful since
Anerystwyth: never cold, never seasick, a walking abomina-
tion of good cheer with odiously bouncing black curls and
eyes so blue one might wince from the brightness.
Summoned from Kells to attend upon the Bishop, Father
Brendan had left his post at the ancient center of Irish
learning and traveled to Wales to meet the senior prelate's

retinue, that they might journey the remainder of the route back to Kilkenny Town together. Not that Bishop Richard de Ledrede had invited his presence. Some bureaucrat in Avignon had decided *for* him that this young scholar, already gaining note for expertise in Celtic history and tradition, would be a valuable advisor to his work as the Pope's emissary to Ireland. Consequently, the crossing was to have been spent tutoring the Bishop on Irish customs. But communication had been seldom and abrupt, limited to exchanges about the Bishop's intestinal crisis, as the gallingly healthy Father Brendan repeatedly aided his superior in lurching from cabin to ship's rail. Now the Bishop sighed again and beckoned to his traveling companion, who swiftly crossed the deck to stand before him.

"*Benedicite, domine,*" the young man said, genuflecting, "*Pax vobiscum.*"

"*Benedicite, filio meo, et cum spiritu tu,*" he replied, proffering his hand. The young priest kissed his ring.

"*Nonne convalescis, domine? Intervenione tuas devotiones?*"

"*Bene.* But English, please, Father Brendan. Latin unites our Church family throughout the world, but in conversation I prefer French, though my native tongue will do. Yes, I feel better—though there seems to be less of me," he mused, glancing down at his rotund body, "and no, you do not disturb my devotions—though perhaps I disturb yours?" He glanced at the young priest's breviary.

"No, my lord. I was simply offering spontaneous prayers of thanksgiving. I have been awake since before dawn, my soul ringing like hammered gold—that eager am I to see Eire again!"

"Nonsense. You have been away for only a fortnight. And you certainly have seemed content—never even *mildly* seasick. Somewhat unmannerly, that."

"Yes, my lord," the young priest grinned, "My apologies. T'is an island nation, don't you know—rich with rivers, too—so we grow up on the water. As for my homesickness, I have traveled little, yet no matter where I venture, t'is a Kilkenny man I am—from the seat of your own bishopric, my lord—the finest place on the blessed earth."

"Well, lad, perhaps you shall miraculously convince me to share your affection for Ireland. But it will be quite a challenge. I can tell you candidly that I have already suffered over a year in your disagreeable country."

Father Brendan could think of no diplomatic response to this, so he tactfully said nothing while attempting a sympathetic expression. The Bishop noted both the silence and the attempt.

"So, you are to advise me, eh? You have a priestly name fitting for this work—Brendan *and* Canice, both missionary saints; my Cathedral in Kilkenny is named for Saint Canice, you know. Well, my son, I need you to acquaint me with the strengths and vulnerabilities of your people in a way no outsider could otherwise learn. You shall be my right arm, to aid me in bringing the Irish back to the Church from whence they eelishly slither away at every opportunity."

"I shall do my best, but—candor warrants candor, my lord. The Irish . . . in truth, they may never come wholly to the Church," the young priest said softly, "yet they cannot but come wholly to the love that is Christ's message."

The Bishop peered at the younger man, deliberating. When he replied, he had to raise his voice above the clamor surrounding them.

"That is all very well, Father," he half shouted, "But I shall now venture beyond candor and be blunt. I do not intend to suffer another purgatorial year on your shores. I no longer *care* if these people come, wholly or partly, to Christ or Christ's message. I care that they come to the *Church*, that they obey Church law. I care that His Holiness cease being plagued by outrageous reports from Ireland: parishioners prancing round maypoles under full moons like cats in heat, priests so permissive they refuse to destroy horn-headed carvings that heathen stonecutters have secretly mounted above the north doors of our own churches! And *denial* of all this! Pretended innocence! As well as *shocking* incompetence. Delay. Elaborate excuses. Faeries. Imps. Enough whimsy to make a sane man gag. Let me advise *you*, Father Brendan. It is neither wickedness nor evil that destroys the world, but *stupidity* and *incompetence*—and the ceaselessness with which most of mankind practices both is awe-inspiring. But Ireland boasts an overabundance of practitioners. No one accepts responsibility for anything. Instead, there is rampant superstition. Superstition is the mother of chaos."

"But surely my lord—"

"What I *care* about is *order*—the foundation for civilizing any country, including this absurd excuse for one. The only evidence of civilization in Ireland is what remains of Roman roads and aqueducts, legacies of what? An imperial *order*. The Roman Empire brought order to most of the world and then, astonishingly, *kept* it. With order comes peace. Not the Pax Romana: today that imperial role falls to our Holy Church. But we bring a broader, more beneficent order, governance temporal *and* spiritual. We teach people how to *exist*. And our influence has intensified during the decades the Papacy has been in France, allied with the French Court. *That* is what I care about, Father. An end to superstition. Respect for authority. People knowing their place. The world united under one efficient system, in secular and divine harmony. *Civilization*."

The young priest frowned in confusion.

"But—my lord... surely the willing heart is brought to God by loving—"

"Father Brendan. Have I said anything about God? This is not about God."

"But, sir, the Irish are a deeply spiritual people who—"

"—flout the Church every chance they get. Spiritual people do not inhabit the real world, Father. Here in the real world, I assure you, temptations are more subtle, blatant, and formidable than wicked banshees or ghostly apparitions. Religious people! The more devout they are, the more they dwell in poesy."

Father Brendan beamed, having found, he thought, common ground.

"Ah, my lord, but who does not love poetry? Erin is the land of poets. Why, the *ollave* were Celtic bards who trained for twelve years to pass a test—the Seven Degrees of Wisdom— before being permitted to write or chant poetry. The *ollave* were powerful sorcerers, too. They could compose an *aer*, a cursing poem to drive a man mad. And the *seannachai*—the tale-spinners! I grew up listening to them. In Eire every village has its tale-spinner and its poet. "

"Well, the world could do with fewer poets and more administrators. Languedoc, Toulouse, Carcassonne—they were also full of poets, along with Cathar heretics. Please. Promise me that you are *not* going to be tediously defensive regarding your quaint local traditions. Your mission, Father, is to the contrary: to advise me on how most effectively papal supremacy can be definitively impressed upon these poor, troublesome, uneducated people."

Father Brendan soldiered on. "Poor, yes sir. And trouble-some, aye—even with open pride, I fear. But uneducated—is that not unduly harsh, my lord? You must know that as far back as the eighth century, Irish scholars were held in the highest repute across Europe. T'was to honour that tradition I first went to my studies at Kells—where surely you must visit, sir! Erin's treasures, Erin's greatest books, the illumined masterpieces of—"

"—the *past*, my son. This is the fourteenth century, not the eighth. Ireland has slipped backward into a mire of pagan idolatry. Your precious Erin—by the by, which *is* it? Erin or Eire? You people seem to use both interchangeably."

"They are interchangeable." Then, wryly, "Why, I am ashamed you could have spent a year here, and no one hospitable enough to teach you that, my lord? Eire is the name in Erse—Erse is Old Irish, early Gaelic. Eire is the older name of the island. But Erin, the poets' name for our land—after Eryn, one of the Celtic Goddess's names?—has itself been around for more than a few centuries." The blue eyes sparkled with amusement. "Of course, you could go back even further, soon after the Great Flood, when the Irish were called The Tuatha de Danaan, the People of Dana—that was another name for the Goddess, you see. Or you could—"

"I could call it *Ireland*. As shall you, in my presence," snapped the Bishop. He might as well discourage this long-winded scholar from such lectures right from the first, or they would never accomplish anything. He had no use for legends. He needed facts. And information on how the local people perceived those facts, strategic information he could *use*. But the young priest babbled on, trying to ingratiate himself and getting it all pathetically wrong.

"Indeed, my lord Bishop, with your gift for languages, you might consider studying Gaelic. A lyrical, rich tongue it is."

"And a minor one. Also too guttural, which is why I never liked German. No *music*. Whereas French or Italian. . . no no, none of your Gaelic. You must do the translating—of words and customs both—for me."

Father Brendan studied his bishop for a moment, then bowed a deferential head. When he looked up, his face seemed almost boyish.

"My lord Bishop," he said, gently but urgently, "My vows bind me to aid you in every manner that I can, and I am grateful for the chance to do so, and will strive to serve you with a glad heart. So I might, if you will permit, explain some of our ways, that you might be more. . . as you say. . . effective. You see, my people truly mean no insult in keeping the seasonal feasts that our ancestors were celebrating even before Christ's great sacrifice for mankind. This is an ancient people, descended from the Celts, related to the Picts, cousins of the Druids. We have a great culture. We— *They* simply want to. . . *mingle* different paths to the Sacred, each path of which they genuinely love—including the newer path offered them by the Church—enriching *each* faith. Nor is this true only of Ireland, but much of Britain. Why, t'is barely twenty years since the Bishop of Coventry openly admitted to being an observer of the Old Religion! So while some of them might—as you note, sir, with wit—sing at the moon, most of them attend Mass as well, and fairly often. The one worship feeds the other. Where is the harm?"

"'*As well*'? They 'fairly often' attend Mass '*as well*'? This is what strict doctrinal obedience now means? My God! The Church is not the savory onion in a stew pot of turnips, Father Brendan! It is not one choice, or even the best choice. It is the *only* choice. Inside the Church, salvation. Outside, perdition."

Father Brendan tried a different approach.

"Perhaps, sir, if you could be mild with them, then? And display some humour? The Irish greatly admire—"

"It is not their admiration I seek, Father, but their obedience, their adherence to doctrine. I am not here to entertain. I am here to educate—and chastise, if need be. For your edification, I *have* tried what you call 'mildness.' For most of last year I exhausted myself. I spent months untangling bishopric finances. I distributed alms. At Christmas and Easter, I knelt and washed the reeking, pustulating feet of beggars. I spent endless hours of what passes for social life with the Irish gentry in Ossary, since most of the English landholders sensibly remain abroad, and I felt my intellect atrophy in the presence of these impressively ignorant gentlemen. I performed baptisms, christenings, and ordinations, celebrated hundreds of Masses, preached scores of homilies, visited every church, abbey, and convent in the entire bishopric!"

"Indeed, my lord, at Kells we heard that you were a model of activity—and I grant some of the gentry *are* uneducated. But not all. There are a few who—"

"Yet *still* blasphemy and debauchery abounded. Peasants would defiantly leave wilting, stinking *salads*—'bouquets of herbs,' they claimed—at the foot of Saint Brigid's statue. The abbesses openly flouted my stiffer rules for their novices. Your precious monks in the scriptorium at Kells continued to insinuate pagan images into the illuminated letters of holy Christian books. Some of my own diocesan *priests* would wink when fires were lit on the heath—with Satan himself knowing what obscene rites were taking place out there!" He paused for a breath. "Perhaps you do not know, Father, that I am English by birth."

Father Brendan bit his lip and raised his eyebrows, hoping to convey surprise.

"Well, I am. It may be impossible for you, who have lived your entire life on this small backwater of an island, to imagine what sacrifice it is for a widely traveled Englishman, educated by Franciscan monks in Italy and France, to demean himself by accepting as his cross the assignment of securing this ghastly quagmire of a country for the Church. When I was recalled to the Papal Court last October, I tell you plainly: I *rejoiced.* I thought I was being rescued. I assumed it was a permanent recall. That, I now realize, was yet another naivete on my part." The Bishop seemed unaware of the bitterness leaking through his words. "The Church Merciful may have sent me to Ireland in the first place, but it was the Church Militant that received me back at Court. There I was reminded that my 'mildness' had worked abysmally. There I was also reminded that the Church has embarked on a great task: bringing Europe to submission—with a firm hand, undeterred by false pity—for the salvation of man."

Father Brendan's rosy face turned pale.

"Oh really. You need not look so terrified. These are merely *inquiries.* Why do people become so emotional about being asked a few questions? When persons suspected of committing heresy are invited to clear their names, what is to be feared? They should be grateful! Indeed, why *are* they afraid—unless of course they have done something wrong? And if they are guilty, it is long past time to scourge the filth from their souls, or else to purge their lives from the community of the faithful. Never forget: *If men do not fear evil, there is no need for them to do good.* In some regions, Church law is now strong enough to overrule degenerate secular courts.

So is the Continent being cleansed of the infestation polluting it—Albigensians, Templars, Kabbalists and other Jews, Moors, witches, sorcerers, all the foul heretics and apostates who prey on Christian souls."

"Aye, my lord, aye.... But Eire—Eire-*land*, Ireland—is a special case. No one here has *ever* been prosecuted for observing The Old Ways, which are so deeply—"

"'The *Old* Ways?' You forget yourself, Father. You would do well to remember it is only a few weeks since I was given instructions by His Holiness Pope John XXII, in a *personal* audience. You are addressing his Emissary, sent with orders to see that the Irish are brought to heel. No more mildness. This time I return not to bring peace but, if Ireland requires it, the sword. Do you understand?"

"Yes, my lord," the younger man replied. His voice held the music of persuasion, but his eyes had darkened to the colour of the waves gently rocking their ship. Serving this Richard de Ledrede looked as if it would be a true spiritual mortification. But somehow he must do it and do it gracefully, winning his release back to the glory of Kells. If he plied sufficient skill, he might yet soften the Bishop's stand for the good of all... but he must keep his distance. He decidedly must not regard this man as his father confessor.

"How came you to the cloth?" de Ledrede asked, gruffly changing the subject. Father Brendan's reveries returned to the conversation with a rush.

"I fear I can claim neither visitation nor early vocation, my lord. It was books. Education.... You see, I come of peasant stock. But I had the good fortune of learning to read—a long tale, that—and loving it, ah, *loving* it. And as I grew older, the great libraries at Kells seemed to me—"

"—paradise pure, on earth," de Ledrede murmured.

Father Brendan was taken aback.

"I feared you might find my story lacking in... religious fervor, my lord. Although surely *since* I have been ordained, my devotion to Christ—"

"You thought I would be distressed because you were drawn to the Church as the greatest institution of learning on earth, in all history? Rather than your crawling to it as some wounded creature, or out of habit, or because of some 'mystical moment,' or simply from not knowing what else to do in life?" To Father Brendan's further surprise, the Bishop smiled. "To the contrary," de Ledrede continued, "you perfectly demonstrate my point. The Church is the sole structure in the world wherein even a peasant can rise. Oh, to be sure, we never lack sons who come to us from the aristocracy or the military, or...the mercantile class. But nowhere else, not even in the finest army, can a lowly man rise from his class so high as in the Church. How? By *merit*, my son! Hard work, intelligence, a healthy ambition. And most of all, obedience."

"And...poverty and chastity...and faith, surely, my lord?" Father Brendan was not going to be caught out twice on doctrinal familiarity.

"I am a Franciscan, Father Brendan, so I know all about 'poverty, chastity, and obedience.' Poverty is dreary. The poor have no power to help humanity; they cannot even help themselves. Chastity...well, yes. But that is no great hardship; personally, I have always lived for my work. Poverty and chastity are greatly overrated virtues. Nor is 'the greatest of these' love. It is obedience."

Father Brendan blinked, unsure whether to be relieved by such frankness or appalled by such cynicism.

"As for faith," the Bishop continued, "let us be honest. Faith manifests itself, after all the flummery is over, in *deeds*. Deeds bring us back to obedience. Do you see?" Richard de Ledrede smiled again.

Emboldened, Father Brendan asked, "And you, my lord? Dare I inquire as to the road that brought you to the cloth?"

The smile faded.

"That is a long tale. Some other time, perhaps."

"And do you never miss your own homeland, England?" the younger man persisted, trying to recapture the moment of warmth.

"Hardly," his superior barked, "Cold. Wet. Populated with almost as many fey eccentrics as Ireland. Now *Avignon—that* is what I miss. You must do whatever you can to visit the Papal Court there one day, Father. It is an amazement. It is..." The Bishop's gaze grew distant with longing. Then he shook himself back to the present. "Look," he commanded, "Off there. The shore-skiffs are approaching. We have dropped anchor. I must prepare to disembark. *In nomine Patri*..." Mumbling a blessing and making a brusque sign of the cross, he dismissed his priest, turned, and strode off to descend below deck. Father Brendan, startled by such abruptness, found himself abandoned. Then, genuflecting quickly to the Bishop's back, he also hurried off, his mind awhirl in anxieties.

Soon the morning was given over to scramble and shouting and rope ladders being dropped over the side and trunks being heaved up from the hold. As the passenger of highest rank, the Papal Emissary was helped to descend, gingerly, into the first dinghy, where a leathery-skinned oarsman sat waiting to ferry him to shore. Once wedged in the small skiff, his hands clutching the sides, his eyes squeezed shut against the damnably lifting and dipping horizon, the Bishop tried to deflect his rising nausea by concentrating on the task ahead. Father Brendan might prove a useful ally, once that youthful idealism was tempered; so they were never fools in Avignon, after all, not even the bureaucrats. He peeked for a second at the detested shore as it drew nearer, then clamped his eyes shut again, recalling the first time he had ever seen it.

Back then, he had been so pitifully enthusiastic to be the Papal Emissary, innocently believing he was being sent to Ireland because of his persuasive powers. Now he knew better. It had been, if anything, a punishment for his presumption.

The dinghy's hull scraped pebbles and sand as the boat heaved. They had arrived.

The Bishop clenched his jaw. This time he would prove his enemies at Court wrong. When next they recalled him, he would make certain it was a permanent recall—for his ceremonial investiture with a cardinal's crimson hat. He stepped resolutely out of the dinghy, reeled for a moment in the surf, then marched up the beach toward the waiting horses. His nausea was already beginning to recede and he was actually hungry. He would bring them a second coming of Saint Patrick, by God.

Excusing himself to stay and oversee the unloading of the Bishop's wardrobe trunks, and promising he would rendezvous with his new master at the Wexford Inn, Father Brendan Canice had remained a discreet distance behind, boarding the third dinghy. So Bishop Richard de Ledrede never saw his tutor and aide step ashore, half-kneel as if to re-lace his boot, and swiftly, discreetly, kiss the blessed soil of Eire.

II

THE RIGHT TO A WINDOW

DAME ALYCE KYTELER ignored the silver snuffer on her bedside table, pinched out the candle flame between calloused fingertips, and slid in under her goosedown coverlet. Slowly, the Lady of Kyteler Castle stretched her left leg over to one edge of the big bed and her right leg over to the other, encountering no obstacles in either direction. She wiggled her toes, cooing small warbles of delight. What *bliss* to sleep alone, after all the husbands. No elbow to intrude into her ribs, no sag to upset the balance of the sweetgrass reed mattress, no icy feet pressed against her calves, no grunts and snores rupturing her sleep.

The bed curtains were drawn back, so Alyce could lean against her goosefeather-stuffed cushions and look out through the narrow window in her turret bedroom. Sir John le Poer considered his wife quite mad for, among other things, having chosen to sleep in a room with a window. Sensible persons, he insisted, knew perfectly well that night air brought evil humours and disease, excellent reason for not having windows. Castle windows, John had more than once lectured her, existed solely for military purposes—as sentinel lookouts, and, if besieged, for aiming crossbows and lobbing arrows through. In response, Alyce had shrugged that military purposes were boring and that fresh air was good for you. Besides, the window was small enough, barely a slit, although during the weeks of Mí na Nollag—particularly near the Winter Solstice, the longest night of the year—even this slit of a window provoked gusty dreams, and that despite the tapestry she had hung to cover it during the cold months. How splendid it would be, she thought, hoisting herself up on one elbow, to work a magick beyond her own considerable powers and create an invisible panel or wall that might keep out the cold yet let in the view. Or, failing that, she thought more practically, persuade the Cathedral masons to divulge their secret for forging those leaded, rigid, colour tapestries set high in church walls, tapestries through which the light glowed. Not that a glimpse of the star-jeweled night sky through her own window wasn't worth a frosty draft or two. . . .

But at present none of that mattered, anyway. It was the month of Júil. She could lie back down in the warm summer darkness and watch the sliver of a new moon glowing through cloud wisps in a celestial game of hide-and-seek. No chilly drafts—and no complaints from John. Savoring the pure luxury of it, she stretched again, gurgling a low laugh of pleasure.

The young moon would be big-bellied and full in time for the coming holy-day, a happy coincidence to make the next sabbat even more distinctive than it already was: the Festival of Grains and First Fruits that the Druids had named Lugnasad, now also called Lammas. Lugnasad, one of the four great Cross Quarter Days of the year, was only a little more than three weeks away, in fact—a realization that jolted Alyce to start mentally listing all the work yet to be done. Pear and ash wood to be cut and dried for the bonfire, new candles to be dipped, chervil seed and pennyroyal to be pounded for incense, kirn dollies to be braided, crescent cakes to be baked from the thousand-year-old recipe. . . and all this in addition to the normal round of seasonal tasks: the first of the summer crops to be harvested, the fresh catch from the River Nore to be salted and dried, the—

Alyce sat up with a start as Prickeare, her plump but distinguished elderly cat, landed on the bed with a thud. Prickeare, whose charcoal grey coat was so densely plush it appeared sable black in most light, was performing the ritual he usually observed around this time of night: abandoning his basket for the company of his pet human's toes. Now he circled his own tail, then settled down with a possessive mew on his mistress's ankle.

"Hullo, Lightfoot." Alyce greeted him by one of the many names she used for her beloved Familiar—this particular one dating back to when he was a lean young catling—as she did so rearranging her legs to make room for this sizeable living pillow that had already begun to purr. The small earthquake of bed-clothes erupting from Alyce having shifted position disturbed Prickeare not a whit; he offered a delicate, coral-tongued yawn as he rode the quilt's ripples and waves like an accomplished sailor wobbling back aboardship after a tipsy revel.

"Been drinking again, eh?" Alyce teased. "For shame, you old sot—*Oh! By the pope's boils!*" she swore loudly to the cat. "The wine! I never finished adding orris powder to the mulling vats! Ah, and I also forgot to wrap sage-leaf layers around those five cheese wheels ageing in the dairy!" Now she was irked at herself. But any state of irritability soon brought to mind her husband, an always reliable target for blame.

"Pah," she spat, "All this ado over John's tantrums and theatrics... I *cannot* let it go on distracting me this way! What a nuisance that man was!" Plumping her pillow with a few vicious jabs, she grunted, turned on her side, and tried to settle down again. Prickeare placidly ignored these agitations, while his mistress tried forcing her mind back toward the sabbat and more agreeable thoughts.

How jubilant Kilkenny folk always are at a warm-weather sabbat, she mused. To be sure, during the winter months it was cozy to have the feasting and dancing indoors—torches aflame, thick candles sputtering, Ieul log roaring in the huge hearth. But there was something... *deeper* about holding the Rituals outdoors at the Covenstead—that circle of massive stones called the Cromlech out on the heath, centered around the dolmen stone—that the Old People had assembled and raised, back before memory. Was it because the Ancient Ones even before *them* had brought the Rituals from a legendary far-off southern isle where the weather was always warm? No matter. Even on this rocky northern island one could celebrate the mystery of new tendrils upgreening through the earth's thaw; one could practice the magick of spinning out giddy chain-dances in summer; one could sit spellbound to watch bonfire flames—red edging orange fluttering into blue—race each other up toward the Moon, hot suitors in love with Her distant, cool, white shadow.

"'No other law but love She knows...'" Alyce quoted to herself, smiling into the darkness to feel her faith freshen through her like a sudden summer breeze, leaving a sense of relief and generalized affection in its wake. The relief was for John's departure. The affection was for her serfs—the men, women, and children of her estate—the people with whom she preserved The Old Ways. There was affection, too, for herself: pride. She was proud of the aristocratic blood sent pulsing through her veins by generations of Kytelers; of her beautiful, fertile lands; of her beloved Eire, the isle sacred to and safe in The Old Ways. Then, too, she felt she had earned the right to be proud, by her own actions. She was proud that she was a skilled healer, and that she did not rule her serfs as other nobles did, but showed generosity to her peasants and cared for their health and well-being. She was proud that her peasants and servants regarded her, she knew, with grateful affection.

Not that she was overly indulgent. She maintained a distance to preserve her authority. But Alyce knew that the peasants' greatest concern beyond their hardscrabble lives was for the future of their children, and it was here she was aware of being most respected, for two reasons. First, she was that rarity, a woman of learning. Second, she had for years been teaching the peasant children to read and write—beginning with the older ones, who in turn would teach the younger, and sometimes even tutor their own parents. The practice was, she knew, a flirtation with danger, but as such it was a thrilling, guilty pleasure. Townsmen and district gentry thought it an outrage that serfs might become lettered; not many townsfolk and gentrymen could read or write themselves. In idle moments, especially after a trip into Kilkenny Town, Alyce would find herself pondering how much of a real threat their surreptitious grumblings might one day present.

Now she flopped over onto her stomach, trying to dismiss such worries. Public opinion had never before stopped her, she reminded herself, so there was no reason to start being concerned with it now. Whoever hungered to learn—nobles, peasants, women—should be permitted to learn. For that matter, Alyce knew that in some of her serfs the hunger itself had to be fostered. There were those whose minds had been famished lifelong, so that the slightest whiff of appetite or hope seemed suffocated by despair. Patient, steady coaxing had to be exercised to elicit a gleam of curiosity in their pain-dulled eyes. But the children, ah. . . they were different.

She burrowed deeper into her bed linen, her thoughts careening back to the work that needed to be done. Soon it would be tupping season, time to put the bucks in with the does and the rams in with the ewes for mating that would produce next spring's kids and lambs. For that matter, she needed to have her women card more sheared fleece for wool so that she could finish her spinning. In the morning she *must* remember about the orris root. And the cheeses. And sketch out a design for the flowered garlands of the sabbat dancers. Which reminded her that she must speak to William, and find a tactful way to suggest that he should not lead the Spiral Dance this sabbat. The last time he'd done so, he had wound everyone up in a mess of confusion, with much kicking of shins and clonking of heads. Dear Will. Her son never *could* remember the difference between dancing deosil, or sunwise, and widdershins, the counter-direction. It worsened when he became excited—certainly an expectable emotion at a sabbat—so that he tended to call out an instruction to circle one way while he blithely hopped off the opposite course, yanking baffled dancers after him in a lurching chain that soon collapsed into a heap of crushed garlands, wildly waving arms and legs, and mutual hilarity.

My own sweet boy, Alyce reflected, realizing anew that at sixteen Will was no longer a boy; he was older than she had been when first she'd been betrothed. "How much younger he seems than *I* was then," she murmured, silently thanking The Great Mother that Will showed few signs of taking after his father, her first husband. For the hundredth time, Alyce hurried her imagination past wondering what life might have been like had her child been a daughter.

She turned over on her back again—this time Prickeare did protest, a bit noisily—and closed her eyes, letting the froth of her thoughts ebb along a wave of drowsiness. Trying to catch that wave, she began an exercise to summon and sweeten sleep. For the sheer hypnotic comfort of acknowledging its dependability, she started softly chanting to herself the stages of The Wheel that drove the year, naming each of the Eight Spokes that radiated from the hub and turned the days:

"The Great Quarters:

Two Solstices—Winter and Summer.

Two Equinoxes—Spring and Autumn.

Intersecting The Great Quarters, the four Cross Quarter Days:

Brigid, the Feast of Returning Light, called Imbolc by the Druids, in early Feabhra, soon after winter's peak;

Beltane, or May Day, the spring Feast of Fertility;

Lugnasad, or Lammas, summer's Feast of the First Harvest;

Samhain, the all-hallowed Eve at autumn's heart, at the end of the month of Deireadh Fómhair—the solemn Feast of the Ancestors' Spirits, the Death of the Old Year and Birth of the New. . ."

What wisdom those primal rhythms held, she thought, as a way to mark time's passage. Her eyelids growing heavy, she blinked in homage to those who had gone before, the Ancient Ones who had studied the moon's phases and the stars and devised the calendar. Then, drifting toward a doze, she gave herself over to the tide of sleep.

*　　*　　*

An insistent knocking at the door roused Alyce to the surface of consciousness.

"Who is it?" she croaked groggily—then heard Petronilla de Meath identify herself in a timid voice from the other side of the broad oak slab.

"Oh, Petronilla. Yes, enter. What is it? Is anything wrong?"

A young woman burst into the room, only to stop short, afraid of its occupant and abashed at having wakened her.

Placing her candlestick on the floor, she sank into a deep curtsey and remained there, her small hands anxiously twisting the ends of her hair—two long braids so light in colour they looked like melting icicles touched by a late winter sun. That extreme paleness framed a plain little face, currently pinched with shyness and trepidation.

"Please an' to forgive me, Your Grace, but—"

Alyce waved away the apologies and inquired again, more sharply, if anything was wrong.

"No Ma'm—yes Ma'm. Well. . . t'is Helena Galrussyn, Your Grace. The babe's not due for almost another moon, y'know. But it comes now anyways, though why t'would willingly rush into such a world is a fine mystery. T'is Helena's first, you'll be kind enough to remember? And her pains—it goes hard with her, m'Lady. I know I feared I'd die with the hurt when my Sara was born. . . so, what with the midwife off to Durrow to be with her daughter through *her* first. . . forgive me, Your Grace, to be bursting in waking you. What must ye think of me! But I was hoping mayhap you might be so good as to look in on—"

Petronilla's last sentence hung in the air unfinished since Alyce, awake now, was already in mid-leap out of bed. The little maidservant watched as her mistress wriggled off her bedshirt in one swift unselfconscious movement, slipped on an under-tunic, and groped about for the brown home-spun gown she'd left casually lying on the floor. Finding it, she yanked it over her head, slung a shawl round her shoulders, and stepped into a pair of hemp sandals. Accustomed to such nightly drama, Prickeare opened one languid jade eye to check on this flurry of activity, then closed it again and sighed himself back to sleep.

"Do stand up, Petronilla. Bring your candle here," Alyce ordered, flinging open the doors to her cupboard of medicines. The maid rose to her feet and carried the taper nearer.

There, inside, were squat jars chiseled from blue stone, bronze boxes with openwork lids, tall brown leather bottles, green pottery bowls, and piles of yellowing muslin bags fragrant with their various stuffings of dried herbs, roots, and flowers— a treasury on shelves pungent with dust, wood, and spices. Petronilla drew closer, fascinated by the disarray ranked in some obscure order on those shelves: the secrets there— balms, potions, and powders mellowing in each jug and dish—waiting for the hand of Alyce Kyteler to apply them properly, so as to bestow the magickal curative properties of sleep or painlessness or health itself. The whole room felt enchanted, Petronilla thought, glancing around at the wall of crammed bookshelves, the small writing desk, the friendly clutter of bound volumes and rolled parchments piled on tables and stools, spilling over into the stone floor.

Alyce was hurriedly packing a small basket with certain vials and casks, muttering as she did so.

"Yes, hmmm. So...belladonna to stop the spasms and halt labor if it seems she might miscarry...ergot if we need to hasten the labor, skullcap for brewing as a tea to ease cramping...another tea we can steep from willow-bark and, let me see, dittany, hyssop, vervain, pennyroyal—if the pains grow really harsh.... Now, what else? Ah, yes. Some hyacinth oil. A massage should relax Helena's muscles, as well as distract her with its fragrance..."

Petronilla stood watching, nervously knotting and unknotting her apron. She felt compelled to attempt another apology for having stirred such a storm in the calm of the night.

"Helena—sure she said I mustn't wake you. Said you were up last night into the wee dawn hours tending to Eva de Brounstoun's bad lungs. You must think me daft, Your Grace, and t'is truly sorry I am. I dinna understand how you manage it all, Your Grace—"

Her mistress glanced up from packing and frowned.

"Petronilla, no ceremony. I have told you before not to call me 'Your Grace.' My peers would eagerly say that long ago I should have forfeit my title by refusing to behave as a noblewoman ought—however *that* is—though they have no idea how their dislike of my behavior delights me. I find the honorifics of rank encumbering. So now I will tell you again, hopefully for the last time: a simple 'Lady Alyce' and 'My

lady,' will do. And *stop* saying Eva's lungs are 'bad.' They are
not. But she *must* cease taking part in the winnow of early
wheat; that is what makes her wheeze so horridly. I have set her
to breathing steam from boiled mullein leaves and cinnamon
camphor, but she must stay away from chaff and pollen. It
has nothing to do with good lungs or bad lungs or any moral
judgment on lungs."

Petronilla blushed, crimson flooding her pale face.

Alyce relented, adding, "I need to keep reminding myself
that you are new to Kilkenny. Can it be only a year and a half
you are with us? And look at you! You have actually put on a
bit of flesh—not nearly enough, but at least you are now
almost a scarecrow, not just a ghost rattling her bones. And
you already a Seeker in The Old Ways! Why, you have begun
to blossom, Petronilla. Out from your darkness. Like a moon-
flower." Alyce touched the younger woman's shoulder lightly.
"So surely by now you must realize that no one around here
has called me 'Your Grace' for a long time—except His
Gracelessness Sir John, of course." Petronilla smiled despite
her embarrassment, not able to take worshipful eyes off her
mistress, who was already moving swiftly to another cupboard,
standing on tiptoe to pull down some lengths of fine linen
from a high shelf.

"That should suffice," Alyce said, folding the cloth into a
second basket. "Clean linen for the bedding, with enough

extra to wrap the infant. . . ." She paused, mentally double-checking the contents of both baskets to make certain she'd forgotten nothing that might be necessary.

Petronilla stood by silently, sending sidelong peeks at her lady, unable as always to find words that might express her admiration for this woman who seemed so fearless, so unlike her timid self. Alyce, noticing her awkwardness, offered the basket of linens for Petronilla to carry. The frail young woman grasped it as if she were being entrusted with a sack of gold.

"You know, Petronilla," Alyce said, peering at the shy face, "You did make the right decision. It would have been dreadful if Helena had been left with no midwifery this night. It was proper that you woke me." She turned and sped to the door, while Petronilla stared at her adoringly.

"Time drags cruelly to a woman in childbirth," Alyce added briskly, looking back at her companion with raised eyebrows. Her glance was like a command.

The two women swept out, leaving the chamber vacant for inspection by the slender crescent moon. It shone in like a smile, serene and satisfied, on the blueblack velvet face of the midnight sky.

III

UNEXPECTED GUESTS

BISHOP RICHARD DE LEDREDE tensed his eminence, a somewhat bloated stomach, producing a loud belch that he tried to stifle behind the stiff silk of his cuff. Squirming with discomfort on the chair's hardwood seat, he shifted his bulk and shook his head vigorously, causing his jowls to vibrate in sympathy with his indignation. This really was unusually rude, even for the Irish. How long must he wait? It was not as though he was unexpected; two days earlier he had sent a messenger informing Lady Alyce that he would call on her today and, though she had not responded, he knew she was in residence.

He had boomed a stentorian *"Yes!"* when the manservant ushering him into Kyteler Castle's Great Hall had asked if he wished for some refreshment while waiting for Her Ladyship. Back then, of course, he had assumed the wait would be the usual brief ceremonial one inflicted on even a distinguished visitor seeking audience with a noble. But hours had passed. He had devoured every crumb of the spiced toast and every morsel of the dates stuffed with eggs and cheese that two serving lads duly brought to him on a small, elegantly laid table. He had drunk every drop of the cider—for which he'd had to *ask*, rejecting the water they'd poured into a silver goblet—though once requested, he had to admit, the cider *had* been quickly fetched. Then he had read his breviary. Then he had slipped off his purple silk pilos, the skullcap that properly should be removed only during certain parts of the Mass, and fanned himself with it in the summer heat. He had paced. He had examined the ornately carved wooden benches set against the walls. He had studied the rich tapestries across which maidens danced alongside unicorns—recalling with unease the heresies that had been uncovered, flourishing like weeds, throughout the tapestry-weaver guilds in Provence. He had admired the gleaming silver candlestands ringing the huge room like sentinels, each taller than a man. The woman undeniably commanded enormous wealth and had superb taste . . . but how much longer must he endure this? It was insupportable that the Personal Emissary of His Holiness should be kept waiting for an entire morning, and by a *woman*.

Richard de Ledrede had more than once found himself wondering why the blessed saints ever considered women a temptation. Along with children and animals, women struck him as the incarnations of pandemonium—although one might excuse children and animals, who existed in a state of innocence, which adult females hardly dare claim. Obviously, men could be agents of disorder as well, but men were complicated. It was a Christian obligation, for example—fortunately parallelling his personal tendency—to loathe men who were Saracens or Jews unless they embraced conversion, in which case they still could never quite be trusted. Scholarly men might be regarded with respect—but respect tempered by vigilance, since too much thinking could dim the most radiant brain to heresy until it might be brightened again only at the stake. Powerful, high-born men were to be suffered but befriended; they were the keepers of societal order, lay generals of the Church—yet they must never be allowed to forget that the Church held the keys for their entrance to Heaven. Wealthy men who preferred to live for pleasure rather than for power—men who had a sophisticated palate for fine food and wines, who relished aristocratic sports and cut fashionable figures in appearance—they were harmless jesters with the sense to leave serious decisions to Church representatives. Then there were the consecrated few, the Pope's chosen sons: cardinal princes, bishops, monsignors, abbots, sometimes even ordinary priests.

To be sure, many men of the cloth were not as disinterested in earthly delights as might be assumed—sport, feasting, drink, and fashion included—and Richard de Ledrede's capacity for irony compelled him to number himself among them. No scrawny Saint Anthony in the desert, he; indeed, he privately harbored a disgust for religious zealots who denounced earthly pleasures God had intended for man's delight. Still, he understood as too many did not how crucial it was to combine such pursuits with a shrewd grasp of what was most important: spiritual authority and temporal power, reflecting and rein-forcing one another. Furthermore, he was wary, having seen more than a few worldly churchmen meet their downfall by a lack of moderation. But such folly was almost inevitably provoked by women, Hell's most reliable servants.

De Ledrede had been canny enough to avoid feminine lures, unlike some of his brethren; his sense of fastidiousness spurned the lazy wantons he found most women to be. Given the misery caused by female lasciviousness and sloth, he thought, how much better would the world be without women! There was procreation, to be sure... but if only God had arranged it so that the tiny homunculus curled inside each spermatozoon might grow to fruition directly and purely, held hostage not even temporarily by the dark, fetid womb. As he had many times before, Richard de Ledrede found himself wondering why God's ways were so much more mysterious than efficient.

* * *

"I canna! I tell you I *caaaanna!*" The vowels rolled out along a wail.

"Yes, Helena, you *can*. And you *must*. Oh, poor dear, poor child. Only two more heaves—just two more—and the babe will be here, I promise you. Petronilla, hold her up, do not let her slump so. Bear down now, Helena, *push!*"

Alyce Kyteler, on her knees in a pool of bloody, watery fluid, kept yelling *"Push!"* as she hunched and strained between the spread, sweat-slick thighs of the woman squatting on the birthing stool before her. It was the seventeenth hour of labor, and Helena was weak with exhaustion. Her colour rose in a livid flush of effort as she bore down hard, then faded to the ashy pale of fatigue again as she relaxed. She moaned softly.

"Good, good, you are doing well, Helena, so well," Alyce crooned, "What a brave warrior you are... and the babe is almost here. I can see the head—I can see fine dark hair. Rest a moment now, dear. Breathe. Breathe deeply. Then one more set of presses, only *one* more, and it will all be over. There will be time afterward, so much time, time to rest, to celebrate, time to sleep. . . ." Hearing her singsong voice echo through her own weariness, Alyce sat back on her heels. *What are you babbling about,* she thought. *Time to sleep? With a firstborn in the house?* But she continued her soothing murmurs while wiping the sweat from her eyes with her sleeve.

"Petronilla, cool Helena down again, will you?" she said. "Yes, her forehead, but also a wet cloth on her neck. . . along her arms, too. And some salve on those lips? Poor dear, poor brave dear. . . ."

There was a timid knock at the door.

"*No*, Sysok, you *still* may *not* come in," Alyce called over her shoulder. "And *yes*, Sysok, Helena is fine, but tired. And *no* Sysok, the babe is *not* here yet. I swear to you that you shall hear it when the time comes! Now leave us in peace or I will set the curse of Macha on you and you will be a *male* in labor—for four nights and five days!"

The father's footsteps shuffled away. Helena whispered something through a throat raw with screaming.

"So . . . grateful, m'Lady. You . . . here . . . like any midwife. So—"

Helena's face contorted with sudden pain.

"Here it is," Alyce said sharply, shifting forward and leaning in. "Come now, child, bear down one last time. Queen Meave is here to midwife you, far better than I could; cannot you feel Her power? The Great Mother Dana Herself is watching over you. Now *press down*—and the babe shall be blessed in Her sight—*press*, Helena, *press*—and your milk will flow more plentiful than Flidais's cow that fed the *push* three hundred in one night yes yes bear down bear down *press press PUSH!*"

A gush of blood and warm slime oozing colours jewel-vivid as rubies, sapphires, and yellow diamonds slid the infant into Alyce's gently tugging hands. One swift stroke on the back brought the first cry. It pierced the dense, pungent air of the cottage like the squeal of a wild goose flying through fog.

"A womanchild!" Alyce exulted, "And though early, she is perfect!"

Helena collapsed into sobs of relief and joy. Petronilla also burst into tears, awestruck, feeling privileged to have been of aid. The afterbirth spewed forth, and the placenta was set aside to be properly buried, as was the tradition with the caul. Sysok, having heard the baby's wail, was at the door and through it before anyone could try to stop him, not that anyone would do so now. Then all was bustle and warm clean water and tears and laughter and cooing and clean soft cloths. Helena waded to her bed, where the child—now cleaned, swaddled, and placed in her mother's arms—squinted tiny eyes on the radiant face bent above her. While the woman and the infant studied each other, Old John, Sysok's father, came limping in, his ancient features creasing with triumph. He announced that never had there been such a beautiful creature in the Blessed Isles as this his own granddaughter and what was everyone waiting for where was the grog.

Only then did Alyce strip off her bloodied apron and indulge in a great armspread stretch.

"What is this wee Maiden's name, then?" she asked Helena.

"Oh, m'Lady," the new mother answered, "I am thinking she must be Dana."

"Well chosen," smiled Alyce. "The One who brought you through an early, long, and hard travail, keeping you in

Her sight. A second birth will likely be far easier, and those that follow easier still."

Helena looked up, startled. "A second!" she exclaimed. "Those that follow! By The Morrigan, I am not at all thinking of *that*! I might do as you did, m'Lady—settle for one and be done with the business for good! Why would any woman go through this more than once, I would like to know? *Even* once, if she knew what was coming?"

"And what choice d'we have, I might ask," Petronilla twitted her, settling a cushion behind Helena's back.

"More choice than you would think," Alyce muttered, with a small wink at Helena. Then she shot a sidelong glance at Sysok—who woke from rapt adoration of his wife and daughter to realize that all three women were peering at him with pursed lips.

His bewilderment set them off. They started giggling, while Sysok smiled back from his daze and Old John, moving about with cups and a beaker, fueled the merriment until the cottage rang with laughter.

*   *   *

Yawning, the Bishop adjusted the folds of his cassock, appreciating as he did so the sheen of its violet-coloured silk, brought to Avignon by heroic Spanish sons of the Church in a raid on an infidel outpost near Granada, an act of militancy reminiscent of the glorious Crusades. He fingered the large pectoral cross of beaten gold that hung round his neck on its heavy gold chain, and admired again the craftsmanship that had so cunningly inlaid five fat cabochon rubies precisely at the five points where Christ's wounds had bled. A taste for exquisite things was a form of worship, he had long ago decided, an esthetic celebration of the beauty of the Church. Meticulously, he centered the ornament on his round front. Squirming in his chair, he glanced surreptitiously left and right, then loosened the cincture girdling his ample middle. Perhaps he *had* consumed too much roast lamb the previous evening—but sweet Christ, that garlic and rosemary crust! No, he thought, God's plenty warranted affirmation. It was this ridiculous waiting that had upset his digestion. Perhaps he had been too mindful of his duty to save this Lady's soul. Now it really was time for him to storm off and. . .

His meditation on rage was interrupted by the entrance of a tall woman who strode toward him across the expanse of the Great Hall. Her red-gold hair hung loose and tousled well past the waist of her wrinkled, stained, homespun gown; its wide hanging sleeves had been rolled and tied up above her elbows, leaving her sun-browned forearms bare. Neither young nor old, she was slender but sturdily broad-shouldered, and the eyes that looked straight into his were green as new apples.

A cat—a black one, he noticed—wove itself between and around her ankles. A small angora goat, fleece lustrous as pearl, clattered in after her, looking bored and bleating softly.

"Welcome to Kyteler Castle, my lord Bishop," the woman said pleasantly. "I hear you have been waiting for some time. My apologies—although I understand that you have had refreshment. I had important business to attend to." The eyes glowed in her tired face. "We brought a baby girl into this life today—tiny, but she will survive. Especially with a voice like hers, strong enough to squall any attention she wants. And the mother well enough, too. Weary she is, but that's no wonder." The woman blew out a sigh of accomplishment and rubbed the back of her neck with both hands. "Ahh, but that was good hard work," she said. "Now. What is it you wish from me?"

The Papal Emissary blinked.

"You cannot be...who *are* you, wench? Announce me to Her Grace at once!"

"The last I looked, Her Grace was standing in front of you," Alyce said affably. Unknotting one of her purse sleeves, she rummaged through its folds, produced a pear from a hidden pocket, slumped onto a nearby bench, and proceeded to sink her even white teeth into the fruit, adding, "Actually, now *sitting* in front of you. Famished."

Her visitor stared. Then he began to struggle to his feet.

"Oh! I *am* sorry," she gargled from a full mouth, "How rude of me." She held out the partly eaten pear to him.

"Would you like a bite? *No*, not *you*, Greedigut," she added, waving away the goat, whose interest had perked up mightily at the sight of a pear. "Please, no ceremony," she added to her guest, "do be seated."

He did, which was just as well because he felt faint. This was a woman of high noble birth he had mistaken for an impudent serving maid. But Jesu, she was too vulgar to be imagined! How to converse with such a creature? Absurd enough that she knew how to read and write and was a scold who'd caused pain to her husband. But running around costumed as a filthy peasant! He could actually see her feet, *naked*, in sandals—and caked with mud at that. Not one jewel on her! Furthermore, though married and an aristocrat, she wore no circlet or hennin, no wimple, not even a veil—she was bareheaded, like an unwed female serf. And actually boasting that she had acted as a common midwife—she must be mad. Or possessed. De Ledrede closed his eyes and took a deep breath. God preserve me from the eccentric whims of the nobility, he groaned inwardly. He had once had to administer last rites to an imperious French count convinced he was already an archangel, thus in no need of absolution. Having succeeded then, he would succeed now.

"My child—" he began.

"Wrong. Grown woman of more summers than you might suspect," she interrupted, "hardly a child. Certainly not yours—unless you know something I do not?" She actually winked at him. "Though I have seen many an Irish priest trying to hide his share of secret offspring under his cassock. Not that I mind their breaking chastity vows. Denying the body's natural joy is as futile a task as Cuchulain battling the tide, I think—ask Greedigut here, she knows all about that," she stroked the goat's head, rubbing gently between the two small horns. "What I *do* mind," she added in a sterner tone, "is refusing to acknowledge the children, and denouncing the women who bear them." She wiped pear juice off her chin with the none-too-clean sleeve. "You are fairly new to Kilkenny, though, so perhaps you have not yet encountered such clerical hypocrisy?"

"I have been Chief Prelate of Ossary and Special Papal Emissary to Ireland for almost two years, Your Grace. I was here all of last year. Then I was away temporarily, attending upon His Holiness at Avignon, over last Christmas. I returned to Ireland in January, six months ago."

"Almost two years—so long as that!" Alyce Kyteler replied genially, adding, "A newcomer by the way we reckon time here. I do know that you have spent many hours acquainting yourself with the district and with your local parishioners in Kilkenny Town."

"That I have, Your Grace. Yet, strangely, I have never had the honour of encountering you among the nobles." He bowed his head with respect, but that brought those muddy toes back into view, so he quickly glanced away.

Lady Alyce laughed heartily.

"You would not likely encounter me among the peers, my lord Bishop. They and I are on excellent terms—so long as we avoid each other. I find them ignorant, pretentious, and boring." De Ledrede's eyes narrowed with interest. "They do not miss my company, nor I theirs," Alyce continued, "I go rarely to town or visit other manors. My days are filled with managing the estate."

"*You* manage the estate?"

"Women manage our husbands' holdings all the time, modestly pretending we do not. I differ only in that I am honest about it—and the estate *is* wholly *mine*, so why would I want anyone else managing it? But such details aside, I am a bit tired at present. I mean you no discourtesy, yet . . . please, what is the point of your visit?" She bit off another chunk of the pear.

The Bishop noted to himself that she was dribbling slightly, which might be a sign of diabolic possession. Yet her contemptuous dismissal of the nobles intrigued him, since her opinion of them mirrored his. He had never met any person, much less any female, like Alyce Kyteler. She was obviously quite clever and well aware of her position, even if she did choose to carry herself like a base serf. He could not work out how to approach such a woman. Not as a parishioner, surely, as she was not one. Nor, despite her cordial manner, did she seem impressed or intimidated by his rank. Dare he position

himself as a friend? An intellectual mentor? Even a confi-
dante? After all, like him, she must be suffocating for lack of
intelligent conversation. He would signal to her that in him
she might find an intellectual ally. That would win her trust.
Furthermore, he realized with surprise, it was true.

"Of course," he smiled, "I would not wish to tire you further.
Although perhaps soon Your Ladyship will do me the honour
of dining with me at the Cathedral Residence in Kilkenny
Town? My chief cook is French, and keeps a tolerable kitchen.
We might then discuss how I tend to agree with your judg-
ment of the Kilkenny gentry." He smiled again, expectantly.

"Not likely. As I said, I go rarely to town. But thank you.
Now then again, the purpose of your visit?"

Astonishing. To deflect an invitation from the Papal
Emissary! To worsen matters, he discovered he actually felt
hurt that she had rejected him—then felt enraged at feeling
hurt, then felt shamed that he had let himself be vulnerable.
He would go on the offensive, then. But cautiously.

"Very well," he coughed, invoking the comforting,
concealing voice of his public self, "Your husband has sought
my advice regarding certain. . . difficulties in your marriage."

"Hah!" Alyce exclaimed, "I'll wager he has."

"Indeed? Sir John seems a distinguished gentleman and
a pious one. He confided to me many concerns that have
alarmed him for some time about your. . . habits. I must confess
to you, my Lady, I was *shocked*."

Alyce Kyteler chewed her pear.

"To, ah, continue." He felt himself start warming to his task. That sometimes happened while preaching a sermon: one might begin awkwardly but gain impetus as one pressed on. Diligence was crucial. He would alternate between the roles of friendly confessor and austere judge. But he would protect himself this time.

"First, I want you to consider me your friend, someone offering—well, we might call it 'fatherly advice.' Forgive the pun," he chuckled. "Well. Sir John has numerous complaints, some of which fall into areas of public as well as private interest. So we—that is, he and I—decided that I should visit you in my capacity as your diocesan authority, but also as your priest. Therefore, this . . . well, mission of mercy." He paused, waiting for a response. None came. So he continued. "I fear, Your Grace, that I must point out to you your errors, that you may be brought to change your ways. It is greatly in your own interest, as an aristocrat *and* as a woman. You know," he lowered his voice conspiratorially, "even if you are innocent, appearance is crucial. It is *so* unfair, is it not, how easily a feminine reputation can be *spattered* with filth!"

Alyce stifled a yawn.

"Forgive me if I bore you," snapped the Bishop, hastily adding, "Your Grace." This woman, he thought, would drive Saint Francis to kick puppies.

Alyce responded only with a meek inclination of her head. Was she mocking him now? Was she trying to *flirt* with him? He felt his grasp of the situation loosening. But he was not a trained diplomat for nothing. He would persist as if he possessed control until he regained it.

"Well then. The errors into which you have fallen. Surely you yourself must know them."

"Why, no, my lord Bishop. Why not tell me? That is what you came here to do, is it not?"

Insolent slattern, he thought. So she was one of those jaded rich women who play at making mischief, having nothing better to do than act outrageously for pure rebellion's sake. They always collapsed into obedience when firmly challenged. Very well, he would teach her the cost of rebellion.

"To begin, it is highly improper that you read and write, being female. A woman is a treasured vessel of life, carrier of man's offspring, so intended for this marvelous task that it is immoral for her to distract herself from it by intellectual pursuits. For a woman to become educated is for her to deny her female *essence*, her life's mission. Her natural knowledge is far more profound than mere education could ever teach. Book-learning taxes the spirit, and women's spirit is inherently fragile, thus readily seduced into the path of evil. You risk your sanity, my dear Lady Alyce. You risk your *soul*." That reliable public voice was heating up now, and he indulged in a tiny sin of pride at hearing himself put things at once passionately yet elegantly.

"For example," he declared, "it is obvious that your knowledge of letters has led you into even more perilous studies. Medicines. Midwifery. But Church teaching is clear on this: as punishment for Eve's sin in tempting Adam and causing the Fall, God The Father sentenced women to bring forth children forevermore in sorrow. *Sorrow*, Lady Alyce. Anyone who conspires to make childbirth easier is acting contrary to dogma. Midwives are barely this side of viperous heretics. But so it is with education. You see? One thing leads to another. It makes the mind *so* unpredictable."

Like her two animal companions, the human member of his audience cocked her head and said nothing, but never took her eyes from his face. While he found this slightly unnerving, it at least reassured him that he had her attention. Now it was time for an illustratory tale or two.

"Just last year in Paris," he went on conversationally, gaining confidence that he was winning her trust, "a woman of noble birth like yourself went about calling herself a healer, and was brought to trial—for practicing *sorcery*. Jacqueline Felicie de Almania was her name. It still is her name, I fear, since she was merely fined and prohibited from practicing—and by now is likely at it again. What do they expect, with such a preposterously light sentence? Then again, she *was* terrifyingly persistent—originally from Germany, which explains a great deal—and she had the temerity to bring witnesses who claimed she was wiser than the master surgeons of Paris.

Nor was she the only one. There was also a Jewess, some woman named Belota, who was prohibited from practicing medicine at the same time. I tell you, we have strayed far from the old days of innocence, when women were chaste in mind as well as in flesh. This is like a plague of Satan's students: lettered females, who can read yet could not possibly understand what they read, who can write yet could not possibly have anything to say. But you? You are a *sensible* woman. I can see that already." He flashed his teeth at Alyce in his most paternal smile. "So. Although we cannot change the fact that you are already infected with such knowledge, we can change the *practice* of it, can we not?" Inspired by her silence, he answered his own question with a chuckle of optimism. "Certainly we can. The medical meddling will cease completely, of course, and at once. But you shall see that I am *not* an unreasonable man, Your Grace. I can compromise. Since you already know how to read and write, you may continue to do so, within limits. Reading for Scriptures, writing for household accounts—these I permit you." This time the smile lasted longer, having made its way through the folds around his mouth. Alyce Kyteler said nothing. She stared at him. He had her now.

"It will be hard at first, I know, Your Grace, I know," he continued, not pausing for a reply, "But Holy Church and I shall help you muster courage for the battle. Because, my dear," he frowned for a more severe effect, "I must tell you there is more. Much more—as you surely know, for it is clear that you are not unintelligent. You have been fraternizing with the serfs. This is out of the question and must stop immediately. I understand your compassion for them, Your Ladyship. A desire to help the poor is commendably Christian, and if you have done so to excess—well, soft-heartedness is actually proof of your womanliness. You see? I do not solely criticize, I can praise, too." Encouraged by his listener's rapt gaze, he forged on. "But one must not burden serfs with affection. It is up to God, not us, to notice their sufferings. Naturally, we must pity them as Scripture instructs—but abstractly—and we must never sentimentalize them. They are hardly better than wild beasts, the least of God's creatures—which is how we must regard them. You, Your Grace, nobly born and nobly wed, *must* carry yourself according to your position. To do otherwise upsets the social compact. So your regard for the poor must be limited to alms-giving. If you insist, I shall allow you to be more generous than others are—but your charity must be channeled through the Church, and *I* shall decide how it is apportioned. Nor must you do anything else to alter the position of these unfortunates. That would be to counter the ways of Heaven, which *intended* that the poor be always with us—as warning and as reminder to praise Him for smiling on our own good fortune and high rank."

Something akin to a small green flame had begun to gleam in Alyce Kyteler's eyes. It went unnoticed by the Bishop, now preoccupied with his own eloquence as he continued cataloging her wrongdoings.

"The subject of your refusing to attend Mass is altogether a different matter. This is not a feminine good intention gone awry, as with the serfs. This is very grave." He deepened his voice. "You trifle with *sin*, Madam! *You provoke the boiling fires of Hell!*"

He waited. At this she should have dropped to her knees. Annoyed, he changed course. Not for nothing did he have a repertoire of styles.

"However, Your Ladyship, even if you chose to be careless of your own damnation," he went on smoothly, "what example do you set for your precious rabble, eh? What about *their* shabby little peasant souls?" He knew these last phrases had emerged with too sharp an edge, and made a conscious effort to regain his elevated tone. "Your husband told me that you did attend Mass with him once, early in your marriage, at his insistence. But according to him—and let me interrupt myself here to say that I can be *fair*, Your Grace, I shall listen to *your* side of the story, too—I know how husbands can exaggerate! Nevertheless, according to His Lordship, you refused to go to Confession, declined to take Communion, were overheard humming to yourself during the sermon, and at the end of the service actually muttered 'Fie, fie, fie, amen.' I pray you will tell me this simply is not true! Oh my *child*!"

Richard de Ledrede had worked himself up to the pitch of sincerity he had been seeking. Now he felt the momentum begin to operate on its own, suffusing him with genuine sympathy for this sinful woman whose eternal life hung in jeopardy. He must save her. He must ride like a hero to her rescue. A desire for her soul seized him; he wanted that soul, he had a right to it. He could feel a holy lust rising in him, and he heard it inspire his speech with conviction.

"My dear, my *dear*, oh will you not let me aid you? Such disrespect for the Church is perilous. These are times when the Horned One walks the earth conspiring with evil-doers and worshippers of false gods! You may think we are safe here on this remote little island. But my priests tell me that Lucifer—or Robin Artisson, as the Son of the Black Arts is called in these Isles—has been seen in these very parts, and not long ago! A black man, wearing female flesh but with horns glowing bright on his hideous head, riding bareback across the heath on stormy nights! You see, my dear, how you gamble with your soul, when you behave so appallingly in Church? These are real dangers of which I warn!"

He paused to grope for his silk kerchief and wipe a film of sweat from his forehead, noting that his listener remained curiously unfazed by the hazards he had so vividly described.

Well then, if she was unimpressed by spiritual admonishments, perhaps he should bolster them with a few practical threats.

"You," he said sternly, as befitted a future prince of the Church, "would have been publicly flogged for such an offense, Madam, were you not a noblewoman. Nevertheless, Christians must be merciful even when sorely wronged. So your husband and I are willing to permit your attendance at Confession and Mass with merely one week's penance of bread and water on your part. And your contrite apology to me. In public."

Richard de Ledrede now felt secure. Laboriously, he heaved himself up from the chair where he had been wedged, and began to stride back and forth before Alyce, waggling a finger at her. Noting that her expression had hardened into something resembling a glare, he was undeterred. He knew that demons resisted most fiercely just before withdrawing from a contested soul.

"These are all ungodly, unwomanly, scandalous acts in which you have been indulging," he thundered. Then, lowering his voice, "Which is not even to *speak* of the more private... intimate problem. This—delicate matter of Sir John's. His concern—that is, his unease—about his own safety in this house. I am informed that you hide forbidden potions in your cupboards! He said he had left you and moved to another dwelling because—absurd as it sounds—he fears for his life around you." He paused, waiting for loud protestations of denial.

There was now a green blaze in Alyce Kyteler's eyes. But she clipped out only one word in answer.

"Finish."

So she would force him to spell it out in sordid detail. The Bishop shouldered the cross of yet another degrading task.

"Well, you *have* been married *four times.* Sir John admitted to me his suspicions about the...departures of his three predecessors. Nor is it only Sir John who accuses you, Lady Alyce. Your stepchildren from previous husbands claim that you bewitched their fathers by sorcery to enrich you with generous gifts of property, and that you then—well, hurried them along to Heaven. But Your Grace, let me say frankly that on this issue I *defended* you. 'Ludicrous!' said I. I said that you—especially you, a lettered woman—*knows* a husband is his wife's lord, and for a vassal to harm a lord—even to disobey him—why, that is *treason.* Men are *hanged* for treason, and women *burned.* So I want you to know that I assured Sir John and your stepchildren that no woman would *dare*—I mean, three adult able men—it is simply too laughable. I also reminded Sir John of the indissoluble marriage Sacrament, and I reproached him for having left you. You see how fair I can be, Your Grace? But his apprehensions, combined with consternation about his own health—worsened, I gather, by ill humours borne by the night air—well, unfortunately he is now so alarmed as to—"

"*Now* you have finished." Alyce Kyteler's voice cut through the Bishop's prattle like a sword through custard.

"I have listened to you quietly," she said, "and without interruption, as my principles are based on courtesy. Now *you* will listen."

Like a wire suddenly uncoiling, she sprang up from where she had been sitting. Never taking her eyes off the Bishop, she tossed the pear core back over her shoulder in Greedigut's direction, and the watchful goat caught it mid-air with a graceful snap. De Ledrede suddenly realized that this woman was his equal in height, and he drew himself up on the balls of his feet so as to loom over her. But that threw him slightly off balance. Taking advantage of his teeter, she shot out a strong hand and pushed him back down into his chair, where he landed with a thump.

"*Sit*," she commanded. "Now *I* will give a sermon."

IV

TWO WARNINGS

SHE FLUNG BACK her mane of hair the colour of rowan berries at sunset, planted her feet apart, stuck her hands on her hips, and began. Flanked by Prickeare and Greedigut, she looked as armored with disdain as a warrior queen about to do battle with a garden worm.

"Last slander first. My husband did not leave me. Difficult as it may be for you to imagine, I sent him away. A pity if he is ill, but t'is not because of anything I—or an evening breeze—did to him. John's hair is falling out from age, not poison. Yet he refuses to admit he is old. He also denies that he has grown stout, and orders his tunic to be laced so tightly that his breath comes short. I imagine he may be suffocating from his own pomposity, too; certainly I was. To put it flatly, the man is sick of himself. Small wonder.

"As for my other husbands, I can easily give you a summary of the lot—how they lived *and* how they died. For one thing, wedlock to one person for all eternity is a Christian notion that has snaked itself into our law. Celtic Brehon law once recognized *nine* types of marriage—only *one* of which was permanent—and even then both parties had the right to divorce. For another thing, I did not particularly want to marry at all, certainly not four times. What, do you think the faerie folk had addled my brains? These were all arranged marriages. Why *is* it most men cannot tolerate a woman who wishes to remain unwed? The sole exception you permit is a nun. Even then, you 'marry' her off to your Church—then afterwards dismiss her as unwomanly."

Richard de Ledrede opened his mouth to reply, but a warning look from Alyce made him reconsider and shut it again.

"My mother died bearing me. My father loved me, in his way. He meant well. But he contracted me into marriage with William Outlawe when I was thirteen, still in the convent— where what *you* might denounce as heretical nuns had raised me and, bless them forever, educated the bright child they said I was. For almost three years, to protect me, those nuns conspired to delay my marriage to William Outlawe, devising various creative excuses. William, as you may have gathered from his family name, was descended from a man who had been in trouble with the sheriff in his youth. But since he had confined himself to the tradesman-like stealing of large sums rather than committing petty thieveries, the lords held him in grudging respect—especially since he could afford to buy their silence. He and his heirs became bankers and money-lenders, keeping the accounts—and the secrets—of highborn men who would excuse anything so long as sufficient gold lit the path to forgiveness. By the time I was betrothed to his great-grand-nephew, the family was regarded as respectable nobility. William himself was a widower, old enough to be my father. Furthermore, even before I was born he was already in love with his lifelong passion. Brandywine. And every *other* wine. The man stank with the odor of drink. I fought him off for a long time—more than two years—which was not all that difficult, since he was usually dazed from the grog. But one night when he was drunk he became angry and beat me—the last time any man dared lay violent hands on me—and he forced me in bed. Nine months later I bore my only child, Will. A year after the boy was born, his father came lurching home in a stupor from some tavern, slid off his horse while crossing the drawbridge, fell into the moat, and drowned. We found him the next morning, still reeking of three wineskins hung round his neck. People said that my fits of laughter at the funeral must have meant I was insane with grief. That sent me into further gales of despair, I assure you."

The Bishop shifted uneasily in his chair, congratulating himself that Alyce Kyteler was confiding in him, yet not quite believing what she said. For her part, his lecturer was gathering her own momentum. Everyone in or anywhere around Kilkenny knew her life story, so she rarely got to relate it.

But she came of a people who lived for the telling of a good yarn, and was discovering that even in her current exasperated state she was enjoying spinning this one. She began to pace as she talked, her voice warming at certain memories.

"I took to widowhood well, I admit it. I enjoyed raising my little boy and running my own estate, and that was when I started my herbal studies. I had become curious about the effectiveness of many peasant remedies in curing sick animals. But I need not have celebrated freedom so soon, because my father quickly arranged a second husband for me. I have neither brothers nor sisters, so Kyteler Castle and all its lands entail to me, and my father assumed, understandably though wrongly, that I needed a man to manage it. This second husband could not have managed a kitchen garden, much more a large estate. He was the sort of man you might have liked, my lord Bishop, to judge from your silks and gems. Adam le Blound was enamoured of his own looks. Well, I confess I was, too; I fancied him at first. He was handsome, and much younger than my first husband, and he knew how to flirt. There were some highly enjoyable moments... I shall always thank his memory for that, since before Adam I knew not one whit about the pleasures of love."

She glanced at the Bishop, relished his embarrassment, and picked up her story before he could interrupt.

"I was still barely out of girlhood, after all, and he *was* quite attractive. Tall, well-shaped, with thick dark blond hair—

always a few rakish curls falling over that broad forehead—
and a sensuous mouth, drawn in a rascal's smile. But once he
opened that mouth to speak—*such* a dullard. Not merely
unlearned, you understand, but impressively stupid. And
absolutely unfazed by his own ignorance about everything
except the quality of a good sapphire and the latest tailoring
cut. Adam could not tell the difference between a doe and a
ewe, but he could ramble on about which was the sleekest fur
for lining a suckeny cloak, and whether tippets should hang
down to the knee or all the way to the ankle. The man once
raved through dinner for four full hours about *sleeves*—wing,
laced, slashed, funneled, hanging, and dagged. As for me,
I have never been interested in the latest fashion, and I could
focus for just so long on his codpiece—so *that* infatuation
soon ended. He barely missed my company; he spent his hours
with tailors, cobblers, hairdressers—yes, that casual curl was
planned. He would do anything to enhance his appearance.
Unfortunately, he discovered that stealing sips of belladonna
from my herbal cabinet would make his eyes shine more lumi-
nously. I warned him that belladonna is a form of nightshade
and can kill when too much is ingested. I even *hid* that flask.
But Adam ransacked my rooms and found it. He drank too
much of the drug, of course—to be more comely at the
Seneschal's ball he was attending that night in town—and
he collapsed while dancing. He certainly was the center of
everyone's attention, though not quite as he had planned.

His eyes shone brilliantly before they closed forever. So I was told. I was not there. I was helping a mare foal.

"I did mourn Adam—but in truth not for long. That is when gossip about my so-called eccentricities began. I came to know my peasants better during this time, which is when I first thought of teaching their children letters and numbers. But my father was not done marrying me off, no matter how I appealed to him for mercy from wedlock. Number three— another widower—was Richard de Valle. This 'gentleman' fancied himself a hero of the hunt. He thought that the greatest pleasure in life was to gallop about with other armed men, shooting arrows and spears into animals. These were not forays for food, I assure you, but blood-sport. Sometimes Richard and his friends wantonly butchered so much game that they left the carcasses to rot because the pack horses were already too laden with trophies and meat. Wild boar was their favorite target. They would mimic the animal's squeals of pain as they closed round it and speared it to death, laughing as they did so. I imagine you do not know our Irish legends, Bishop—like the tale of the wild sow, sacred to The Cailleach, The Old One, She who in one of Her many guises is also Goddess of the Wood. She brings justice. Once, when Diarmid, the Sun God, offended Her, she sent Her great sow to kill him. Well, I believe that Richard de Valle offended Her so many times by slaughtering Her creatures that the only wonder was why She waited so long to set revenge on him.

For that is how he died. The hunted turned hunter—and one day my third husband was borne home by his servants on a litter, blood streaming from two deep wounds where he had been severely gored. Not all my medical arts could save him. Justly, *he* had become a trophy—for a wild sow fiercely defending her piglets."

The Bishop of Ossory cleared his throat as if to speak.

"Oh, I would advise against it," said Alyce politely. "I will inform you when I am done. This is *my* sermon, remember? You have met Sir John, so I need not describe him. Suffice it to say that he became unbearable, with his multiple imaginary illnesses—which he would never let me properly examine, diagnose, or treat—and his prejudices and his whining about all the things serfs *must* do and all the things women must *not* do. Then one day I found myself thinking, 'This is intolerable. I am not a girl any longer. My father is dead. I can read and write. I can heal. I am perfectly capable of managing my own lands and inheritance; indeed, I do so more effectively than any of my husbands ever did. I really need not put up with such foolishness one hour longer.' So I asked John to leave my estate—and remember, it is *my* estate, Bishop, and always has been. He laughed. I repeated my request. He ignored me. When it became clear that he would not go with gallantry, I threw him out. Well, not *him*. I had his clothing packed up and placed, along with his armor and collection of weapons and favorite bench and other goods—out into the fields, well on the far side of the drawbridge. I sent his two personal menservants—the poor lads didn't want to go—and his favorite luckless horse and another horse and cart out there, too. This time John noticed my request. He followed his possessions within the hour.

"So much for my marital history. I am certain, my lord Bishop, that good men do exist. I have known a few such men, even among your despised serfs, and my son William bodes to become one—despite his having endured a childhood around unfortunate examples. But my experience with husbands has cured me of marriage. A drunkard, a fop, a brute, and a bore. I never chose one of them, never truly loved one of them, and can honestly say I do not mourn one of them. *But*—" Back in the present, recalling that she was being forced to defend herself from slander, Alyce found her good-humour dissipating, "but to think I would *murder* any of them, or stoop to harm John! I am too busy with *life*, with feeding the bellies and brains of the children on Kyteler lands. I do not imagine you can be expected to understand *that* preoccupation."

Prickeare, alert to the mounting indignation in Alyce's tone, decided to punctuate this last sentence with a hiss, an arching of his spine, and the full fluffout-tail treatment; Greedigut, following suit, pawed the ground, snorting. Their mistress nodded in acknowledgement of their support, and pressed on.

"As for the accusations of my stepchildren? They are still the spoiled whelps their fathers insisted on raising—despite my efforts to teach them that tradition and knowledge carry more value than gold—but they are grown whelps now. Wealthy in their own right, they crave still more. *I* know that *they* know if they can make anyone take their absurd charge of murder seriously, then my estate—lands mine by right before I ever married at all—will be forfeit to *them*. I also know that if I am charged with sorcery, my estates will be forfeit to the Church—to *you*, in effect. I am not a fool, my lord Bishop. I know that the Church intends to change our Irish customs so that when a woman weds, she becomes a *femme couverte*—legally dead—no longer able to inherit or possess land in her own name. "

Alyce paused for breath and de Ledrede saw his chance.

"Your Grace, if I may I offer my opinion—" he began, careful to use an conciliatory tone.

"Pardon my discourtesy, but you may not," growled Alyce. "I have been forced to countenance others' opinions for most of my life, whilst no one asked for mine. Were I a man possessed of my education and inheritance, my opinion would be sought after. But the Church views women as temptresses while the world treats us as property—a stifling choice, *in my opinion*. Yes, I did whisper 'Fie, fie, fie, amen' at your mass. Frankly, your masses weary me, with priests droning on and *on* and no dancing or laughter in your worship. I meant no disrespect to your faith or to those who follow it. But you seem a bit... *primitive*. The wine and bread I can understand easily enough: a celebration of the earth's gifts—the vine, the grain. But the way you claim it to *be* the body and blood of your god, and then *devour* him—like cannibals." Alyce permitted herself a small shudder. "It is not for me. I observe The Old Ways, the tradition that began before time was charted, when the world was newborn from The Great Mother."

The Bishop recoiled as if he had been struck.

"*Pagan!*" he spat in horror. He crossed himself. "You are a heathen Devil worshipper! Dear God, you state it openly! You *are* a witch!"

"Well, I do choose to live on the land. 'Pagan' is from *paganus,* for rural dweller—can you have forgotten your Latin? And 'heathen' is similar—meaning one who lives on the heath—though it comes from the Greek."

"I know my Latin and my Greek!" he shouted, getting red in the face.

"But with all the languages you have studied—yes, you need not look so startled, I know something of your personal history—did your scholarly monks never teach you that the word 'witch' comes from the old Saxon 'Wicca,' which means 'wise one'?"

"It is unseemly for a woman to—to so flaunt her learning! It is—"

84

"Have no fear. I shall not try to educate you further. I teach only where I am wanted and never inflict knowledge on the willfully ignorant, but—"

"Your *Grace*, I must *protest*! You insult my—" Yet she plowed on, a scythe leveling a field of grain.

"—but your accusation of 'devil worshipper'! How absurd. The devil is more real to you priests than to any of us. Come, come, we really are quite simple. We celebrate the earth and the seasons, cherishing each moment, living not for the promise of some afterlife brandished from afar to make us more willing to tolerate suffering in this one. We dis*like* suffering, you see— which is why we do not deny the flesh as you do, and why the Irish have risen up more than once against tyrannical lords. But we are wise enough, usually, never to *seek* conflict. Leave us alone and we will leave you alone. Though that is not your way, is it, my lord? You even martyr your own followers if you catch them actually believing in the love you preach, do you not? Crucify them first, sanctify them later?"

The Bishop stared at her, mouth agape, incredulous.

"Ah, yes. That was quite a superb performance you put on for me just now, Bishop—concern for my marriage, my reputation, my soul." She clapped her hands in mock applause. A manservant immediately appeared in the archway of the Great Hall, but she dismissed him with a wave, turning back to her guest. "Now let us discuss what your visit is really about. You consider us here in Eire ignorant dolts living in a backwater. But you forget that I can read, and I have means. I employ personal scouts in England and on the Continent, a few trustworthy people who send me news in private reports. I keep up with your Holy Inquisition, you see. I know that your John XXII has issued new papal bulls calling for an outright war against those you accuse of sorcery. I know the Church has its own new blood-sport. I follow all your slaughters, wherein you hunt down and burn alive scores of people, mostly women and girls."

"Not without provocation! For being hideous heretical—"

"For being healers or teachers or weavers, for questioning, for studying star constellations, for wishing to marry whomever they chose or perhaps not marry at all, for seeing visions, for having dark skin or a mole, for disobeying a father or husband or brother or even son, for being too smart or too simple, too rich or too poor, too plain or too pretty. What have women ever *done* to you but bear, nurse, raise, and love you? Does our existence so unman you that you feel compelled to imprison Divinity in a single shape—reflecting *yours*—and then destroy all who disagree? Is *that* not why your pope sent you to Ireland, Richard de Ledrede? To carry your plague of accusation and massacre here? To hunt witches? I see it in your face as if written across your forehead, like a stain."

Energy rising in her from the passion of her argument, Alyce began to tremble. But she stood her ground.

"Hearken to me now, Papal Emissary. These people you call rabble have never hurt you or your church. When your priests threaten them, they peaceably *go* to your mass—but they still attend their own sabbats and hold to their own ways. They are poor, these peasants, but they are also not fools. I give you fair warning. *You shall not harm these people!*"

De Ledrede blinked hard and repeatedly, like someone trying to urge himself awake from a nightmare. The stone walls rang with Alyce Kyteler's words, yet her tone grew even more combative.

"My lord Bishop, you are what we in the Craft call a *cowan*—an outsider—so you would do well to conduct yourself with humility. You are English *and* from the Papal Court, neither of which will gain you many friends here. We Irish have long memories. T'was only two hundred years ago Pope Adrian IV granted overlordship of Ireland to Henry II of England, and we have not forgotten. You are on an island where most people still worship many faces of Divinity, female *and* male, but above all, The Great Mother, She of One Thousand Names, Queen of Heaven and Earth. Here, the leaders of Her Craft are *women*. I am one."

The Bishop tried to shake himself into action, but he did not know where to begin. Yet he could not just sit there, idiotically silent, as if in her thrall. The Church must be defended. Womanhood itself must be defended.

"The Queen of Heaven—" he sputtered.

"Oh yes," she said wearily. "You are about to offer your queen of heaven as proof of how the Church respects women. Actually, one of the few good things about your religion *is* the mother of your god. But Mary is a more...*domesticated* version of our Goddess, and you observe only two of Her three phases—the Virgin and the Mother. Be warned, it is unwise to ignore the Crone, the most powerful of all. In sum, we prefer our original to your imitation. Oh please, do stop looking so perturbed. You need not feel embarrassed that you poached the idea from us; yours is not the first religion to do so—nor, I imagine, will it be the last. I have given hospitality to Kabbalists fleeing from your flames on the Continent, and from these Jews I have learned of their ancient Goddess, also called by many names—Ishtar, Binah, Shekinah. So fret not. She who gives birth to everything belongs to all of us. You cannot steal a freely shared gift. But do not think you can steal our *souls*, or put our bodies to the fire you have so devoutly carried here from France. Best to return to Avignon or Rome or wherever you keep your pope these days, Bishop, and tell him to leave the Irish in peace. And return to John and tell him to leave *me* in peace. There. I have finished. Now you may go."

The Bishop of Ossory staggered to his feet, edged past where Alyce stood glowering, and scuffled toward the archway in furious silence. Only at the threshold did he pause and turn, groping for the right remark to dignify his exit. But he became distracted—unable to help being impressed again at how the high-vaulted ceiling rose firm on thick stone walls around the Great Hall's vastness, how the room's shadows were cornered by the gleam of torches flaring from bronze bowls and from creamy fat candles guttering in the tall stands of polished silver. The harridan standing in the Hall was unkempt, mad, and heretical—but she was also the richest landholder in this and all the surrounding counties. And she was dangerously intelligent.

With supreme discipline, he marshalled his features into a mask of diplomacy. It was time to exert his own rank by addressing her intimately, as an equal.

"My dear Alyce—" he ventured, "let us not part as—"

"*Your Grace*, the most noble *Dame* Alyce Kyteler to you, Bishop. Daughter of Celtic Queens, Healer of the Sick, High Priestess of the Craft of the Wise. That is how you may address us."

De Ledrede's composure deserted him. This *she*-wolf, he thought, this... he cast about for a reply sufficiently withering to trump hers. Instead, he felt the blood seethe to his head, and heard himself swearing through clenched teeth.

"By God, you will regret the words you dared speak today, woman. The Bible commands 'Thou shalt not suffer a Witch to live!'—Exodus XXII, verse 18! So *you* be warned, Madam—you *and* your serf followers!"

She did not flinch. Rather, she took a step toward him.

"Actually, that phrase is likely a mistranslation of the injunction 'Thou shalt not suffer a *poisoner* to live'—but perhaps you do not read Greek that well?"

He felt his dignity shatter. Worse, in its place he experienced a bitter admiration for his opponent. At this moment, he would trade his eternal soul for the right riposte to devastate her. His diplomacy dwindling into honesty, he surprised himself by speaking aloud his real thoughts.

"You hold me in disdain, Madam, that much is clear. Yet for my part, I think it a pity you choose to squander the bounty of a mind so learned as yours on superstition, sorcery, and cheap, self-flattering beneficence to the serfs for whom you claim to speak. You profess to save their grubby little bodies while I profess to save their scruffy little souls. I wonder. Which of us, do you think, patronizes them less?"

For a moment, they stared deep into one another, and he thought he saw her blanch.

Then she clapped her hands again and the manservant reappeared.

"The Papal Emissary is leaving us. Show him out," she commanded, adding, as if in an afterthought, "Oh, by the by, my lord Bishop. I can see that you suffer from dyspepsia and choler. Chamomile leaves brewed as tea, sipped thrice daily, would ease that, you know—and cider vinegar mixed with honey at meals instead of wine. Chewing fresh mint would also comfort the stomach, and might sweeten your breath."

Unable to determine whether she was being condescendingly solicitousness or deliberately humiliating, and feeling further diminished by either choice, he wheeled and stomped through the archway in a blur of purple robes and purple face. After him drifted Alyce Kyteler's now calmer, almost bemused voice, with her maddeningly relentless prescriptions.

"Hulloo? Bishop? A mild tincture of wormwood flowers—only a few drops a day—would lessen the indigestion and all that wind you break. Also, a less rich diet? And some physical exertion would certainly..."

The bang of a far door and the subsequent clash of gates told her he was now beyond hearing.

She looked down at Prickeare, fastidiously licking his left front paw, then at Greedigut, who had folded her legs under herself and settled down for a doze in protest at this tedious human conversation.

"I," Alyce announced to her companions, "am in dire need of a nap."

Hurrying from the Hall, she sought and found Petronilla, instructed her to take charge of that afternoon's planned berry-picking for the holy-day pies, and added that she herself would oversee the other Lugnasad tasks later. Then, wearily, she climbed the stairs to her tower.

Once in her room, the lady of the manor kicked off her sandals and sent them skimming across the floor. Then she flung herself down on the bed fully dressed, groaned once, and instantly fell asleep.

V

KITCHEN CONSPIRACIES

DURING THE WEEKS that followed the Bishop's visit, Lady
Alyce was so busy that she all but forgot him and his threats
of revenge. The keep of Kyteler Castle was a village in itself,
and every corner of the estate was being cleaned—from turret
to stables, from the central castle buildings to the free-standing
peasant cottages in the adjacent fields. On the chance that it
might rain on Lugnasad and force the celebration indoors, all
the castle rooms and halls had been thoroughly swept, washed
down, and sprinkled with clover and fresh rushes; the tapestries
had been lugged outside and beaten free of dust, then brushed
with care before being rehung on the scrubbed stone walls.

In the dairy, fresh butter was being churned, and crocks of
potted cream were being stocked in the unused dungeons that
Alyce had converted years earlier into cooling pantries. In the
brewhouse, the air was heady with the scent of malt and hops
from fresh beer being steeped and golden ale recently hauled up
in kegs from the cellars below, where it had been mellowing
along with the elderberry wine that still waited down there,

chilling. In the larder, where the winter meats were aged, the bacon cured, and the catch of fish from the nearby River Nore salted down, the usually full salting tubs had been given over to the dipping of special candles for the Ritual, as no flesh—fowl, fish, or mammal—would be handled or eaten during this Sabbat or the days just preceding.

The bakehouse was steamy with aromas of cinnamon and honey, as batch after batch of crescent pastries—plump, dense, crushed-almond delicacies—emerged from the ovens and were set to cool. Alongside them rested still-warm loaves of parslied oatbread heaped in crisp piles on the worktables, ready to be carved into trencher-platters. Since Lugnasad was the festival of grain, a variety of breads were being mixed, kneaded, and baked. There would be barley cakes and wheat crisps, oat fritters, rye muffins, and bran pie-crusts. This Sabbat honoured Lugh, the ancient Celtic Sun-God who in his many-staged life cycle was child, brother, and consort to the Goddess; he was the Green Man who added his powers of fertility to hers to ensure that the grains grew tall.

All the inhabitants of the manor had been bustling about for days, preparing for the Sabbat.

Henry Faber, the blacksmith, had stopped by, together with his wife, also named Alyce and herself a smith as well as a skilled craftswoman at working with precious metals. They had come from their forge to fetch Alyce Kyteler's ceremonial dagger, the Athame, for sharpening and polishing, and to deliver a cask of their specially steeped vinegar for burnishing the pewter wine flagons.

Alyce's son William and his best friend Robert de Bristol had finally finished stacking ash and pear logs in tottery pyramids inside the shed for drying, later to be hauled out to the Covenstead for the Sabbat bonfire. That task, like every other for which the two lads were responsible, had taken twice as long as necessary, because the performance of each chore apparently required much jesting and argument about which of them young Maeve, Will Payn's bonny black-haired daughter, preferred. Then, under Alyce's watchful eye, the two reluctant lads had been assigned to wash the ceremonial red garments to be worn at Lugnasad. The linens had to be boiled, the light wools scrubbed with lye cakes, and the silks soaked overnight in warm white wine and water. Already some of the garments flashed, brightening and bellying with the wind—as tunics and kirtles, shirts, cloaks, gowns, and leggings danced on the drying ropes—a spectrum of scarlet and murray, ruby and vermillion, maroon and cherry.

Children ran errands every which way, gathering baskets of wildflowers—a gaudy harvest of velvety blues and greens soft as summer shadow—for weaving into garlands and dancing ropes; the littlest ones dashed about, playing and giggling. The air shimmered with energy and laughter.

By the day before Sabbat Eve, all this hustle had accelerated to a delirium of excitement. The whole manor was in motion, and at the hub of the whirl pulsed the castle's central kitchen. There, three women sat around the long oak table, relishing the periodic breeze that cooled them from the open door, and talking while their hands flew about their work.

Helena, recovered from childbirth, perched on a stool at one end of the table, her baby comfortably strapped to her back. Little Dana burbled contentedly while her mother worked at a leisurely pace, braiding what had once been a large heap of straw, wheat-stalks, flax, and wild grasses into many kirn babies, the grain dollies given as favors to Sabbat guests. Each Lugnasad, the previous year's dolls were cast into the bonfire for good luck, to be replaced with fresh ones who would stand guard yearlong on humble home altars, honouring the crops born from the Goddess's joyous mating with the Green Man.

Across from Helena, Annota Lange, a widow with a droll wit who was the manor's most talented spinster-seamstress, was making house-protection sachet charms as additional gifts for the guests, some of whom would be coming quite a distance from other counties. Spread out before her on the table were fragrant piles of powdered cloves and orris root, sandalwood shavings, dried lavender flowers, figwort, rue, ground allspice, and various oils and gums. The recipe was a simple one—eight parts of this to three of that, the whole wrapped up in a small square of unbleached muslin and tied round three times with red yarn. Later, Lady Alyce as High Priestess would hallow the sachets, invoking the name of Hertha, the Goddess in Her role as protector of home and hearth.

Petronilla de Meath sat next to Annota, her pale braids twined into a knot and bound up out of the way of her busy hands. She had been shelling peas and was now blending basil and sage leaves with a mortar and pestle, trying at the same time to keep watch over her daughter, Sara. That two-year-old sat on the floor with a wooden bowl and a small stone she wielded like a toy mallet, cracking hazelnuts and mixing up the shells with the nutmeats in an endearing if ineffective manner.

Petronilla, as she did lately every chance she got, had turned the conversation to her growing fears about Richard de Ledrede. By now, everyone knew of His Eminence's skirmish with Her Ladyship, and how she had bested him. But he had not left Ireland. On the contrary, he was ordering frequent parish assemblies in the Cathedral, summoning the townsfolk so that he might deliver speeches against evil-doing Jezebels in their midst. He peppered his sermons with references to signs of the Devil evident all around—claiming that Satanic eyes could be seen staring out from the circles on peacock feathers, warning that hair the colour of fire likely meant a person was marked for Hell, and repeatedly retelling the biblical stories of Bathsheba and of the whore of Babylon and their many husbands. Since Alyce Kyteler kept a pet peacock, had auburn hair, and had been multiply married, all of Kilkenny— indeed, all of Ossary—knew who he meant.

"That Bishop's after having Her Ladyship's soul in his pocket or her head on a pike," Petronilla declared. "One or t'other. I be telling you, the man is up to no good." She pounded the sage as if it were named Richard.

"M'mm, I dunno," mumbled Annota, breaking a strand of red yarn with her teeth. "I canna take him seriously. I mean, he, you know, he is so...*solemn*." She pulled a long face. "Hard to take seriously someone who canna even laugh."

Petronilla glowered. She was growing impatient with her friends' complacency. She was also concerned about what she perceived as her mistress's blithe indifference to danger.

"I dinna know much about anything, but this much I know. A body who canna laugh may be just the person you would want to take all the more serious. Are we not to care, then—about him calling these big meetings and firing up all the priests and people against Her Grace?"

"Dinna scold us, Pet," Annota protested mildly. "Her Ladyship keeps watch in her own way."

Helena blew off a few clinging kernels of wheat from the last kirn baby and placed the poppet into a large wicker basket along with all the other finished dolls. She rubbed her hands and frowned.

98

"T'is a fact," she murmured, "that the Bishop is calling a meeting with all the abbots in the diocese, aye. And when I brought the plums to market in town, I heard he now has all diocesan priests and monks attend on him in group audiences— pity the dears—to hear him lecture on 'the crisis of the Irish soul.' But Her Ladyship says t'is probably him just showing off— 'theatrics,' says she."

Helena and Annota exchanged glances.

"And by Holy Mongfhinn, Her Ladyship knows about 'theatrics!' " Annota laughed.

"What is there to laugh at, about Her Grace?" demanded Petronilla, ever defensive on behalf of her adored lady.

"Nothing, child," Annota replied. "T'is just that. . . well, Her Ladyship—like all nobles—knows how to show off, too."

"I dinna know what you mean. She dinna dress in finery or act like gentry folk—"

"Nae, she shows off different. By ignoring 'em. Pleasures herself showing how she *not* be one of 'em. And in her way, shows off for us, too. Pleasures in acting like one of us, some-times. Oh, naught *bad* about it, just funny if you—"

Petronilla leapt to her feet.

"Her Ladyship is the *kindest*—"

"There, there, Petronilla," Helena soothed, in the voice she used with Dana. "Sit down, sit down. We all know our good fortune to live under Lady Alyce's hand. T'is is only that . . ." she glanced at Annota again, who came to her rescue.

"T'is only that the great ones of the world strut their stories large, Pet," the widow said, "and t'is best we humble folk keep well out of their way. Our mistress, sure she's the best of her kind there be, aye. But when her kind does battle, t'is people like you and me can come to harm."

"But this Bishop dinna want to harm you and me, Annota. T'is Lady Alyce he wants to hurt!"

"This Bishop dinna even *see* you nor me, Petronilla," Helena chided, "He sees *her* because—well, t'is hard not to, round these parts. T'is what Annota means by using Her Ladyship's fancy word, 'theatrics.' But you need not worry much. A lot of what passes between highborn folk—even threats—be just talk. They have the time for it, dinna you see."

"Nae, he's plotting something," Petronilla scowled. "Something dreadful. I'm sure of it."

"Perhaps not," put in Annota, "Might be that the Bishop is lonely, wants for a bit of company, and canna admit to it—so he goes about calling assemblies. Have you considered that, then?"

"My thoughts exactly, Annota," chimed a hearty voice behind them. All three women rose instantly, then dropped to the floor in curtseys as Alyce Kyteler, enveloped in an enormous apron with five deep pockets, swept into the kitchen. "It might be that this pompous, blustery little man needs to feed his sense of self-importance. Up, up, on with your work," she continued, motioning for them to rise,

"It might be that his convocation will dwindle into one of those nostril-flaring rituals so many of the fellows like. Even if they *are* supposed to be chaste, priests are men nonetheless, you know. Ach, I want a bit of a sit-down."

She drew up another stool and sat down at the table, fanning herself with her apron; the women sat, too, returning to their tasks.

"I have been running about so much I hardly know how to stop," sighed Alyce, "I sampled the crescent cakes for the right texture, tasted an herb butter to correct the flavor, oversaw the last of the candle-dipping, and made myself hoarse shouting at William that he and Robert must at least *try* to pay attention to what they are doing, and secure those cloaks more firmly or the wind will carry them away like so many rosy clouds. That lad . . . I worry about him. He is *so* agreeable—yet he evades his tutors and idles when he should be learning oversight of the estate. It cannot have been easy, having all those fathers and not one of them a fit man. I thought young Robert would be a good influence, but now I wonder . . . . Will ought to be more respon-sible at his age. We must all keep an eye out for him, eh? I do not want him misleading Maeve Payn with false promises into some irresponsible act that she believes will end in wedlock. . . ."

Petronilla, unbidden, had fetched Alyce a cup of cool water. She drank it down, then smiled at her three women. They all smiled back.

"Not that I lack for critics who think me incapable of *recognizing* an irresponsible act," she chattered on, circling back to the previous subject, "Our Bishop, for instance.... Well, perhaps if these priests meet and preach and rail at each other long enough, they will tire themselves out and go play their games elsewhere." She shrugged. "This is *Ireland*, after all. No one in Ireland has ever been executed, or even prosecuted, for practicing The Craft. This Bishop, apparently bereft of a sense of humour, seems to forget that most priests here are Irish, so do not share his failing. Like dear young Father Brendan Canice, for instance." Helena and Annota chorused agreement.

"I think you've not yet met him, Petronilla," Alyce mused, "but he used to come round often. Such a sweet-faced man! Hearty laugh, strong arms, good heart—hair black as midnight and eyes blue as cornflowers. . . now *there* is a waste of a comely chap! Ah, what celibacy squanders!... His mother— she has parted now—was a Wiccan Lore and Legend Keeper. Wondrous Tale Spinner of the Seannachai she was, too! A Biddy Róisín story would shine and ripple like a waterfall in starlight. And that woman could raise fluffy curds from new milk with just three swirls of a red-hot poker in the churn! She would say, 'What today calls Magick, tomorrow calls Science.' Nice, eh? Well, Brendan—of course we'd known him as Sean Fergus—went off to study at Kells in Ceanannus Mór, and he was such a fine scholar they snapped him up to

be a priest. But on visits home he would still attend sabbats—
in secret, of course. He would arrive in this comical disguise,
having darkened his face with charcoal—you know, the way
the Morris Dancers used to do?—and having pulled his hooded
cowl way down over his eyes and having stuffed half melons
under his robe against his chest, as if he could masquerade as a
woman! Róisín would call out, "Thanks be! T'is my daughter,
the priest!" and we would laugh until our ribs ached with it.
Once here, though, he'd be grinning like a gnome, kicking out
the liveliest steps to be seen! He has not been to a sabbat in
several years, more's the pity. But I fear even if he did try to
visit, the Bishop watches his priests' comings and goings like a
hawk spying every twitch of the field mice below. Well, let him
spy all he wishes, if he has nothing better to do. . . ."

Petronilla blinked at the older woman, awed at how Alyce
was able to change a mood of fear into one of good humour. It
reminded her of tales she'd heard about alchemy, the skill of
turning dross into gold. If only Sara could grow to womanhood
learning such self-confidence, such indifference to what other
people thought—qualities her mother knew she herself could
never imitate. If only Sara might grow to be like this oak tree
of a woman—rooted strength against her enemies but leafy
comfort for those seeking shade from the world's glare. Even
Lady Alyce's rare melancholy or pain seemed to Petronilla
lofty, compared to her own vulgar troubles. The maid was

ashamed to admit that she might envy so much as the way
Alyce suffered—and it was clear to her that Sir John had made
her mistress suffer—since Petronilla loathed how she herself
cringed before her own pain. Not that her life had taught her
to do much else.

Petronilla was an orphan—her mother dead in the act of
birthing her, her father unknown. She had been a servant
since earliest memory, always trying desperately to please
others: first in the scullery of the convent where she'd been
raised from infancy, in Inistogue, a neighboring village to
Kilkenny and the place of her birth; later as kitchenmaid to
one of the gentry in the nearby coastal town of Wexford. At
the order of Cook in the kitchen where she labored, she'd married a man who had taken her by force one Twelfth Night, an
assistant flesher whose hands always seemed to bear the faded
red stains and gluey smell of the sheep and pigs he butchered.
He frightened her. But she tried hard to gratify his desires,
hoping that together they might create the family she'd never
known. She clung to that hope until the day she ran away from
him, taking Sara with her. Petronilla had grown used to the
beatings her husband regarded as both husbandly duty and
pleasure—but when he started striking their baby daughter,
she found within herself a courage she'd never known she
possessed. With the clothes on her back and her child in her
arms, she fled to the sanctuary of the Wexford parish church.

There, confident in her religious devotion as only someone with no other comfort can be, she threw herself and her child on the protection of her priest, Father Donnan. But Donnan was not one of Alyce Kyteler's jovial Irish clergy. He was a cleric who believed fear to be the greatest form of worship and punishment the sole excitement flesh deserved. He denounced Petronilla as a sinful wife who had abandoned her husband and betrayed the marriage sacrament. Then he instructed her to do penance: to say fifty Paternosters, return home, kneel and beg forgiveness from her husband, endure his anger in whatever form it came, then fast and flagellate herself for three days and three nights.

Petronilla de Meath lingered long hours in that little Wexford church that night, but she was not saying Paternosters. She watched her child sleep peacefully in her arms while she considered her life. She sat still, listening inside herself to something she could not name, something that felt like a shifting, a swelling, a crack opening in her heart. When she finally walked out through the church doors, she knew that now both husband and priest must be left behind—whatever else might lie ahead.

She sought shelter with Lady Alyce Kyteler of Kilkenny, a stranger whose name she'd remembered hearing from another kitchenmaid. That forlorn woman once had gone to Kyteler for a potion to free her from her eighth pregnancy, and had blessed

Alyce's name ever after. Indeed, from what was whispered about Alyce Kyteler by more than one woman, she sounded less like a noble lady than like a possible friend—even an *amchara*, the cherished soul-comrade ancient Celtic culture had celebrated, the parent of one's best self, trusted intimate of one's secrets, reflection of one's truest spirit. And Alyce Kyteler had in fact changed Petronilla's life.

Not only her physical existence but everything she had been taught to believe without questioning—everything—had been transformed at Kyteler Castle. She had thought the Church merciful, yet found her priest pitiless; she had believed the aristocracy cruel, yet, arriving as a stray, found a noblewoman who treated her like a guest. Now she had as much food as she might wish to eat; she had a clean bed and two small rooms all to herself and her daughter, with her own fire—of real wood, not peat—in her own hearth; she wore warm dry woolens in winter and soft muslins in summer. Now she was learning numbers and letters, music and laughter and friendship. After a year and a half, she was still struggling to adjust to this way of living: days and nights with no fear, the emotion that had defined her entire existence. Most miraculously, she watched Sara growing into these freedoms early enough so that the child might never acquire the scars her mother bore.

But now there was danger. Now Petronilla was terrified that the Bishop might harm this woman who sheltered them.

Now she was cold with dread that the violence of her former world would collide with the safety of her current one. With a sudden ferocity, she realized she would do anything to protect what Sara and she now had.

Such were the notions flickering through Petronilla de Meath's mind as she sat grinding herbs with a mortar and pestle at the kitchen table on the day before Lugnasad Eve. But she kept these thoughts to herself, glancing at her mistress and saying only, "Well, my Lady, may our Holy Saint Brigid grant you be right about the Bishop and his boyos doing no hurt to nobody."

All four women chuckled at the joke. Brigid was one of the oldest of all Irish names for The Mother—in Her capacity as Goddess of fire and keeper of poets, healers, and smiths. When the people of the Isles refused to cease their devotions to Her, the Church had created a new saint named Brigid— who quickly became the people's favorite. It was an ideal Irish solution, one with a wink: the congregation could now be good Catholics while still offering devotions to their older deity, and the priests could pride themselves on the conversion of so many souls.

"Yes, well, I admit the Bishop and his fellows are a devious bunch," Alyce agreed. "And if I seem unafraid, Petronilla," she added, "t'is because in times like these a witch learns to hide her feelings. De Ledrede was so wroth about my delivering a baby—

can you imagine what he would have thought if he suspected how many women I have helped *not* to have babies?"

"Here sits one—and glad of it," cackled Annota Lange, "four was three too many."

"So do not worry, Pet," Alyce continued, "I am on guard against the Bishop and his monks. I suspect he would like nothing better than to burn me as his first Irish witch."

"*No!*" Petronilla shocked herself by shrieking. "They canna have *you!* Never *you,* never! I canna let 'em!" She clutched her pestle like a club and glared across the table.

"Well let us not be so military about it!" Alyce laughed. "Truly, I would swear there must be warrior strains in your blood—not only that Anglo-Norman name, but the Viking ice glittering in that hair! Did you know, Pet, that the whole of Wexford county, where you were born, was settled by Vikings more than five hundred years ago? Perhaps you do come from warrior people!"

Petronilla knew that her mistress was trying to smooth the conversation toward another subject. But she could not stop circling, like a moth the flame, her own anxiety.

"I dinna know aught about my people. I dinna even know how old I am. My name—I dinna know if t'was my mam's or my da's, or if the Church give it me when they took me in as a foundling to raise me—"

"Well, you belong here now. They shall not get you back."

"But the Bishop—" Petronilla began again.

"The Bishop will not get you, either, Pet. You shall go on being safe and content, and raise wee Sara here to a happy womanhood."

"You could raise her for me. Better'n me. T'is a fact," Petronilla murmured, a tinge of jealousy shadowing the admiration in her voice—though whether it was jealousy of Alyce or of Sara she could not tell.

Alyce shot her an exasperated look.

"What kind of dismal talk is this for the day before a Sabbat Eve? Could we please forget bishops and plots and miseries, and concentrate instead on the holy-day? Much has yet to be done! We need to consecrate the Working Tools for the Ritual— which means that someone must go to fetch the Athame from Alyce and Henry. William could do it—that is, *if* he and Robert ever finish pretending they are knights jousting with those menacing billowy red clothes hanging out there SARA!"

Alyce let out a screech and dived to the floor where Sara sat silently turning blue as a Pict painted with woad. She had a nutshell fragment stuck in her throat, having begun to chew the shells once she had dispatched the nutmeats. One thwack on her shoulders brought the shell out, along with a fit of coughing. The delayed wail that followed worked beautifully: it maneuvered her onto Alyce's lap to be cuddled and successfully averted a scolding from her mother for her reckless eating habits.

As the crisis subsided, Annota brought out a gift for the little girl. It was to have waited until the following day, but seemed a helpful diversion now: a tiny kirtle embroidered with yellow thread—stalks of wheat against a deep orange background the shade of peachblush. Labor paused for everyone to admire Annota's needlework—which naturally had to be tried on and displayed by Sara at once, although intended for wearing at the Sabbat festivities. The child twirled around the kitchen, receiving applause from the four women and curtseying like a tiny queen accepting her subjects' fealty. Then Helena brought forth a snack of boiled oats and cream and hung a kettle on the fire, while the conversation turned to cheerier subjects than the Bishop's intrigues.

But Petronilla de Meath—stooping to clip fresh mint leaves for tea from the herb garden just outside the kitchen door—was not so easily distracted. She stood upright again and sighed, staring off into space, indifferent to the fragrant sprigs in her hand. Well in the distance, beyond the sunlit gardens and, further on, the paddocks, a small mass of clouds let loose a local rainfall; it advanced slowly, as a silvery column of mist, across the heath. But Petronilla did not notice it. She found herself imagining the Bishop of Ossory huddled in consultation with Father Donnan of Wexford Parish. One face was florid and fleshy, the other bony and pinched: greed complementing denial. In her mind's eye, these uneasy allies were conspiring with a common purpose as well as a common power. And despite Alyce Kyteler's reassurances, she was not consoled.

VI

THE SABBAT CIRCLE

IT WAS LUGNASAD EVE, the night of the Sabbat.

The heath was dimming toward summer darkness as Alyce Kyteler dressed herself. She did so slowly, with attention to each detail. Having dismissed her maidservants, she had bathed in warm water scented with rose petals, then blotted herself with a thin sheet of fine wool. She had brushed her damp long hair dry until it flamed in the candlelight, then left it hanging loose. Finally, standing alone and naked in her turret chamber, lit by the gleam of three candles—one red, one white, one black—she ceremonially anointed herself with Sabbat Oil.

"Blessed be my brain, that I may conceive of my own power," she whispered, touching the tip of her left-hand third finger first to the small clay bowl filled with heated oil, then to her forehead.

"Blessed be my breast, that I may give nurturance," she continued, again touching her fingertip to the liquid gold and then to each nipple point and to the hollow between her breasts where her heart had begun to pulse more strongly with excitement.

"Blessed be my womb, that I may create what I choose to create," she murmured, touching the warm oil to her naked belly.

"Blessed be my knees, that I may bend so as not to break." She grazed each kneecap with the oil, which had begun to give off the fragrance of the herbs and essences steeping in it: flakes of saffron, poplar leaves, hemlock, moonwort, cinquefoil, crushed almonds. . . .

"Blessed be my feet, that I may walk in the path of my highest will." She anointed the arch of each bare foot.

Then she stood still, the Five-fold Blessing complete, and inhaled the perfume of her own body.

Moving deliberately, she slipped into loose linen trousers of her own design and Annota Lange's tailoring, similar to but less restricting than the hose and breeches men wore. Then she donned a pleated linen gown with slender wrist-length sleeves, the whole dyed a rich strawberry red. She slid over her head a shorter crimson silk tunic embroidered at its collar and its hem in gold thread, with tiny pomegranates exquisitely worked in scarlet against the gold—Annota's artistry again. Last came an open, sleeveless, light surcoat of unbleached linen the colour of young wheat. Then she stepped into the soft leather soles of her best sandals, and strapped the thongs around her ankles. The Ritual Jewels would come later. For now, she took up a casket of rosewood inlaid with red enamel, lovingly carved with runes surrounded by spirals, cones, and whorls—the recurring images of Celtic art. With this secured under one arm and her graceful but stout ash staff in the other hand, Alyce was ready. She emerged from her turret chamber and descended the Great Stairs to join the others for the procession to the Cromlech.

It was a perfect summer night, clear and balmy, with the full moon agleam so that people barely needed their staffs to aid them in making their way across the fields. Leading the column from the castle to the Covenstead, Alyce smiled to herself at how foolish were Church accusations about witches flying on broomsticks and staffs. Let a priest try walking over the fields on a moonless night, she thought with grim amusement, lit only by candles carried in hollowed-out gourds as makeshift lanterns; let a priest move across hillocks and rabbit holes and other wee treacheries underfoot—and see if *he* can manage not to break his neck without something sturdy on which to lean. Although she did have to admit to herself that a sabbat made her so light-headed with pleasure she *felt* almost air-borne. Each time she approached a Ritual, she did so recalling in her heart the passwords with which she, like every Neophyte, had long ago entered her first Circle: *Perfect love and perfect trust.*

From all directions, people were moving across the heath, approaching the Covenstead. As they converged at the gently sloping mound inside the curve of standing stones, they embraced, their calls of "Merry Meet!" ringing through the night's stillness. Children scampered about, eager to show off their holy-day finery. Familiars and family pets—cats, dogs, now and then a lamb, a kid, or a tame robin or wren—circled, sniffed, perched, and were vocal in adding their various greetings.

Finally, when everyone seemed present, when the feast had been assembled but not yet unpacked from the hammocks and baskets of transport, when the infants had been bedded down cozily on quilts and the children had settled from frenzy to mere delirium, Alyce signaled to William.

That young man was torn between nervousness (about performing well in the dances), pride (over his dashing new leather hose), longing (that Maeve Payne would notice how well the hose set off his calf muscles), and jealousy (that she was watching Robert twirl his new mantle about). Consequently, he didn't notice his mother's signal until she repeated it: a second, firmer nod of her head, this time accompanied by a sharp look. Sheepishly, he drew from its silk wrappings the Horn of Lugnasad.

Three blasts young William blew upon the curved bronze throat of the trumpet, slow and stately—and something about the instrument transformed his breath into three calls, each one primeval, vibrating with mystery.

At the first call, the entire company, including the animals, fell silent.

At the second, they arranged themselves in a circle around the heap of pear and ash logs layered over straw.

At the third, Alyce Kyteler appeared, taking up her position on the southern point of the Circle. She bent and placed her staff at her feet. A sigh of satisfaction rose from the crowd, in welcome of their High Priestess.

She stood before a low stone altar—a broad, flat rock resting on two upright plinths, a smaller version of the great dolmen towering behind her, that massive capstone balanced on twin stone pillars. On the altar sat the casket, its red enamel seeming to glow in the moonlight. Alyce opened the box, and a low murmur of expectation rippled around the Circle. One by one, she brought forth her Tools of Art.

The High Priestess's Necklace she raised in dedication to the moon, then fastened around her throat: a crescent torc, a massive collar of thinly hammered gold incised with a rim of interhatched triangles. It framed her face like a ruff of light, giving off moonglow from above and her own flush from within. This was the Lunula.

Next she lifted the Talismanic Ring, its bevelled crystal stone winking like a star caught and clasped between the jaws of two serpents—one gold, one silver—whose intertwined bodies comprised the ring itself. This she slid onto the third finger of her left hand. This was the Ring.

A plain length of braided red yarn came next, to be wound and knotted about her waist. This was the Cord to bind the spells.

Then came the Moon Helmet of the High Priestess, its skullcap of burnished gold forming the base for two silver crescent points that arched upward. This was the Crown.

The other Tools appeared, more and more swiftly, as if in time to the quickening drum and tambour rhythms beat out by Will Payn.

A white cloth of fine linen, embroidered with a red and black Pentacle—the encircled five-pointed star—was laid directly on the altar stone.

The Bell, a small masterpiece of bossed silver with filigree of thistles and wild roses, was placed on the cloth.

The three-legged copper Brazier was then stood atop the stone. It would be lit with Elf-fire—flame struck from no metals—and sprinkled with incense, so that aromatic clouds wafted across the assembly.

The Athame, gleaming in its amber-studded scabbard, was placed upon the altar.

Then the last two, most powerful Tools of all, were brought forth.

With a loving touch, the High Priestess lifted her book shrine, its compartments of yew-wood nested inside silver that was nested inside niello nested inside bronze, all embracing her Grimoire, the volume of bound parchment leaves that comprised her notes, recipes, rituals, cures, meditations, and spells. This contained both personal and ritual secret lore, knowledge passed on and added to, Witch to Witch, generation to generation, from time before understanding—since, it was said, the Blessed Days of the legendary southern isles of Krete or Thera, called by some Atlanthis. This was her Book of Shadows. She set it at the corner of the triangular stone, to one side of the cloth.

Last came a small three-footed bowl of silver, rimmed with red gold and inlaid with black enamel. This was placed carefully on the Pentacle cloth, facing north. Here was the Cup.

It was the consecrated Cup of the Witches, the vessel of a hundred names: Cauldron of Cerridwen to the Welsh; to the English, Gwyneviere's Chalice; to the Christians, The Grail.

The High Priestess lifted a flagon and poured an arc of elderberry wine into the silver Cup.

She rang the Bell three times. The Coven held its collective breath as if in a single lung.

Then Alyce the Priestess grasped the Elf-fire taper offered her by Alyce the blacksmith. Touching the wick's spark first to the Brazier, she raised it high—and then with one swift movement cast it at the pyre. There was nothing. Then there was a feather of smoke, then a flicker spreading to sporadic flames, then a sudden rush of heat, and the lit bonfire blossomed heavenward.

"All mortal presences not Seekers! Leave now, or never enter here this night," the Priestess cried her warning.

No one departed.

Instead, one by one, each member of the assembly came forward and dipped her or his candle into the central blaze. The whole Circle sprang into clarity, a wreath of faces reflecting the light.

"*Spirits of Air, we welcome thee!*" Alyce's voice chimed through the silence. The entire assembly turned to the east, and Petronilla de Meath, acting as Coven Maiden, walked to that point of the Circle, bearing the Brazier now billowing its plumes of incense, in honour of the element of air. At the eastern point she set it down.

"*Spirits of Fire, we welcome thee!*" cried the Priestess. And the company turned to face the southern point of their round, where Alyce herself lit a torch from the bonfire and thrust it into a crevice in the towering stone behind her, one of the thirteen that loomed protectively around the frail human inner ring.

"*Spirits of Water, we welcome thee!*" she called. And watched with pride how a well-practiced little Sara, after a glance of reassurance from Petronilla, toddled diligently to the western point of the Circle, carefully bearing a wooden beaker of water dipped from the River Nore no earlier than dawn of that same day. Annota Lange, standing near the western edge, helped Sara put the beaker down without spilling a drop, after which the small celebrant beamed and hopped up and down at her own success—then suddenly was overcome with shyness and raced back to bury her face in her mother's skirts.

"*Spirits of Earth, we welcome thee!*" Alyce's voice rang out once more. Her son William stood forth at the north point, opposite from his mother, representing for this night young Lugh himself, the Shining One—Son, Brother, and Consort of the Goddess. He knelt, placing there a polished oval rock shaped like a stone egg, over which he poured a handful of salt, as symbol for the earth.

Slowly Alyce Kyteler drew the Athame from its scabbard. She held it before her, its point aimed downward toward the earth, as she stepped to the Circle's outer perimeter and, muttering softly, began to glide around it, like a fuse burning behind the backs of those gathered facing the center, enclosing them. When she reappeared to her people at the southernmost point, she sheathed the Athame, and rang the Bell again three times.

"*The Circle is sealed,*" she proclaimed. "*We stand in Sacred Space.*"

The night itself seemed to pause.

In the forest that ringed the heath, owls halted their pursuit and hares checked their flight. The breeze fell still. . . .

How long did they stand there, hand in hand? What has time, or even timelessness, to do with such a moment? All the time or timelessness that mortals can imagine strains simply toward the moment when hands clasp against the night.

They stood there long enough to reassure the wood creatures who ventured to the heath's edge, watching the scene with unalarmed curiosity, furred and feathered heads cocked to peer at this distant circle of other animals, all clad in sunset colours, their flower-garlanded heads nodding and murmuring to one another, sometimes together, sometimes individually; their upright animal bodies sometimes swaying as one, like a living garland of human flowers encircling the uncombed flames that shook themselves out, wind-tousled, at the center.

Now the people stood, arms linked, chanting to raise the Cone of Power—their words pealing in unison as if from the vaulted splendour of a single throat, resounding in waves through the charged air.

Danu, Macha, Badb, Morrigan, Cailleach, Brigid, Hertha, Artis, Astarte, Diann, Sybil, Tana, Hecate, Kore, Lillit, Andred, Rhiannon, Magog, Eryn, Scotia...the Names of the Goddess breathed through the forest, a freshet of energy....

Evoe! Evo Kore!...Night of the Waiting, between the first ripeness and the late harvest.... Days of the tall wheat, the graceful grain leaning into sweet summer winds.... As the Moon waxes in the Letter Tinne, as the star of Red Belligerence rises.... As this is the time of the Compact, the Ritual, the Door....

Clouds of incense turned incandescent by the moon's rays rose in puffs and streaks, silver flowers of fragrance nodding on silver stems of air.

...Chant the Word and let it free: as my Will, so mote it be! Do what thou wilt, an it harm none! For the Law of Three will return to you whatever you send against another thricefold.... Deflect all harm.... Protect. Protect. Protect....

The moon was now poised directly above the Circle, as if to listen to these observers of The Old Ways name Her waxing and waning. And so they did, murmuring The Charge of the Goddess:

Hear My words and know Me.

You call me by a thousand Names, uttering yourselves.

You call Me Eternal Maiden.

You call Me Great Mother.

You call Me Ancient Chaos.

Moon, I answer you, my opening and closing eye, the regenerating shape, the Possibility. This to remind you that You are yourself The Virgin, born always now, new, capable of all invention and all creation.

Lotus, I answer you, lily, corn-poppy, centripetal rose: the Choice. This to remind you that You are yourself The Mother, who unravels from Her own body, brain, and spirit each thread of the net that sustains You.

Earthquake, I answer you, flood and volcano flow: the Warning. This to remind you that You are yourself The Old One who holds the Key, The Ancient who knows the secrets that you know not yet you know, The Crone to whom all things return.

So shall I be the Goddess with No Name, The Nemesis, shrouded in Mystery, yet recognized in every heart.

Whenever ye have need, then shall ye assemble. To thee will I teach things yet unknown.

First, ye shall be free of all slaveries. Ye shall dance, sing, feast. Ye shall make music and praise and love. For Mine is the spirit's ecstasy. But Mine also is the joy on earth.

Love unto all things is My law. Keep pure your highest desires. Let naught stop you nor turn you aside.

Know that I am the Universe that ever spins.

My feet stamp on the brown earth, dancing, My breasts bring forth the milk of reasoning thought. My throat sings low the thunder. From Me springs all life, all death. I am rain-rush and mud-suck, sun-sear and drought-dust. I am the tidal ebb. I am the tidal wave.

I am Form.

I am Energy.

I am the Abyss from which all things proceed, to which all things return.

I am the rapture of being. I am the rapture of nonbeing.

Call into thy soul. Hear and know Me. Offend Me not with sacrifice or bargaining. Venerate Me only with a heart in gladness, never in fear.

For behold, all acts of love and pleasure are My Rituals. Therefore, let there be beauty and strength, power and compassion, honour and humility, mirth and reverence within you. And you who wouldst yearn and search for Me, know that thy seeking and yearning will avail thee not, unless thou knowest the Mystery: If that which thou seekest thou findest not within thee, thou wilt never find it without thee.

For behold. I have been with thee from the Beginning.

And I await thee now.

The stars seemed to freeze and focus, unblinking for a moment in their cosmic indifference, as if gazing across the empty vastness to this shred of matter, a watery world where on a small island a knot of mortal intelligences stood concentrating their powers.

Then a familiar voice rang out.

"Spirits of Air, we thank thee."

This time the entire assembly echoed gratitude.

"Spirits of Fire, we thank thee." Again the people's chorus.

"Spirits of Water, we thank thee. Spirits of Earth, we thank thee." And again the community.

"Mother, make of each of us a safe and secret island, sacred unto Thee. Mother make and keep us whole. Mother, make and keep us free."

This from Alyce, as she lifted the Cup and sipped the first drops of ceremonial wine. Then she passed it to her left, saying as she did so, *"The blood of the Old Ones courses our veins. The Forms pass. The Circle remains."*

Then Petronilla de Meath as Coven Maiden approached the altar, bearing a tray of crescent cakes. Alyce bowed to her in tribute, then broke the first cake, ate, and passed the tray to her left. One by one, each member of the Circle drank and ate, murmuring, "*Blessed Be grape and grain*," then passing along the Cup and the cakes with the words, "*Blessed Be thee and me.*"

There was still wine to spare at the Cup's return to the High Priestess, and there remained one last cake.

This she crumbled into the Cup, and these dregs were poured out onto the ground as libation to the earth.

Then the final words of the Ritual rang from Alyce Kyteler's lips:

"*Blessed Be, one and all. The Circle is opened. . . . Let the Feast begin!*"

VII

DIFFERENT HUNGERS

THE TOOLS DISAPPEARED, nestled safely back into their casket—except for the Necklace and the Ring, which Alyce wore still.

And the feast began.

There were platters of anise-flavored pancakes, and cheese-stuffed boiled eggs, and fried baby artichokes sprinkled with rue. There were creamy leek-and-walnut pastries and crusty pies secreting honey-raisin filling spiced with galingale and nutmeg. There were various butters—some flavored with sage, some with basil, some crunchy with filbert nuts—to spread on various breads: wheat, rye, oat, and bran. Cauldrons and tureens offered choices of warm and cool soups to sample: cabbage and almond, turnip and parsley, sorrel broth with figs, barley-fruit consommé. But the certain favorite was Petronilla's heated gourd and fresh pea concoction: a smooth, strained blend with onions, saffron, and cream; Will Payne announced that he would willingly drown in this brew. Cups, beakers, and bowls were filled and passed around, and into these were dunked lentil crisps, and delicately fried squash flowers.

Guests milled about and squatted or sat on the grass to eat, having piled their trenchers high with chunks of hard cheddar cheese, beet relish, dried apple rounds, and currant dumplings—amid dollops of freshly ground mustard and pinches of precious salt imported from across the sea in Lincolnshire. Beer and ale, mead and wine washed all this down, and there were ewers of pear cider and almond milk.

The confectionery was the stuff of dreams—and had been the subject of the children's dreams for weeks. Gilli-flower puddings, tansycakes with prune jellies, stewed compotes of bogberries, hazelnuts, cherries—and there were doucettes: sweet tarts of wild plums marinated in cardamom and sugared vinegar. Each new dish was met with applause and sighs of pleasure: a cheese custard called an arboletty, and tricreams—the plain cream whipped and carefully folded in with the quince-and-honey-flavored creams to form red, gold, and white spirals, an enchantment for the eye as well as for the palate.

The children writhed in agonies of indecision. Which to choose? Strawberries and rosebuds sautéed to a crisp in chestnut flour? Or a confectionery made from honeyed hawthorne flowers called a spyneye after the hawthorne's prickly spine? As drunk with excitement as their parents were tingly with wine, the children finally reached a point when they could not swallow one more bite. Which was just as well, since it was time for the feast to pause until song, dance, and digestion permitted

enjoyment of the menu's crowning moment: the Spectacle—
what cookery masters called the Subtletie, or the Illusion Food.

First, though, to settle the stomach and pleasure the spirit,
the music began. Pipes and drums, rattles and tambourines,
cymbals and shawms took up their rhythms, and for the next
hour or two, roundels of singers and braidings of dancers
celebrated their Sabbat and themselves—with young William
making a fine accounting of himself while leading the Spiral
Dance. Then, when throats were almost sore from singing and
laughter and when feet needed rest, the party assembled in a
looser circle around the bonfire, which had now subsided to a
steady, comfortable flicker. Certain couples had gone missing—
young lovers who'd paired off during the dancing and then
slipped away to enjoy the summer night rather more privately
and intensely, on a bed of moss or fragrant pine needles in the
nearby wood. Goddess and God they felt themselves this night,
and so they were.

But it was to the children, drowsy now with dance, sweet-
meats, and the late hour, that the Vision of Lugnasad would
appear. So, as the conversation grew mellow, the children
gathered in a smaller circle inside the large one, waiting,
sitting rigidly with the effort to stay awake.

Then, from behind one of the Cromlech standing stones
where it had been hidden, the Spectacle was borne toward
them. William carried it with painstaking balance on a silver

charger: the Illusion Food, the magnificent sculpture built of gingerbread, marzipan, and spun sugar. It towered almost four feet high, this statue of Lugh, the harvest's Green Man—a jolly poppet of sweetness. He was dressed in a short tunic of heliotrope leaves and candied rose petals, his features skillfully molded and adorned with bright, edible paints: lips red with sandalwood and alkanet, eyes lavender with crushed candied violets, flesh sun-yellow with dandelion powder, and hair green as any proper vegetable god's should be—a curly confusion of mint, mallow, and hazel leaves. In one chubby hand this Lugh held a sheaf of wheat, and with the other he seemed to point toward his own bosom, from which a cascade of ripe raspberries flowed, a painless heartstream of bittersweet fresh ruby drops.

The children gasped with wonder and Alyce gasped with relief as Will lowered the Subtletie safely to the ground. Now even the adults might crowd around to admire the handiwork, and to agree that never had there been such a superb Illusion Food at any Lugnasad. For its creator, Petronilla de Meath, applause and hurrahs broke out. She had for years in Wexford eavesdropped from her kitchenmaid's pallet and watched from her kitchenmaid's corner how Cook and others built such spectacles for the gentry's banquets, sculpting food into mythical beasts, heraldic coats-of-arms, and the figures of saints. Now she had combined that knowledge, along with her new learning of The Craft, creating this triumph. After her gourd soup, this! Of all the cooks present—everyone had prepared some part of the feast—Petronilla was the undisputed success of the evening. Her pallid face glowing, she seemed to grow less frail, more substantial, as Alyce Kyteler honoured her by handing her the chaffer and parer with which to carve and serve the masterpiece.

So intent was everyone on this dramatic moment, all faces turned toward the mouth-watering statue near the Circle's center, that no one noticed a stealthy band of intruders approaching: ten men swathed and hooded in black cloaks despite the warmth of the night. They advanced steadily across the heath, moving through the tall grass like phantoms, the moonlight trying to drag them backward by their shadows.

Meave Payn saw them first, as she turned to slap Will's hand from her thigh. By then they were only a few yards away.

"Cowans!" she cried. Then again, louder, "*Cowans!*"

People wheeled in confusion, their circle curling back into a crescent as the invaders penetrated it.

There was no need for an introduction. In the bonfire light the identification was clear. It was Richard de Ledrede, Bishop of Ossory, with an escort of nine priests.

The Coven and its guests parted to permit their High Priestess passage. Alyce Kyteler strode forward to stand between her people and the Bishop.

Four steps behind de Ledrede, a troubled Father Brendan Canice found himself realizing that it had been a while since he had last seen Lady Alyce. Now he stood awkwardly in the Bishop's train, facing a scene he knew he had rightly feared would put him in conflict with his priestly obedience, because it roused his Celtic loyalties in blood-surges through his veins.

Holy Saint Patrick, he thought, staring at Alyce. *She looks like a fever-spirit! Or like one of those gold-leaf capitals in the illumined books the monks at Kells spend their whole lives trying to paint.* Her people were clustering densely behind her, their ritual garments a layering of scarlets and sun-golds, as if they too were letters—of a script more ancient than Ogham runes, more powerful, more mysterious—letters Brendan had once been able to read with ease, though now they felt locked, secret and silent, against him. He noticed a few hostile looks directed at him from some of the folk who had known his mother well, and he hazarded a small smile back at them—but was met with stony, closed expressions.

"Hellions! Devil's whelps! Heretics!" It was one of the priests, screaming like a soul in torment.

"Blaspheming heathen!" yelled another.

The Bishop gestured to his men, and they fell silent. Then, in a voice of authority, he proclaimed loudly,

"Satan, *begone*! I cast you out! This defiled, barbaric gathering is hereby disbanded! Nor shall you blasphemers ever convene again!" He made the sign of the cross over the crowd.

"Bishop, *you* blaspheme *our* Rite," Alyce Kyteler replied, her tone of command matching his. "Who then is the barbarian?"

He took note of her necklace and her ring.

"Madam," he said stiffly, "You do your followers ill service by leading them to worship false gods. Have a care, Madam, to openly flout the Church and all that is holy." He looked past her to the assembly. "Have a care—*all of you*—for your own spiritual salvation!"

"So we do," Alyce replied coolly, "Have a care for *your* spiritual salvation. See to it now. Depart in peace."

Richard de Ledrede had never in his career faced public opposition and dismissal from a layperson, much less a woman. He was livid at her calm, condescending manner.

"These idolatrous rituals shall cease *now*, this moment! *All* of you—return to your homes at once!"

No one moved.

"This is my final warning," he declared, "I have been patient with you people. But I cannot show you lenience when you deliberately offend Heaven! *This apostasy stops now.* Else I cannot hide you from the wrath of the Lord! I cannot protect you from the condemnation of the Church!"

"Perhaps not," Alyce said. "But you can *count*."

Accustomed to plots that raveled slowly and in stealth at Court, de Ledrede was unused to making swift tactical decisions in action. Now he realized that she was again, infuriatingly, right. He and his priests were considerably outnumbered. He needed time to think. . . .

But the other Wiccans, taking courage from Alyce, began to edge forward.

"T'is a two-faced turncoat coward *ye* are!" Sysok Galrussyn suddenly bellowed at Father Brendan Canice, "Is this what ye learned from all the fine books? Ye know damnable *well* what Wicca really means to—" But Eva de Brounstoun silenced Sysok with a stern look that reminded him never to betray to cowans the identity of anyone who was or ever had been Wiccan.

Then a tall monk, so thin he was almost skeletal, lunged toward the bonfire. He pointed his bony finger contemptuously at the remnants of the feast, his mouth working, so filled with spite no words came forth.

With a sudden frost at the heart, Petronilla recognized him. It was Father Donnan, her old parish priest from Wexford.

"Gluttony!" he finally hissed. "You gorge as of the forbidden fruit. You eat your way into sin. You chew sin, savor sin, swallow it, digest it, defecate it! You store up food for the worms of your rotting flesh! Filth to filth you add! You cram your maw with death—"

"That will do, my son," the Bishop interrupted. But Father Donnan, unhearing, ranted on.

"It is the Apple, the Original Sin! That is what leads to every debauched pleasure of the vile body. All other sins—pride, wrath, envy, sloth—are vices of the mind, lesser than those of the putrid flesh: gluttony, greed, lust! *You must kill all appetite!*

Starve the flesh, thrash out its hunger! Fasting and flagellation alone lead to salvation! We must all fast or be damned!"

"My son! *Silence*, I say!" The Bishop barked, feeling himself slide into the sin of wrath while defending that of gluttony. Still, his order had its desired effect. The zealous priest fell back, muttering.

But his outburst had been sufficient to provoke an implosion in Petronilla de Meath. She now flung herself forward, like a spark from the fire, to step between Alyce Kyteler and the Bishop. Her spindly body was shaking, and her words came shuddering out.

"Ach, Bishop, *Bishop*," she cried in a trembling voice, "whate'er else you may or mayn't be, t'is a consecrated leader of the Church you stand—an' that before Heaven itself. How then can you call that man 'son'? He be a cruel one, oh Bishop! He be a man with no droplet of Christ's compassion in all his starving soul. *He* be the man, Bishop, who did drive me from the Sacraments! *He* be the man who did drive me from the Church!"

Richard de Ledrede studied Petronilla, then glanced at Father Donnan, at Alyce Kyteler, and back at Petronilla. Slowly, he extended his hand with the Bishop's ring toward her, as if baited with a blessing. Petronilla swayed toward him dizzily. Cursing, Henry the smith leapt forward to restrain her. But Alyce Kyteler's arm shot out, *her* Ring of Office still gleaming on her hand, and Henry stopped mid-stride.

"Freedom is our law," she murmured to him, "As her will, so mote it be." Yet her tone was as tense as his body.

"Daughter?" coaxed de Ledrede to Petronilla, his voice now rich as whey, "How can I help you, my precious lost lamb? How to wrap you in my keeping and bear you safely home? How may I rescue you, my child, from the peril before which your soul wavers?"

Like an aspen tree in a storm, Petronilla de Meath stood quaking under his gaze, bending to the enchantment in his voice.

Alyce Kyteler's raised hand bound the Coven motionless.

Father Brendan watched, riveted. He felt as if they were all suspended in this moment, a single moment lasting as long as the *brevima dies*, the eternal Sacred Day that Stands Outside the Year, at the Winter Solstice.

"Dear daughter," the Bishop crooned, "You know where you truly belong. Dearest daughter, baptized child of the Church. You are in error. Let not error keep you from salvation. The man you accuse is a consecrated priest. You must not question his actions. Nor must you let a single stern pronouncement, intended for your own good, drive you to damnation. Reward yourself with the great mercy of the Church. Come back to your own people. Let the community of saints welcome you. Little lost lamb, let me shepherd you home. . ."

Like a woman walking in her sleep, Petronilla staggered one step toward the Bishop.

Alyce swallowed to keep the tears from rising, but her uplifted hand still held the assembly in check.

Woodenly, Petronilla took another step.

Then, as if from far off, safely behind the Wiccans' ranks, a faint, sleepy voice piped out.

"Mumma? Mumma, *where* you? Mumma!"

It was Sara.

Her voice broke the Bishop's spell.

Her mother began to speak again—slowly, disjointedly, yet gaining confidence with each word.

"Shepherd me? Home? To you? I am home. Your Eminence, I be home here more than any place in all my days. These be my people now. Kind people, honest folk and generous. What they do—what they *be*—lets me. . . know hope. Aye. Lets me *hope*. Fitting t'is they be called the Wise Ones. To me, *they* be holy." She began to cry, drifts of tears like moonlit diamonds strung across her face.

"Ach, Bishop," she shook her head sadly, "Reared in your Church I was. Reared *by* your Church. I dinna know no world for all my days *but* your Church. I believed. I obeyed. I *loved* your Church—t'was the one thing in the world I loved till Sara came to me. I dinna understand much, yet ready was I to sacrifice *all* for love of your Church—that deep did I thirst for divine mercy." Her words began flowing more swiftly. "But I found no mercy there. And now I be knowing something. I be knowing ye have a power. Ye get a hold on a person's spirit.

I be knowing *him*"—she jerked her head toward Donnan—
"for a foul hater of life. There be a meanness of soul in him,
like some wound afestering. And if ye excuse him and clasp
him as one of yourselves, then nae, nae, *none* of ye are worthy
of Jesus Christ—who was also the Hanged Man on the
Summer Tree, like the Green Man Lugh. Aye, Bishop," she
mourned, "t'is you who are the barbarian. So now I too say
what others be saying about your ways—and I say it proudly."
She drew in a quavering breath, and spat out all her sorrow
and fury with the words, "*Fie, fie, fie, amen!*"

Then she whirled and sped back through the crowd to
her child.

But the Wiccans, catching fire from her heat, began to
shout at the priests in anger. Alyce Kyteler lowered her
restraining hand. People started to surge closer to the
clerics, yelling.

Richard de Ledrede, frightened at the possibility of being
crowded round by rabble, struck out blindly in the nearest
direction, and hit Eva de Brounstoun hard in the face. Father
Brendan heard himself cry out in indignation at the blow—
but even as he leaned to catch the falling woman, he saw in
the passing instant that Alyce Kyteler appeared transformed
before his gaze, as if into the warrior goddess Morrigan—
carved staff in hand, hair streaming, vengeance whistling
through her teeth and dazzling from her eyes.

"Holy Mother!" he called out—too late.

Alyce smacked her ash-wood staff deftly at Richard de Ledrede's substantial target of a stomach and he went down like a struck tent, all silk panels flapping.

Then, as if by signal, there was uproar.

Henry grabbed one of the monks in his brawny arms and tossed him playfully, as one would a ball, into a hillock. His wife Alyce grasped the Athame she'd so proudly sharpened and swung the large dagger in a wide arc around her head, creating a circle all her own upon which no one, priest or witch, was eager to intrude. Young Will was charging about, swatting at anything that looked like a cowan. Helena and her husband Sysok were thrashing two monks with whips of roped flowers, but their anger was so energetic that the clerics seemed not to realize what gentle weapons were being used against them. Eva de Brounstoun, wheezing with rage, crowned another priest with a pastry coffyn, the last drips of its blueberry filling staining his surprised face azure as a Celt's painted for battle. Even little Sara, wide awake now, joined in what she took to be a jolly adult game and began pelting cassocks with juicy plums that often hit their targets with a satisfying *splat*. She had a talent for catching one cowan in particular: the stringy zealot, Father Donnan, who by now was so decorated with fruit and crumbs, so streaked with creams and butters, as to qualify for a Spectacle himself.

At last Richard de Ledrede and his pack retreated across the heath, pursued for a while by Wiccans yelling, "Blasphemers! Intruders! Barbarians! Go back to Rome or Avignon! This is *Ireland!*" Limping along with his fleeing colleagues, Father Brendan furtively scooped up some quince cream staining his cassock and licked his fingers, grateful that the night and his cowl hid a huge grin he could no longer suppress.

Finally, the last of the Wiccan pursuers straggled back to the Covenstead. More wine was passed round. Alyce moved steadily through the crowd, stooping to inspect any scratch or bruise, though no one was seriously hurt. Slowly, people regained their breath. A few tried to resume the celebration.

But the conversation was now mere chatter, and the feast felt soured by violation. Then Helena saw that Dana was fast asleep at her breast, blissful mouth still clamped on her nipple, so she signaled to Sysok to gather their things. That seemed a sign for others to start packing up and preparing to leave. One by one, family by family, they did so, murmuring their farewells.

"Merry Part until we Merry Meet again."

Will Payn ambled among the departing guests, sweetening their spirits with the music of his small harp. At last he settled down amid the remaining few and leaned against a stone to softsing the words of *The Song of Amorgin*, older than memory:

"*I am the womb of every holt,*" he sang, echoing the poet who had imagined the words of The Goddess, "*I am the blaze on every hill, I am the queen of every hive.*"

Alyce Kyteler sat quietly beside the dying bonfire. She was deep in thought, her fingers turning the Talismanic Ring round and round on her finger, her eyes fixed on the glimmering garnet embers that occasionally erupted in a few last tongues of flame.

"*I am the shield for every head,*" sang the harpist, the ancient words reassuring in their eternal indifference, "*I am the tomb of every hope.*"

Watching her mistress so withheld in silence, the Ring turning and turning, Petronilla de Meath felt chilled by a night wind that sprang up from nowhere. Clutching a drowsy Sara in her arms, she shivered and drew closer to the fire.

VIII

FRIENDS AND ENEMIES

BABY DANA ITCHED. Her howls left no doubt about that in
the mind of anyone within earshot. Baby Dana definitely
itched, and Alyce had been lightly rubbing her rash with a
cooling salve—soured cream in which had been steeped
leaves of savory, calamint, and tarragon, together with finely
ground salt and pulverized cucumber—to prevent infection
and ease the itching. Now she was murmuring nonsense words
of comfort as she cuddled the babe in her lap, feeding Dana
sips of weak burdock-and-chamomile tea. Alyce had spiked
the tea with a drop of fermented apple cider, so that the
infant—and her parents—might eventually get some sleep.
The two were sitting on a stone bench in front of the Galrussyn
cottage, waiting for the child's parents and grandfather to
return from Kilkenny Town where they'd gone to sell surplus
vegetables at market.

Dana was cranky and restless, so to make the waiting pass
until the tea took effect, Alyce rocked her slowly, and sang
the old *Song of the Running Seasons:*

I shall go as a wren in spring
with sorrow and sighing on silent wing
and I shall go in the Mother's name,
Aye, till I come home again.

They shall follow as falcons grey
and hunt me cruelly as their prey
and they shall go in their master's name,
Aye, to fetch me back again.

Then I shall go as a mouse in May,
in fields by night, cellars by day,
and I shall go in the Goddess's name
Aye, till I come home again.

And they shall flow as black tomcats
and chase me through the kirn and vats,
they shall go in their master's name,
Aye, to fetch me back again.

Then I shall go as an autumn hare,
with sorrow and sighing and mickle care,
and I shall go in the Mother's name,
Aye, till I come home again.

But they shall follow as swift grey hounds
and dog my tracks by leaps and bounds,
they shall go in their master's name
Aye, to fetch me back again.

Then I shall go as a winter trout
with sorrow and sighing and mickle doubt,
and I shall go in the Goddess's name,
Aye, till I come home again.

But they shall follow as otters swift
and snare me fast ere I canst shift,
they shall go in their master's name,
Aye, to fetch me back again!

The song was usually sung as a round, with the opening verse recurring at the end—but Alyce was trying to ignore a sense of foreboding as the theme of pursuit continued, so she was relieved when Helena, Sysok, and Old John could be spotted approaching, down the path. Their cart was drawn leisurely by Maude, their old mare who stolidly refused to be rushed. But today Maude's passengers seemed impatient to get home.

Helena jumped down before the cart had completely stopped. Bobbing a curtsey to Alyce, she rushed to pick up her daughter, hugging Dana and inquiring about the rash.

ROBIN MORGAN

"Better, I think," smiled her mistress, pushing a strand of hair out of her eyes. "The salve seems to be clearing it up and the tea helps numb the itch." Dana's eyelids had finally begun to droop, but as her mother laid her across one shoulder, patting her back, she offered a contented burp.

"Actually," Alyce confided, "I think she is tipsy from the drop of cider. Looks ready for a nap. I will leave the rest of the cidered tea with you for using tonight if she turns fretful. You all need some sleep. You look a bit overwrought."

At a glance from Helena, Old John took his granddaughter from her, worshipfully cradling the baby in his arms, and carried her inside for her nap. Meanwhile, Sysok unhitched the mare while Helena flung herself down on the grass near Alyce.

"Produce sell well at market?" Alyce asked, stretching like a sun-warmed cat now that she was relieved of her bundle.

"Aye, m'Lady," replied Helena, fanning herself in the heat with her wide-brimmed straw hat, "though we'd so much summer squash I feared we'd never be rid of it. Yet it sold off right away—as did the pears, and every one of the lettuces. But never no mind to any of that. There be news we heard in town— grave news and much of it. I dinna know where to start."

"At the beginning is a customary place," smiled Alyce.

"T'is hard to know where that is, M'am. Our troublesome Bishop has not idled away this past week since the Sabbat. He took himself off to Dublin—to the Lord Justice. To demand that a writ be issued. For your arrest!"

"My arrest, is it now?" Alyce laughed. "Well, this bodes to be interesting. The Lord Justice is Roger Outlawe—kinsman to my son Will."

"Aye, M'am, that he is," replied Helena, "and he flat out refused to oblige the Bishop. Said such a writ could not be issued until—ach, how was it now?"

"Until the accused parties have been proceeded against at law?" Alyce asked.

"Aye, aye, that's it!"

"Indeed," laughed Alyce, "thanks to what remains of our Celtic Brehon law."

"De Ledrede oh, he dinna like that one bit, Your Ladyship. There was raised voices. People say he stormed out from the meeting, shouting and all, saying that the Church was above, you know, regular law, nonreligious law—how do they call it—"

"Secular law. Well, you have to admire the man," Alyce said mildly, "He does not give up easily, does he? And him not even Irish!"

But that, as Helena explained, was only part of it.

Sysok, having released the mare to graze, now reappeared, eager to participate in telling the news. Granted permission by Alyce to sit, he joined his wife on the grass. Then John emerged from the cottage. He eased his aged body down onto the stone steps with a few grunts, then reached for some thin strips of soft wood from a pile beside him and swiftly started bending and binding the staves for a barrel. Everyone knew that Old John was unable to sit still without doing something, but his gnarled cooper's hands knew his materials of wood, tin, and leather so intimately after a lifetime of cask-making that he worked by touch, not needing to look at what he was doing. Nor did he glance at it now, intent on watching the others and being included in the conversation.

Apparently the Bishop, rejected by the Lord Justice, had left Dublin and taken his personal crusade to the Seneschal of Kilkenny, Sir Arnald le Poer. This gentleman, though a relative of Alyce's most recent husband, nevertheless had also defied de Ledrede. He had refused to prosecute.

Alyce blinked with amazement.

"You cannot mean that John's family is actually *supporting* me after all this time? Oh, that is simply not possible! The le Poers regard me as a shrew and a hag!... Though if what you heard has any truth to it, then I would wager it can only be because Arnald has always disliked my husband—his cousin—intensely. Some old family fight about inheritance. So Arnald might see this brawl as a chance for revenge at John, with me as the pawn in his game."

"Aye.... Or else t'is loyalty to his own," Sysok ventured— adding, half under his breath, "Nobility hangs together in the end, whilst the rest of us plain hang."

"Oh *Sysok*," Helena interjected, seeing a blush shadow Alyce's face as she overheard him, "these people be not regarding Lady Alyce as family or nobility for years now."

"I dinna believe that," he mumbled, with a cautious glance at his mistress, "I dinna believe 'these people'—though I dinna mean *you*, Your Ladyship—*ever* be forgetting who shares their blood-lines."

"*I* believe," Helena persisted with a frown at her husband, "t'is not blood relations nor marriage bonds nor any such connections mattering in this rebellion against the Bishop. *I* think t'is a certain well-known Irish willfulness at work. Bless us, when the troubles come, we turn *more* stubborn, and somehow stand together. The troubles *bind* us, heathen and townsfolk, even the nobles, say I. All we need is something to be *against*— and sure the finest thing of all to be against is a foreigner who dares to meddle in our ways."

"*That* threat on occasion has even tempted us to ally with the Scots—an extreme remedy," Alyce grinned.

"Aye," Helena laughed.

"Howsoever that may or mayn't be," Sysok interrupted, annoyed at the drift into international politics when local matters right under everyone's noses were in need of attention, "I be *trying* to tell Her Ladyship some more *news* here, the Scots aside. See, m'Lady, not only did the Seneschal throw the Bishop out, but then he be declaring in public that de Ledrede—he calls him 'this vile, rustic, interloping priest'—had. . . oh, some words like. . . "

"'Exhausted his patience and outraged his sense of honour,'" Helena prompted.

"Aye, t'is close enough," Sysok said, "I knew outrage and honour were there somewhere." Then he mumbled, "Always are, with gentry and nobles."

Alyce chose to ignore the mumble and clapped her hands with pleasure.

"*Good* old Arnald! Perhaps this pawn of his should send him a cask of wine! Considering that he has dared to—"

"Please. Dinna be celebrating yet, Your Grace," Old John put in quietly, "There is more, and t'is *not* good news. The Bishop was publicly shamed, M'am. That makes the man more dangerous. Now he has gone to rally support— from the filthy English knights who stole those lands 'round Kilkenny."

"But John, there are so few of them. And they are never *here*. They all live abroad—thanks be."

"That matters not," Sysok all but snapped. "Pardon me, Your Ladyship. But what matters is he's sought them out and written to them and got their pledges to aid him. And here's the black heart of it: with their support of men and arms, he has—ach, how'd they say it—gathered—"

"Convened," interjected Helena.

"Aye, that's it. 'Convened' an—an. . . a church court—"

"An ecclesiastical court?" this from Alyce.

"Aye. And whilst himself was lording over that—"

"Presiding over it," Helena corrected.

"—*presiding* over it," Sysok shot a glare at his wife, "and whilst himself was presiding over it, he excommunicated you, Lady Alyce. Just like that."

"Summarily excommunicated! I *am* crushed," the lady said dryly. "Now I cannot attend mass anymore. Oh lackaday."

"*Will* you be taking this seriously?" Sysok complained, "Oh—again, begging your pardon, m'Lady, for my being too. . . but t'is *daft* to be lighthearted when—"

"Your Ladyship, on this point Sysok be right. *T'is* somber news. And t'is not the worst, by far. Hear us out, please," Helena added, urgency rising in her voice. "Through that court, the Bishop. . . M'am, he has accused you of *sorcery*. Formally. Seven charges."

"Seven!" said Alyce, "Rather excessive. I should have thought one would suffice."

"*Seven*," repeated Helena. "You stand accused of renouncing your Christian faith, of mocking the Church and the Sacraments, of making pacts with the Devil to swear obedience, of possessing magick powders and poisons, of practicing divination and medical sorceries—wait, how many is that?"

"Five so far," Sysok said tersely. Then he added, with embarrassment, staring down at his large, calloused hands, "Sixth is the charge of—pardon me, m'Lady—of, ah. . ." he cleared his throat, then forged ahead, ". . . consorting with the Devil in the shape of a black man who was Robin Artisson.

The Bishop claims he has witnesses who saw you, together with the Devil, more'n two summers ago, in a lewd dance—"

"What? But no Moors have visited me in—why, it must be almost a decade. That is *pure* imagination! There is not even an acorn of gossip from which to grow such an oak of a tale! No, *wait*...unless...that's it! It has to be! My having danced at some sabbat with Sean Fergus—you know, Brendan Canice—a priest, to boot, in his foolish charcoal-covered disguise!"

"Aye, well your precious Sean-Brendan not be sabbat dancing now. Too busy scuttling after his Bishop like a pet rat."

"Now Sysok, be fair," Alyce chided, "Sean Fergus was ever a decent man. T'is not his doing, this madness. Though when I heard he had been sent for to wait upon the Bishop, I admit I hoped his presence might soften de Ledrede."

Sysok was not one to be charmed out his denunciation nor deflected from reporting his list of Church accusations.

"May that turncoat rot in his Christian hell. Now where was I? Six?"

"Seven, dear," put in Helena, now trying to keep track of both the list and her husband's temper.

"Oh, aye, the seventh charge. Well, t'is...pardon me again, M'am...t'is about your having, ah...intimacy with the Devil in the shape of your Familiars, a black cat and a white goat—"

"Holy hell!" exclaimed Alyce, immediately realizing that her oath was, in the circumstances, not the wisest. "Now Prickeare and Greedigut are my paramours? Poor beasts!"

"*And*," Sysok continued grimly, "of making charms and ointments with—ach, beastly stuff. Dead men's fingernails, animal innards, flesh from dismembered babies. They say you boiled it all up in the skull of a beheaded robber.... Begging your pardon, Your Ladyship."

Silence descended, as the group sat, taking all this in.

"Oh. And he also charges you with murdering your first three husbands," Helena whispered, as an afterthought. "He demands you answer every charge, m'Lady."

Alyce roused herself as if from a daze.

"Answer every charge? Answer even a *single* charge? I shall do nothing of the kind. His religious court is not empowered to judge *me*. About the charge of murder he *will* get a reply—of sorts. I shall *sue* that madman for slandering my character and the Kyteler name. Pacts with devils! As if it is likely I would swear obedience to another male, human *or* inhuman! Nothing personal, Sysok." Alyce threw him a glum smile. "But truly, who *does* de Ledrede think will believe such lies? He himself cannot believe them! "

Helena bit her lip, reluctant to add more details yet knowing she must.

"Well, he be claiming he personally witnessed the devil-worship."

"Oh? And where was that? In his Cathedral, where he keeps his devils stored?"

"At our Sabbat, M'am."

"Then we *know* that he is simply *lying.* Helena, I have talked with this man at some length. He is a servant of the Church, yes. He goes in his master's name. And he is certainly full of himself. Keenly ambitious, I suspect. I am sure he is capable of doing harm. But I have glimpsed in him a sophisticated mind. He *cannot* genuinely believe that at our Sabbat he saw—"

"He says everyone was garbed in Satan's colour."

"Oh, and red is not the shade worn by archbishops?" Alyce sputtered.

"And he be claiming he saw a small girl forced to caress the Devil, who went sniffing about in the form of a shaggy black dog—"

"Who could he possib—you mean the way Sara rides around on Tyffin as if the little hound were a pony?"

"More," Helena went on. "He says the wine casks were abrim with a poison liquid. He says bats and frogs were swimming in it."

"Feh," Alyce made a face, "The vintners will not appreciate his compliments. Or is he blaming it on your casks, John?"

"And," Helena added, "he claims you pointed a sorcerer's wand at him, m'Lady, and then he was sent flying through the air without being touched. Aye, aye, *t'would* be funny if t'weren't so demented. But most horrid of all, he be swearing he spied the burnt remains of newborn infants he says had been thrown into the fire—he swears he saw a dismembered child, bleeding from its chest, lying hacked to pieces by the stone altar. There. T'is the whole of it." Finished with her list, Helena sat back, breathless.

Alyce pondered the last items.

"Now where could his fevered brain have conjured *that* from?" she muttered.

Then she had it.

"*The kirn dollies,*" she whispered, "*And Petronilla's Spectacle.*"

"What?" chorused her companions.

"Yes. Of course!" Excited now, Alyce began speaking rapidly as she thought aloud. "That *must* be the answer. The Bishop saw last year's discarded kirn dollies lying in the embers. . . and when he and his priests came upon us—just *think* about it—we were beginning to carve up Petronilla's marzipan Green Man. . . and de Ledrede—de Ledrede's perverse mind turned that into a human sacrifice. The kirn poppets: burned babies. The Spectacle Food: a dismembered child. But surely he *knows* that we would never—wait. . . wait. *He* eats the body and blood of *his* god, so he actually might assume that we. . . Great Morrigan, the man might *believe* what he is saying. . . ."

The four of them fell silent again as the full impact of the Bishop's accusations sank in.

Then Alyce broke their reverie. But she spoke with new resolve.

"It is time to move against this man, I think," she declared. "We must adapt with the seasons—be a wren or a mouse, a hare or a trout—when we find ourselves pursued. It is time to unpack the gowns and the jewels, and masquerade as a Lady. It is time for me to travel to Kilkenny Town."

*   *   *

Early the next morning, an increasingly peevish Alyce Kyteler sat and stood, and sat again, and stood again, in her chamber. She was being attended on and attired as befitted the Dame of Kyteler Castle—"being arrayed in my armor," as she put it. The procedure required five hours, three of her women—Petronilla, Helena, and Annota Lange—and layers of preparation, decoration, and clothing, all of it accompanied by a running commentary of intensifying irritability from the subject of these ministrations.

First came a white silk chemise. Then there was the "ordeal," as Alyce groaned, of sitting still to have her hair dressed: the long thick carroty mane brushed, combed, pulled, twisted, and gathered up into a silk net studded with pearls; the sides tightly braided in ten tiny plaits from each temple and then wound in whorls and pinned with silver clasps; and the front held back by two high amber combs that, she snarled, "feel like tiny pikes jousting at my scalp."

Little did it help that Annota kept trying to distract her mistress with chatter about how much worse it could be: wearing the old cone-shaped hennin headdress with the floor-length hanging veils, for instance, or that new-fashioned turban all the ladies were beginning to copy that took half a day to coil properly, or the latest style from Burgundy, the houppelande—a heavy, pleated skirt so voluminous its wearers could barely stand up straight. As a seamstress, Annota tried to up with such things. But Alyce's mood grew still more sullen when the wimple—of pure white linen, as befitted wives and widows—was wound around her head and tightly under her chin. A small, opaque, white silk gorget was draped over it—"I may as well be back at the convent," she muttered crossly—and a third white veil, this one long and of translucent silk, over that. Atop the whole, a diadem of beaten gold was firmly pressed, "to keep me from sailing away in all my cloth flappings."

Grumbling with disbelief that she could ever have worn such "adult swaddling clothes" daily, Alyce was then laced into a bodice embroidered in gold thread with the Kyteler crest, but Helena's energetic lacing made her lady swear in a most un-ladylike manner. The bodice was followed by a wide skirt of heavy dark blue silk that hung to the floor and pooled there, ending in a three-foot-long weighted train, its border patterned with Irish thistles worked in silver thread. Separate lemon-coloured sleeves of stiff brocade reaching to the middle of her hands were then fastened to the bodice, buttoned with pearls at the shoulders and buttoned again, tightly, all the way down to the wrists. They made her feel, Alyce growled, as if her arms were carved from willowwood, incapable of all but the smallest gesture.

The cyclas—a knee-length, sleeveless, open-front tunic of dove-grey silk banded in tissue of silver—came next, topped by an additional long sur-coat of pale blue brocade with crystal beads sewn along its edges. There would also be, before departure, a full-length wine-coloured cowled mantle of thin wool—although Alyce had flatly refused to wear the fur-rimmed cloak proper to her rank even in summer. For now, however, all that remained to be done was gird her waist with the belt of indigo-blue-dyed leather, from which hung the aumoniere—the leather purse "containing the bribes," as Alyce sourly noted. The transformation was completed by decking her with a heavy gold necklace chain, two waist-length strings of pearls, two bracelets of gold and one of silver inlaid with garnets, and a large ring on each hand: emeralds embedded in gold on one, a walnut-sized ruby clasped in silver on the other. Petronilla knelt, holding out the gold-embroidered black velvet slippers with curled toes for Alyce to step into, since, so attired, her mistress could not bend.

"*No!*" that lady shouted. She tried to turn her head to face her women, but could only rotate stiffly, from the waist, and her face was bright pink with frustration. "*Not* those evil shoes! I have been pinched, laced, and combed. I have a headache from so much weight on my skull. I can barely move, and I am *suffocating* under so many layers in this heat. But some things I will *not* do. I will *not* wear furs in Lúnasa—t'is late summer! And I will *not* wear shoes shaped like no human foot and designed for a woman who will be carried everywhere in a litter. And no, no, *no*—I can see it coming in your expressions—I will *not* ride to Kilkenny in a covered horse litter, no matter what gossip is fed by my traveling in an open cart! I would ride Tissy, as usual, if I could—but the poor horse would perish under all this weight! But *no* litter!" She paused, braced for argument. Her women said nothing. They bobbed curtseys, exchanged glances, and stared intently at the floor, trying to stifle laughter behind pursed lips.

"That settles that, then," Alyce announced. "I shall wear my hemp sandals. At least my feet will be comfortable, even if the rest of me feels so cramped. No one can see my shoes anyway, hobbled as I am in fabric stretching for counties round my ankles." She huffed and drew herself up to sweep haughtily across the room. But the train threw her off balance, destroying any attempt at dignity. Wobbling, her arms stuck out to steady herself, she was reduced to pleading, near tears, like a petulant child.

"Will someone please find my sandals? And help me maneuver myself downstairs?"

And so they did, enduring at every step her rancorous denunciations of the Bishop for being the cause of her having to suffer such a wretchedly fashionable state.

But it was no petulant child who arrived that evening in Kilkenny, accompanied by a small party of retainers and—shockingly enough to the townsfolk—riding in an open cart, drawn clattering through the narrow streets that rapidly filled with onlookers. It was Her Grace, the Most Noble Dame Alyce Kyteler, in full splendour.

Annota Lange and Petronilla de Meath attended on her ("to help resurrect me tonight and then re-inter me in a different set of shrouds tomorrow morning"), and young William rode his prized stallion, looking very adult as her formal escort. She brought four men-at-arms with her, and succumbed to Sysok's plea to go along as a member of the retinue; once in town, he was joined by burly Henry Faber, who insisted on leaving the smithy and accompanying them for further protection. Touched by their concern, Alyce refrained from telling them that she was quite certain her purse, clanking its beckoning melodies, was the most reliable protection of all.

Indeed, when they disembarked at the inn, taking all of its rooms, the reception was royal. It was as if the legendary Queen Diedre had alighted—in full panoply, with baggage, ceremony, and personal court—in Kilkenny Town.

IX

DAME ALYCE wasted no time.

The first afternoon, in full grandeur, she swept through the Seneschal's palace, calling on Sir Arnald by surprise, thanking him for his support, and genially expressing hope that, "Since your cousin, my husband, our *difficult* Sir John" was no longer in residence at Kyteler Castle, their families might again be "close and loving," as if they ever had been. She also brought "a humble symbol of sisterly affection" for his wife—twelve generous lengths of clover-green crushed velvet imported from France. Lady Megan, flattered by the thought and delighted at the lavishness of the gift, became an instant ally bent on ensuring that her husband would help their kinswoman-by-marriage in all ways possible, and who would remind to do so him until he did. His aid was further secured when Alyce confided to him that she had found several documents her husband had left behind, writs apparently in Arnald's favor regarding his and John's old quarrel about contested le Poer property.

By the end of the following day, due to several judicious disbursements to district administrators, Alyce's purse was lighter. By the next day, those officials and their clerks had become eagerly cooperative—providing her with access to county documents covering the previous two years, including records of all civil and criminal proceedings at law—with their silence about such cooperation as part of the purchase. A further lightening of her aumoniere resulted in the heavy registers and ledgers being (somewhat illegally) carried to her at her lodgings, since she felt it would be both impolitic and uncomfortable to sit poring over papers in public at the Registry—not to mention the fact that she would have to be attired in full state if she left the inn but could wear a cool linen gown if she did not.

Thus ensconced in her rooms, Alyce spent the hours from early morning to late at night scanning entry after entry. She slept little and ate little, despite special meals that Petronilla insisted on cooking in the kitchen of the inn, bringing trays to her mistress of, she sniffed, "better fare than any public lodging can present," thereby offering the innkeeper's wife a mortal insult.

Petronilla went early each morning to the Kilkenny marketplace, to buy the freshest goods she could find. There, strolling with her basket among the stalls of vendors—privately scoffing at the idea of purchasing what she was now accustomed to plucking fresh—she also tried to pick up whatever gossip she might overhear. But there was a new tension in the air, and women hawking their wares or bargaining to buy them seemed unwilling to chat. Indeed, some of the marketwomen, recognizing her as a member of Dame Alyce's retinue, clucked at her, making the sign of the Evil Eye, a pair of horns, with their fingers. At that, a group of small boys began trailing her steps, whispering, laughing, and tossing pebbles at her until she hurriedly finished her purchases and left the market. She told no one back at the inn about these encounters, and refused to let her own timidity deter her from returning to the market each day, sweating with nervousness, to do the shopping she insisted was important for her mistress's diet and health. But she recognized that amidst the pungent, friendly market smells—freshly caught fish, ripe melons, imported cinnamon spice, live caged ducks, crisp-baked meat pastries—was the distinct odor of fear.

Meanwhile, hour after hour, head aching, eyes stinging, Alyce read on, despite pleas from Annota to rest and bathe her eyelids with cucumber juice. She had no fixed notion of what she was looking for, but she felt confident that something would emerge, and certain that she would recognize it when she saw it. So she made her way through the lawbooks, growing angrier with each page as she encountered cases where imposed English law or imposed Church law had been used to manipulate or flatly overrule Celtic Brehon or indigenous common law. She had known that this sort of thing happened,

ROBIN MORGAN

but abstractly. Now, reading through the records, she saw faces in the lawsuits: the man whose hand had been cut off for poaching a goose later found to be his own—as he had claimed all along—yet to whom no reparations had been paid by the accuser; the woman who had been denied a Church marriage annulment and then was sentenced to be publicly whipped for fleeing the husband who had beaten her almost to death. . . .

Then, one midnight, when all her people were asleep and she was alone, hunched over a table peering through air smoky from constantly burning tapers, *there*—the third-to-last page of one of the few ledgers left—she found it.

It was an old deed of accusation, still unsettled, in the criminal records of Kilkenny. It charged Richard de Ledrede with having defrauded a widow of her inheritance shortly after he had first arrived in Ireland.

"*Checkmate!*" she whispered fiercely. "*Now* I have you, little Bishop! Scuttle in any devious diagonal you choose. But never forget that a queen can move as far as she likes in *any* direction."

* * *

Richard de Ledrede knew that his adversary had been in Kilkenny Town for days. He even expressed anxiety about her "dark purposes," as he put it, to Father Brendan—who had now taken to staring at the wall and saying as little as possible,

162

in hopes of being judged stupid and sent back to Kells. But the Bishop, too canny to believe the young scholar a dolt, kept him at his side, waiting for the opportunity when he might actually prove useful. One midnight, pacing the floor in his apartments, trying to calculate what Alyce Kyteler might be up to, the Bishop thought of just such an opportunity.

Early the next day, he dispatched a desperately reluctant Father Brendan to attend on Her Ladyship at the inn, to find out her plans.

"Sean Fergus! Merry Meet!" Alyce exclaimed, when the priest was announced and then ushered into her rooms by a disgruntled Annota Lange. Rising from her worktable, Alyce moved to embrace him. But he knelt before her, his usually genial face a portrait of distress.

"Lady Alyce," he pleaded, "I *beg* you to believe me when I tell you that I have had no part in leveling these hideous accusations against you! I hope and pray you do not blame me for—"

"Sean, Sean! Of *course* no one blames you!"

Annota, standing warily by the door, registered disagreement with a harrumph.

"That is sufficient, Annota," Alyce said, "Thank you, you may go. " Once the widow had stalked out, Alyce turned back to her guest. "Do get up, Sean, and have a seat." He rose to his feet but remained standing. "Have you breakfasted yet? You look thin. Your mother would have said you want feeding."

"Thank you, my Lady. I have no appetite."

"Oh dear! Are you unwell? I can—"

"No, no, I am well enough. Merely miserable. *He* sent me—though I admit, t'is truly glad I am to see you."

"And I you, my dear," Alyce replied, not needing to be told who "he" was. "Poor Sean Fergus, how painful it must for you, caught betwixt as you are. I saw you at the Sabbat and I knew you would rather be feasting with us than spying and decrying with him. Can you not get away, back to Kells?"

"T'is not for want of trying, I can tell you that."

"Well, I suspect it will all be over soon enough. Will you have some mint tea, at least?"

"No, my Lady, thank you. I cannot stay long."

"But do sit *down*," she commanded, "I must apologize for such clutter—" deftly sweeping the books off her worktable, and throwing a quilt over another pile of ledgers on the floor "—but you know how absurd I am about books! It seems I cannot even come to town to visit relatives unless I bring along a small library!" She located a bench from under another pile of books, slid the volumes behind a tapestry, and pointed him to the seat.

For the first time, a smile warmed his face, and he sat down.

"Oh, I remember well enough. I am the same now. I caught the disease from you, and a fine contagion it is. Lady Alyce, I want you to know that I shall never forget—and I shall be eternally grateful to you for them—those long soft-blue summer evenings when you sat with me so patiently and first opened my eyes to the wonder of books, the miracle of reading and writing."

"Well, the lessons were mutual. You were my first student. From you I learned *how* to teach. From you I learned how much I *loved* to teach."

The priest blushed.

"I—I was a tad touched, y'know. . . . With you."

"Ah, Sean—or should I say Father Brendan? No? Sean it is then, and always shall be, to me." She also coloured slightly. "Adam was dead but a year then. And me in my mid-twenties. And you but three summers younger. . . . "

"Aye."

"Well. . . . Well, t'is all long, long ago."

"Oh, aye. That it is. Aye."

"T'is indeed. Aye."

"Aye."

Neither knew what to say next. Finally, Alyce rescued the conversation.

"A fast learner you were, too! I mean," she added hastily, "about your letters. I know not which of us was prouder of you, Róisín or me."

"You changed my life. My mother knew that, and it pleased her so. Though t'is glad I am that she never lived to see me in *this* predicament."

"How can I help you, Sean?"

"T'is the reverse, my Lady. How can I help *you*? I have tried everything I can think of. I have pled with His Eminence so often and so long that now he largely refuses to hear me. I have counseled him that The Craft poses no threat to Christ's teaching. I have told him that what we saw at the Sabbat were not murdered bodies but cut up cheeses and burnt kirn poppets, that Wiccans do not keep animals as lovers, that your healing has brought health to many and harm to none. He must *know* in his heart that you sent him flying through the air at the Sabbat not by pointing at him but with a hearty blow from your staff; he *must* know that—he probably still wears a bruise from it! I have spent nights through trying to work out what *drives* the man. Does he actually *believe* the charges he lodged against you? I still do not know. Is he mad? I think not. Is he a religious zealot? Possibly, although I doubt it. Can anyone be so cynical as to wreak such damage simply because he has been told to, in direct opposition to Christ's own teachings? Why, I ask myself *why*?"

"Sean, the answer is simple. *The answer is that it does not matter.* I too have spent nights trying to scry his motives— which are probably a mixture of many things, since he is human, like you and like me. What I have come to is that ultimately his motives matter not. His actions do."

"But surely intention is a great part of—"

"—yes, but if I remember accurately what the nuns once taught me, the Church places as much or more emphasis on intention as on commission. The Craft, on the other hand, regards the two as one—the same, a seamless cloth."

"Then what—"

"My dear. Richard de Ledrede is merely a symptom of a greater sickness, and while I may be able to treat the symptom, the sickness itself is one for which I know no cure. We live in dangerous times, our lives ruled by men far from us, far from our lives, our experiences. They are men who love to hold power over others, who *live* to do so, and who doubtless have convinced themselves that what they do—no matter how cruel—is for the good of those who suffer and perish from their doing it. This much I know: almost no one committing evil *believes* he is committing evil. T'is an interesting quirk of humanity—one that, could we ever learn enough about it, might one day save us all, since it must mean that at heart even the worst villain *wishes* to do good."

"Hearing you reminds me how greatly I have missed our conversations, Lady Alyce. But I am here to—he sent me to *spy* on you, my Lady! I am so ashamed!" He buried his face in his hands.

"Why need worry, when you shall fail in your mission? What is there to spy on? I have come to visit with the le Poers—surely that is permissible. You and I spoke about your dead mother, who was my friend. You did not even break bread or take tea with me."

"My Lady, please. You must flee. He—he. . . he plans to make an example of you, to prove his diligence to the Pope. These charges are. . . no one in an Ecclesiastical Court will ever find you innocent. I know you care naught about being excommunicated. But you will be *condemned*. You could be burned alive!"

"Nonsense."

"No! T'is *not* nonsense! You *must* get away, to Wales or—"

"I shall *never* be driven from my home and lands, Sean Fergus. But *you* must flee. Get away, my dear, keep trying to get back to your studies. I could send you a potion that would convincingly make it appear as if you were mortally ill for a few days, so perhaps he might let you—"

"But now I *must* stay here. Only I can testify to your innocence before his Ecclesiastical Court!"

"And thereby endanger yourself to the charge of heresy? I think not. However, I also assure you that such a trial shall never take place." He groaned, and Alyce chuckled. "Nor am *I* mad. Or a religious zealot. Although I confess to a tincture of cynicism at times. . . ."

"But now—"

"Now you must go. Return to the Bishop. Inform him that Her Grace has thought deeply on the charges. Inform him that I will attend on him later today, before noon, at his Residence."

"You will attend on...*why?*"

Alyce stood and held out her arms to him, saying nothing.

"Holy Brigid, my Lady! To recant?"

She did not answer him directly, but she smiled, "Well, if recanting would stop such viciousness, it might be worth it, Sean Fergus, might it not? Mere words, after all? Words offered with the *intention* of making peace?"

In a confusion of relief, dismay, and bafflement, the young priest leapt to his feet and rushed into Alyce's embrace.

"I cannot—I will help you any way I can—but I know not what to—to..."

She held him a moment. Then she murmured,

"Now be on your way. And fear not, my dear. Róisín watches over your ways, even as The Mother watches over *all* our ways. Go. Bring your bishop my message."

He bowed and kissed her hand, then walked to the door.

"And...Sean?" He turned.

"Blessed Be."

He bowed again, and smiled.

"Blessed Be, my Lady."

Then he turned and was gone.

Annota Lange, in the door before his footsteps on the stairs had faded away, demanded to know what he had been after. But Alyce assured her that the meeting had merely been a courtesy visit between old friends, a teacher and her very first student, and that underneath his cassock Father Brendan Calice was still the Sean Fergus they had known and loved. The widow was not satisfied with that answer.

But her dissatisfaction could not compete with the Bishop's, when his priest returned to the Residence bearing at first somewhat similar, innocuous information. Nevertheless, Richard de Ledrede was greatly mollified and even more greatly excited to learn that Dame Alyce would be calling on him before midday, possibly—although his priest could not proclaim this for certain—to discuss recanting.

As for Father Brendan, while neglecting to tell his superior that he had confided numerous details to Lady Alyce, he realized he could honestly report that *from* her he had really learned nothing at all.

X

BISHOP TO QUEEN'S PAWN

TRUE TO HER WORD, later that morning, attended by her full retinue, Alyce Kyteler descended on the Prelate's Residence at St. Canice's Cathedral.

When word was brought to the Bishop that Dame Alice actually awaited him in his reception chamber, he felt elated. A recantation from so prominent a rebel would surely sweep other Irish apostates in its wake. He might be able to return to Avignon sooner than he had hoped, in triumph!

Enjoying himself, he poured a cup of wine and sat savoring it, deliberately keeping his caller waiting as long as he dared. But in less than half an hour, his manservant informed him that Her Grace was about to depart, so he rushed to his reception chamber, fearful that he had gone too far and might lose his prey.

The noblewoman Richard de Ledrede encountered was as different from the peasant wench he had first met as she was from the infidel priestess he had later confronted. He was taken aback, for a moment thinking that perhaps the witch actually could *become* three different females. Yet there was something recognizably consistent in her expression, although certainly *this* woman—arrayed according to high rank and station—was more to his liking than either of the others. Impressed by her taste, her jewels, and the cut of her watered-silk pale rose gown, he decided that he could afford to be magnanimous. After all, he had her in his power. She was here, alone, a penitent about to recant and submit to his authority in public contrition.

"Your Grace," he said, bowing formally, "Welcome to Kilkenny Town and to my Cathedral. It is a prudent action that you take, and you shall discover that I am not a man of petty revenge. We will find ways to set your penance so that it is tolerable and not as harsh as some may—"

"For you," she said. She neither smiled nor rose to greet him. She simply held out a scroll of parchment.

"For me? Me?" he stammered, confused. "If you have written out your recantation, that was unnecessary, Your Grace. You could have dictated to my clerks any—"

"Read it."

She sat there so regally that he felt diminished, a petitioner in his own house. He scurried to where she had enthroned herself, took the scroll, and backed away as he unrolled it. But one glance at the parchment script was enough to send his heart pounding. He looked up at her, then back again to the scroll, then back up again at her.

"My lord Bishop," she said coolly, "You issued ultimatums when last we met—when you brought disrespect and violence to our Lugnasad Sabbat. I come bringing neither disrespect nor violence. But I do bring a reciprocal ultimatum."

He felt fear rise and wash over the residue of his jubilation.

"You. . . are not here to recant?"

He looked so genuinely devastated that Alyce found herself pitying him. She chose the gentlest tone she could muster in the circumstances.

"No, my lord Bishop. I am not here to recant."

"But, but. . . why. . . what has *this* to do with—" he waved the parchment at arm's length as if it might curl closed with a snap, devouring him.

"I am here in the hope that you and I can solve our dispute in peace, between ourselves. If you give me your word that you agree to cease persecuting my people and my person, then that paper will be quietly returned to the county annals to gather more years of dust. Well, in truth, the parchment you hold is actually a fair copy—but I have the original in my safekeeping, which I will then return to the Registry. Afterward, you may re-convert as many of us Irish as you can catch—or at least you can try. But not here. Not in Kilkenny. Not in all Ossary. "

The Bishop groped toward the nearest chair and sat down heavily.

"If you do not agree, then I must tell you that I intend to revive the charge, and have public proceedings opened against you."

"This is extortion!" he whispered, incredulous.

"Perhaps. Or perhaps it is a case of a woman who has means pursuing justice almost two years late on behalf of a woman who lacked means."

"You actually would—you would—"

"I would. Doubt me not."

"But I could have you arrested *now*, right *here*! I could—"

"No. You could not. For one thing, my women wait just outside that door, and they can be rather fierce. With them are a few of my brawniest 'followers,' as you would put it. *And* my men-at-arms. *Your* men-at-arms, by the by, are off enjoying a leisurely early luncheon at the tavern, with unlimited tankards of ale—at my invitation and expense. They were so pleased to be offered such a treat, and this not even a saint's day."

The Bishop stared at her.

"Come, come, my lord. Why look so ravaged? This is a good bargain we might strike! You are left your reputation intact, and in exchange, we are left our lives in peace. As I recall, you care greatly about reputation—an understandable concern for a man well on his way to becoming a cardinal prince of the Church, perhaps one day even Pontiff? Why not?"

Rigid with anger, de Ledrede could not yet reply. Unfazed, she continued. As she talked, she removed one of heavy pearl necklaces from around her neck and stripped off the emerald ring, placing them both on the small table next to her chair.

"You once invited me to dine and implied that we might become friends, my lord Bishop. I should not necessarily dislike that."

His eyes on the jewels, he bit out each word:

"You dare try to bribe me!"

"Why no, my lord. What a thought." She tugged a silk kerchief from her sleeve and serenely began fanning herself with it. "I merely feel warm. As you know, I am at heart a country lass, unaccustomed to being indoors in summer heat—and unused to town finery." She left the jewels where they were, but picked up her earlier thought. "Were we to forge our own peace, I might prove a powerful friend—one who could support your ambitious crusade for advancement at Avignon."

"You know nothing of me or my ambitions! And what can an admitted witch possibly know of politics at the Papal Court?"

"That they are not much different from politics at any other court," Alyce shrugged. "With sufficient finances, a cardinal's red hat would be well within your reach. As for knowing you, I am a diligent student, and have managed to learn a bit of your history. You are a fascinating man. I know that your mother died when you were a child, and that your father was given to express himself in blows rather than words. I know that he often filled your home with his strumpets; t'is little wonder you think all women whores. I know that one of your older brothers died in a tavern brawl and the other became a tanner and saddler, that your sister had scrofula and died young, and that your father assumed you would follow him in the family trade."

She paused, watching him flush dark red.

"Yes, my lord. Trade. I know that he refused your pleas to become a scholar. I know that you surrendered your hopes and made a disastrous attempt to follow family tradition. . . as a petty merchant."

"You know. You *think* you know, Your Ladyship. You know nothing. You were born to privilege and you wallow in it, unaware, free, so free that you can afford even the ignorance of not realizing you wallow in it. *Look* at you. How could you possibly know what it feels like: to squander your intellect on London tradesmen in tawdry commercial scuffles over a few sordid pence; to be forced to do business with Jew moneylenders; to compete for a clientele of fine lords and ladies who scorn you; to grovel for the patronage of nobles like yourself!"

"So you rebelled. Well, I applaud you. You ran away and took religious orders: rather a dramatic rebellion, that. Tell me, did you choose to become a Franciscan and adopt the most altruistic vows of any order—"

"—the better to serve suffering humanity—"

"—the better to distance yourself from grimy commerce?"

"You *are* a devil!"

"Oh dear, back to that again, are we? Why *does* your kind always attribute insight to a demonic impulse? As if obtuseness were a holy value? Were all your saints idiots, then? Unlike you, sir, I do have faith—faith that not all good people need be stupid."

The Bishop smiled grimly at his guest.

"What a clever woman you are, Your Grace. I know not how your informants ferreted all this out from the long-buried past. But it matters little. I can tell you the rest, so you need not exhaust your spies further."

"Not spies, my lord. Scouts. In your case, I requested information that might be helpful to a student of human nature, like myself. But for some time now, my...curious couriers have proved useful to me as a lone woman managing the affairs of a great estate. They tell me of trends and markets and wars on the Continent. They ask questions, speak with neighbors, sift through public records. They listen. They read county registers and district annals, craft-guild member lists, law proceedings, birth and death rolls. Not so different from the Church's information-gathering arrangement— but for three exceptions: mine is infinitely smaller; my couriers do not accept slander as fact; and no one in my employ tortures people."

"No need to, eh? The nobility simply has them murdered outright?"

"My lord Bishop, if you insist on—"

"Oh no, Madam. You wanted my personal history, and you shall have it. I fled to Italy, but I am sure you know that. There I encountered a banquet of learning—theology, philosophy, languages—all within my grasp. You were not the only intelligent student in the world, Your Grace. The Church *noticed* me, while everyone else ignored me. I applied myself. And so I rose, gradually but steadily, from priest to monsignor. In time, I was judged worthy to be sent to France, to the Papal Court. There I was…it was as if I had been transformed. The place itself…the south of France, with its golden light—"

"—and golden opportunities? With the realization of how many occasions there were for a shrewd young man to seek advancement in the Church?"

"Your sarcasm, Madam, is unwarranted. You have not been to the Court at Avignon, or you would not speak of it so dismissively. It is an earthly paradise. There, fountains dance in sunlight throughout lush gardens, and the larks sing counterpoint to Gregorian chant. There, peace is no longer an *idea* but an *experience*. There, exquisite art, sophisticated discourse, and sumptuous feasts are all daily devotions celebrated as often as Mass—and every part of this is accomplished in a seemingly effortless manner. There, daily life is miraculous."

"Due to great wealth, which is never effortless. While daily life is always miraculous. So. In Avignon, you discovered how heady earthly power could be, and the myriad ways it might be obtained—"

"—to work all the more effectively for mankind's redemption! Although I do not expect you can believe that."

"Oh but I can," she said slowly. "None of us becomes who we intended to be when. . . when we first chose the path to a then-certain destination. We are fortunate if the path approximates any resemblance to what we originally thought we were selecting. . . . Nor is it possible to decipher when, where, or how one began to change, subtly, along the way—since one has no vantage point from which to perceive the entire terrain."

The Bishop raised his eyebrows in surprise. For a moment, he found it difficult to remember that he was facing an enemy. Rarely had he felt so recognized.

"Yes," he admitted, "What you say is true. I discovered a new universe—one of delicate moral shades, more challenging yet more soothing than the simplistic blacks-and-whites of my youth, when I was so pathetically straining to live as a parody of Saint Francis. But no matter the path I chose, the Church was there before me, with answers to all my questions. I found my salvation, in this world as well as the next, through the one institution wherein a man might move from impotence to

power, to live and act as the equal of those who are born—
callously, unjustly entitled—into it."

"Like me," Alyce said softly.

"Like you," he answered, nodding. "Yes, Madam, those born
to power like you. You can afford to play at being a peasant, you
see. I was only a step up from *being* one. I know you as well as
you know me, though with fewer specifics. I have met your type
before among the nobility; ones who act beneficently toward
their inferiors, but always for their own purposes—beguiling
them in the process, as you did with my obviously corruptible,
incompetent men-at-arms. You personify the ideal mistress to
your serfs—but one day you will get bored with them, or the
peasants you have indulged will actually begin to take themselves seriously. Then nobles like you fling the wretches out,
back on Church alms again, which they need to augment the
pittance you have allowed them, just to stay alive."

Alyce flinched. But she chose to ignore this remark,
pursuing her own strategy instead.

"Yet we have something in common, my lord. As you
noted, we both struggled to become lettered. We both—"

"And we both became lettered. Highly educated, in fact.
But here is the bitter joke, Madam: we were both educated *by
the same institution*—one I embrace and you deny. What an
ingrate you are, Your Grace! What a hypocrite! You would
champion your allegedly defrauded widow—but if I *relent*, you

stand ready to abandon her *and* her case, summarily. Or will you seek her out and bribe her, too? You posture, you extort, you threaten, you bribe. A true noblewoman! So arrogant, indifferent, and immoral that you deign not even recognize your own malevolence."

Alyce's eyes flashed.

"Hearken to me, Papal Emissary. You and your Church leave a blood-soaked trail of forced conversions in your wake—and you call *me* arrogant? You hunt down people; you accuse them on evidence of rumours based in spite or envy; you torture them to extract confessions—and *I* am immoral? You coerce them to name other innocents, more victims for more condemnations; you condemn as a heretic anyone who dares dispute an Inquisitor's verdict; you spill human agony from your cornucopia of conquest—and *I* am malevolent? You burn *alive* living human flesh—"

"Have you ever actually attended such an execution?"

"*Never!*"

"I have." The Bishop rose. He walked slowly to the large bronze crucifix hanging against the far wall. There he paused for a moment, then turned and walked back to stand in front of his visitor, his hands clasped in front of him.

For a moment, Alyce glimpsed Richard de Ledrede as a young boy—a beautiful, somber child, all large eyes and hurt—and the image blurred disturbingly in her mind with Will's face.

He stared at his hands and spoke quietly, intimately.

"You look on me with horror and contempt, Madam. Well, so be it, so you may—though I think that is a sluggish intellectual conclusion. But I do at least insist you acknowledge that I have not come to where I stand easily. I am no simpleton. I can tell you personally that the theologians and the poets need not imagine the Inferno. An execution *is* Hell. Livid, in life, *now*. Conceivable. Actionable. Unspeakable.... Although it becomes more...endurable with familiarity. Like any other hell, I warrant." He suddenly lifted his head and muttered fiercely, "I vowed to be an instrument of the Lord's *peace*. I vowed to *serve* people, to bring comfort, to end suffering. I stood ready to sacrifice my life for the Church.... That was naive. What was required was my soul. The Church was honest, admitting all along it craved my soul. But I did not yet comprehend how demanding the Church could be, how ensuring its survival outweighs *all* other concerns—for who else can be trusted to bring salvation to the world? *No matter* the sacrifice, the cost, the horror. No matter the terror I read in others' eyes or the sorrow I wear carrying out my work. The Church is more important than my discomfort. Or *yours*, Madam. If in seeking out fiends to slay them, I become a fiend, so be it. Your denunciations are not new to me, I made them once myself. If I could care about anything but the Church, I still would not care that you judge me monstrous.

But sweet *Jesu*, woman! At least use your mind! You also are not a simpleton! Do you think I *enjoy* being trapped in such a—*grotesquerie?*"

There was silence as Alyce sought her answer.

"No. Yes. . . . I know not. I know only that there is no rationale on or off this earth that can justify such inhumanity. I hear your confession. But seek not absolution from me. Morality! How dare you claim you have faith in anything sacred, including in any god?"

"I have faith in the *Church*. God . . . God is an argument. I believe in what I can *see*. Satan too is an argument—except that Satan's works are everywhere visible around us. Sometimes such evidence must be simplified, in order to educate man's boundless stupidity—but you can certainly *see* it. . . I believe in what I can *see*. I believe in the honour and purpose of the *Church*." He seemed to have found his old voice again. "This is the most efficient structure man has devised to establish order and peace, to address the yearning for a universal family beyond one's tribe or nation. Miraculously, it has endured. Kings and conquerors come and go. But the Church *lasts*—a living record of the finest qualities of humanity. It *must* last, for another thousand years and *more*."

"If the Church is living evidence, as you claim, of humanity's finest qualities, it is also evidence of humanity's capacity for acting with greed, corruption, violence—"

"—all of which are stages along the path to civilization. I do not claim the Church is a perfect structure. Divine Plan may have established it, but fallible man sustains it. Still, it is the best humanity can do."

"The best! You truly *believe* we cannot do better?"

"I believe we *can*. But not yet. I believe this is the best we can manage so far. We need *centuries* to alchemize such a vision. Which is why I would do anything—*anything*—to protect the Church."

"I am trying to understand you, my lord Bishop. Can *you* in turn understand: so do I feel about protecting my people?"

"Your people! Your people are doomed! By *you*, Madam, and by your superstitious traditions. You and your people will vanish, while the Church will prosper and conquer the world, including those lands where now only infidels roam." He stiffened with pride. "Impugn my integrity no longer. Take your bribes—of support and of trinkets—" he strode to where the ring and the pearls lay, picked them up and flung them into her lap, along with the scroll "—and take your threats as well. Return to your fiefdom. But not, I assure you, for long."

"Then there is no way that we can—"

"There is no way. The Church does not bargain."

"The Church bargains all the time, my lord—even with your own god."

"Not with heretics, apostates, or infidels."

She rose and looked him in the eye.

"I have tried. You know that from here there is no turning back."

"There is no turning back from anywhere. *Iacta alia est.* It means—"

"'—The die is cast.' I know what it means. *Immo, domine. Vale.*"

"*Vere. Vale, domina.*" He bowed.

She wheeled and swept out, the rustle of her train whispering in her wake.

Alone, Richard de Ledrede sank into a chair, breathing heavily. Only after some minutes did he straighten up to sit, staring, unseeing, at the crucifix. He was frightened of her next move. Yet he was also strangely excited, as if filled with the energy of his devout youth or the energy of battle—what he imagined warriors felt, preparing for attack. He had defended the Church. If martyrdom of his reputation was the cost, so be it.

This resolve helped buffer the blow when, the following afternoon, he learned that Lady Alyce Kyteler was formally reviving the charge.

The process did not take long. She dipped generously into her purse to hire a few well-connected legal advocates and numerous ink-stained clerks who scurried about, filing the proper writs. She did not even have to appear at the lawcourts.

Two days later, Richard de Ledrede—the Papal Emissary to Ireland commissioned with the task of rooting out heretics—found himself a prisoner in Kilkenny Castle. In full regalia, wearing his gold mitre and carrying his jeweled shepherd's crook, he had stared straight ahead as he was escorted from the Cathedral and borne through gaping crowds to the rooms set aside for his confinement. At least power still respected power somewhat: he was not to be lodged in the dungeons with common thieves. But the civil authorities refused to permit his cook to attend on him—punishment in itself, considering the fare. Nonetheless, he would continue to carry himself as a martyr ought, with dignity.

Meanwhile, leaving matters in the hands of her newly hired lawyers, Alyce Kyteler returned home and changed back into comfortable clothes.

In her tower chamber, surrounded by piles of crushed and abandoned finery littering the floor, she savored her physical freedom. Yet she felt tired—too weary to plunge into all the manor work that awaited her attention.

She slumped down onto the low wooden chest at the foot of her bed. There she sat, legs dangling, eyes closed.

"What we call victory," she sighed, and shook her head.

XI

FAMILY CONNECTIONS

ONCE CONFINED with the time to think about it, the Bishop discovered that he was, after all, not a man to welcome martyrdom, not even of his reputation. Reputation was ultimately a matter of history, and history was written by those who survived. So better to fight back—and better still to win. Nor was Richard de Ledrede a man to languish in jail, and he was nothing if not resourceful. Even from behind bars, he struck back.

Although imprisoned, he could not be denied visits from his priests and monks, to consult on bishopric matters. Alyce had miscalculated in overestimating the independence of Irish priests by basing her model on Father Brendan. The rabid Father Donnan was not alone in his zealotry; there were other priests closer to his temperament than to Brendan's, and there were abbots and friars quite willing to use and be used by the powerful prelate from abroad. Consequently, de Ledrede—employing a repertoire of indulgences literal, figurative, and spiritual—had over two years built himself a loyal clerical following.

Through these intermediaries, and still wielding his diocesan seal and the signet of his bishop's ring, he placed the entire diocese of Ossary under religious interdict. Every inhabitant was now in danger of excommunication and no one was allowed the full services and ministries of the Church.

To the heath-people this mattered little. But to the townsfolk it was cause for considerable unease. They had long grown accustomed to observing a combination of the old rites and the new, and now were confused and frightened by the open schism. Like most people, they disliked anything unfamiliar, disliked being trapped in the middle of a fight between powerful adversaries, and disliked having to choose sides. They found the situation particularly upsetting because Church affairs were intricately bound up with financial matters, tied to customers, favors, jobs, and land holdings. Consequently, the markets and taverns of Kilkenny and environs were loud with argument. Some people blamed the Bishop for this misfortune, some blamed Lady Alyce, and some began to blame the Wiccans. But whomever they chose to denounce, everyone felt cut adrift—as if a storm were about to break, with themselves shelterless in the open sea.

Meanwhile, Lady Alyce remained calm. She kept watch from a distance to ensure that her lawyers in town pressed the lawsuit through the courts, but she stayed at Kyteler Castle and threw herself into estate matters.

*   *   *

The late summer shearing had come and gone, with its attendant sorting and baling of different wools by crimp, lustre, and colour. The goats had suffered a temporary outbreak of foot-rot, due to soggy paddocks caused by summer rains, so Alyce spent hours pulverizing zinc to a powder for mixing into a foot-bath solution that was poured into low troughs of her designing. But then came the real challenge: cajoling, pushing, and bribing (with apple cores) the goats to enter the trough and stand for a few moments *in* the solution. Since goats, like cats, are serenely disinterested in not going where they ought and equally intent on going where they oughtn't, the foot-bath procedure alone produced quite a few exhausted heathens. Then tupping time had filled the paddocks with randy goats and sheep—the does and ewes tripping along, glancing backward over their shoulders bemusedly at the bucks and rams who raced after them, nostrils flared, sniffing, snorting, and "Having at it," as Maeve Payn archly observed, "with even more braying then certain lads I could name, *if* I chose."

One of those lads, the young lord of the manor, found himself lately engaged in frequent heated argument with his mother, about precisely such behavior.

"No, Will. I am *not* saying you cannot be a friend to Maeve," Alyce repeated, her irritation rising as she and her son sat at the large kitchen table with the manor account ledgers spread before them. "But then you must *act* like a friend. You must be honest with Meave. You must not mislead her."

"Mislead her where, into what?"

"You know into what. Into thinking that marriage lies in the future. Which it does not."

"Because? Merely because—"

"William. You *know* why. Maeve is a good-hearted lass, smart, fair to look on. Will Payne and his family have lived on Kyteler lands since they arrived from Boly, oh, decades ago— well before she was born. But Maeve and you. . . Will, you are not merely an Outlawe heir; you are sole heir to the Kyteler estates, here and elsewhere in Eire. Never forget: you are not free to follow any road you choose. It needs be, lad, that you wed someone of your station. Nor would Maeve, a musician's daughter, be happy with. . . she would feel like a fish in the air, like a wren underwater. You know this. You have known all this since you were five summers old."

"It seemed . . . so far off then," the young man muttered glumly.

"Time runs more swiftly each hour we use it. That, my son, is called growing up. Later, t'is called growing old."

"But I cannot see why. . . why should some girl I have never *seen* become lady of Kyteler Castle someday? Why should a stranger—"

"I have sworn to you I will do my best to ease the arrangements in your case, Will. I promise you will be allowed to become acquainted—even friends—with your future wife before you are betrothed. For her sake as well as yours."

"You have already gone and chosen her then, have you?"

"No, dearest, I have not. But you should know that there are many who look at me askance for *not* having done so by now. A goodly number of young lords are wedded fathers by your age, you know. Oh, Will. Perhaps I overindulged you. But I wanted you to enjoy your youth in ways I had not been permitted to enjoy mine. . . " She rubbed her forehead. "And t'is not as if I have been idle, you know. I have been somewhat preoccupied with other matters."

"Aye, and there's the real reason. You are always preoccupied with other matters, Mum."

"William."

"Truly. I think I fall near the bottom of your thoughts— after the land, the healing, the Craft, the estate children, the serfs' welfare. And now declaring war on the Church."

"*William.* You know you are my *most* cherished concern."

"I know I was when I was little. But that was before you started the healing studies, and the teaching and all."

"My love, I know we have quarreled on and off of late. These are difficult times for all of us. And I admit I am weary.

Then, when I find you are not doing *your* share of work on the estate, Will, I—oh my dear, life is not all jousting with Robert, nor flirtation with maidens. You are not a child any longer, nor are you a peasant lad without responsibilities. *Look* at these accounts, Will. You swore to me you would keep them up to date. Yet now I discover—"

"Mum, you already manage everything. You did in secret even when all the stepfathers were around, but now everybody sees it. You and I both know you do it better than I ever could. So why should I pretend to try? *You* command here. There's naught left for *me* to do." He shoved his stool back from the table in a sulk, and made as if to rise. His mother put out a restraining hand.

"William, wait. You know that I cannot give you authority until you prove worthy of it. Our people's livelihoods, their very lives, depend on decisions made by me—and someday by you. I cannot bear to think of you acting callously and greedily, as do most lords. I cannot bear the thought that—"

"So you do *not* trust my judgment, then. Is that not what you really mean?"

"No, my dear, no!"

"How pleased you are when one of your maidservants, or the Galrussyn men, or the Fabers, come to you, asking to be heard. Even visitors from afar. You listen to *them*. But not to your own son. Anybody can just—"

"You are not anybody. You are in a special position. And I do listen to you. But Will. . . look around us. We have begun something different here on Kyteler lands. Our serfs know it. Everyone knows it. The preserving of what we have managed to accomplish so far requires great care. You are young, Will, still somewhat of a gangling, awkward—"

"*Lad*? Though others my age are already husbands and sires? Robert is thinking of joining whatever remains of The Bruce's Scots troops off in the Fermanagh mountains with the Ulster chiefs—regrouping, people say, to rise against the English. I might go with him, then. There is no need for me here, a useless wee boy acting like a daughter, clinging to his mum's skirts."

Exasperated, Alyce sprang to her feet and slammed the table with her fist.

"You will *not* go off on some doomed adventure to get yourself heroically, witlessly slain. *Damn* Robert de Bristol *and* Robert of Scotland—who, let me remind you, sold out his own people *and* the Irish, which is *why* those fools will still be hiding in the mountains when your grandchildren walk on Kyteler land! You will remain *here*. You will work at your studies with your tutors, and you will work at learning how to run the estate with me. Enough of this foolishness!"

He sprang up, too, looming taller than his mother, glowering down at her.

"And just *wait*? Wait for you to choose my wife? Wait for you to die before I come into my full title? You are already old. What if you live for *years*?"

Alyce winced, and her son bit his lip with instant regret. But he was too firmly held in the grasp of resentment to stop.

"And meanwhile I cannot even have a bit of fun with Maeve? Her father is thinking of wedding her to Robert! You think I will stand by and let that happen? Well, I will *not*. I will claim my rights. I will claim *droit du seigneur*!"

"*Never*," Alyce spat at him. "No son of mine will rape a maid on the night of her wedding to another man, no matter *what* right is yours!" Standing on tiptoe, she reached up and boxed his ears.

Head ringing, William spun and ran out through the kitchen door. His mother started after him, crying after his receding shape, "William! Come back at once! I never meant to. . . William?"

There, standing at the door peering into the empty air, was where Annota Lange found Alyce some moments later. She curtsied, then bustled about in silence. She could not pretend ignorance of a quarrel whose shouts had been audible throughout the courtyard, nor could she dare proffer advice to her mistress. But noninterference was unthinkable to Annota, so she settled on abstract observation, pointed in its transparency.

"Ach, Your Ladyship," she cooed soothingly, "I was pondering the other day . . . getting old, t'is hard. But t'is not so difficult as being young. Especially for the lads, eh? All temper and ears. Girls grow more swift and smooth, dinna ye think?"

But her mistress did not answer. Instead, she returned to the table and buried herself in the account books without a word.

*   *   *

As days passed with no sign of the Bishop's interdict being lifted, nervousness already rife among the townsfolk began to be shared by some of the heathen, chiefly Petronilla de Meath, who now acted like a bird poised to take flight. She remained at Kyteler Castle, but all her former anxieties reasserted themselves. No longer the young woman shyly testing her confidence at the Lugnasad Sabbat, she now clung to every sympathetic listener, pouring out her fears and interrogating others about what they thought might happen. When some of the heath-folk finally grew vexed with her babbling, she drew back into herself, saying little, but reviving her old habit of unconscious fidgeting, her tic of ceaselessly twisting and untwisting those silverblonde braids.

One night, Alyce, unable to sleep, started down to the kitchens to brew herself a cup of skullcap tea. Padding along the lower hall, she overheard Petronilla pacing in her room, talking aloud, half to herself and half in an address to the listener she could not possibly have known was so near, standing just outside her door. Over and over, Petronilla anguished, arguing with her invisible *amchata* Alyce:

"Are ye daft then, m'Lady? Canna ye see? Ye think t'is easy, ye think we won. Ye canna *know* them as I do. Ye dinna understand the *power* they get over a body. They got ways to make your *spirit* afraid. None can stand up to 'em. *None.* Ach, why, why t'is ye canna *see?*"

Forgetting her tea, Alyce returned to her turret room and sat for a long time, staring out the window toward the Covenstead. Then she went to her writing table, pulled up her stool, and sat down. She drew a fresh sheet of parchment, shaved a new quill nib, unstoppered her ink pot, and began composing a careful letter to the Lord Justice.

It began with jolly news about his kinsman her son William, boasting as any mother might about young Will's looks, intelligence, recent growth spurt, and remarkable physical grace (she chuckled as she wrote this); clearly Will took after the Outlawe side of the family, she added, wrinkling her nose with distaste at stooping to such bald flattery.

Then she got to the real point of the letter.

Next, she drew a second parchment and wrote similarly to the Seneschal, praising *him* as a man of conscience, and sending her personal regards to Lady Megan.

Then she got to the real point of *that* letter.

The real point of both letters was an appeal: that the Lord Justice and the Seneschal journey to Dublin and wait upon the Archbishop, who was also the Dean of Saint Aidan's, and that they inform him (and whomever else they in their vastly superior wisdom deemed necessary) of the Bishop's interdict; that they take particular care to apprise the Archbishop-Dean as to how this interdict was disturbing, dividing, and provoking the people—even toward possible civil unrest. Alyce delicately wondered of both men whether they might also wish to remind the Archbishop-Dean that it was a Kyteler, one of her forebears, who had more than a century earlier commissioned the famous Crozier—the bronze reliquary of gilded silver with gold filigree, inlaid enamel, and millifiori beadwork—and donated it to Saint Aidan's Shrine at Dublin?

By the time Richard de Ledrede was released on bail after eighteen days, his cincture hung loosely around his middle, and he felt himself a famished man. But just as he was finally sitting down to a long-anticipated dinner of a whole roast suckling pig accompanied by numerous flagons of malmsey, he was infuriatingly interrupted by a courier, just ridden in and bearing letters with official seals.

It was not appetizing news. He found himself commanded to appear before the Lord Justice of Ireland as well as the Archbishop of Dublin, to answer charges regarding his having dared place the diocese of Ossary under interdict.

At first, he fell into a fit of pique, stamping about his chamber and flinging his wine cup at the wall the way his father had done when in a rage. These *obnoxious* Irish! *How* had they put him in the position of the accused, when his proper role was as the accuser? This primitive marsh of a country had ignored him, then flouted him, then humiliated him. Now his career was at stake. And all because of one damnable bitch.

Richard de Ledrede walked to where the wine cup lay, stooped with some effort, picked it up, and placed it carefully on the table. He clapped his hands and, when the servant appeared, sent for more malmsey. Then he sat down again, determined to enjoy his dinner.

Some leisurely hours later, in better humour and surrounded by fresh candles and more wine, he reread the summons, snorting in admiration of Alyce Kyteler's influence and the skill with which she wielded it. How he had missed political swordplay with an equal! Yet how gratifying it would be to defeat and destroy her utterly.

He called for his writing materials. Then he wrote back to Dublin in an unctuous tone, deeply regretting his inability to appear there and making ingenious excuses for refusing the "kind invitation." He pled ill health, citing—with a smile to himself—a medical diagnosis of dyspepsia and choler. He added that it was, moreover, gravely unsafe for him to travel such a distance, since he had been warned that violent pagans would surely waylay and murder him en route. He rolled the parchment, waxed and sealed it with the signet of his bishop's ring, sent for a courier, and dispatched the letter.

After three more rounds of malmsey, he slept soundly that night.

*   *   *

But the besieged prelate was granted only a few days respite—plus pheasant, partridge, custards, and brandywine—before the responses ricocheted back from Dublin.

His excuses were not accepted.

Instead, he received a sharp reprimand from the Archbishop. That affront was compounded by an accompanying missive from the Archbishop's highest deputy that denounced him as "a truant monk from abroad" zealously bent on carrying out papal commands about which no one in Ireland had ever heard.

But there was a crowning insult.

Dublin overruled him, and lifted the interdict.

De Ledrede's wrath at what he now termed "this affliction called Ireland" was apoplectic. But beyond his own circle of loyal priests and monks, the rage was not shared. On the contrary, the Bishop was further maddened at hearing happy shouts in the streets. People learning the news were flocking to the Cathedral, seized by a sudden piety that inspired them to resume brisk business dealings in Cathedral Square.

Back at Kyteler Castle, the release of tension was palpable. In spontaneous revels, the wine and ale flowed freely to everyone in residence, and to everyone who passed by or dropped in to visit. The children drew a rough portrait of the Bishop in the dirt and practiced pitching stones at it.

"T'is true we are not the world's most graceful winners," Alyce remarked wryly, "With traditional Irish mercy, when we have an adversary down, we kick him into the ground."

It did seem that the foreign witch-hunter was in general disgrace. It further appeared that Celtic loyalty and courage were flowing strongly through the Irish—peasant and noble, Wiccan and Christian alike.

Meanwhile, Father Brendan Canice, having wheedled himself a temporary leave from the Bishop's service, had set off to journey back to Kells. Stopping on the way north at an inn for the night, he heard the news about the lifted interdict from another traveler. At dawn the next morning, he slipped out onto the heath and gave joyous thanks to Brigid, cheerfully scolding himself for being unsure in his heart whether he was praying to the Goddess or to the Saint, but confident that his good intentions would be divined by *Some*thing sublime.

XII

HARVESTING SOULS

INDIFFERENT TO THE JOYS AND GRIEFS of humans, their fears and hopes, forthright lies and secret honesties, the wheel of the year revolved, steady on its seasonal cycle. Two periods in that cycle were, for the heath people, times of intensive labor: spring planting and, near the Autumnal Equinox, the reaping.

Those fields that had been left to rest, ungrazed and unplanted, had been gleaned for haymaking, and now towers of sweet-smelling, prickly sheaves were piled high inside the barns and sheds, ready for winter use as fodder. Meanwhile, the second, late harvest had grown ripe. The grains had largely been garnered but other crops remained, so most everyone spent long days in the fields, picking and sorting. The estate beehives were being gingerly unburdened of their honeycombs by dexterous elders, while children went on forages for treefalls of chestnuts, almonds, and hazelnuts.

Work was intensive indoors, too, sometimes continuing late into the nights, which had begun to crisp with the first frosts as darkness drew down earlier. Halls echoed with the clang and clatter of reaping hooks, drying grapnels, croppers, and sieves, and courtyards hummed to the rhythmic snap of winnowing sheets. Brimming baskets were hauled back to the kitchens so that pears and quince could be stewed into compotes before they overripened to rot. Grapes were spread out for shriveling to currants under the autumn sun, in courtyards where peas and lentils had already been strewn to dry. More grapes were boiled into jellies, pressed into verjuice and into clear liquid for fermenting as wine. Beans, marrows, and cabbages were being soaked in vats of spiced cider vinegar for pickling, along with a quarter of each day's egg yield from the generous hens, since pickled eggs and vegetables would be staples throughout the cold months. The root foods—parsnips, radishes, beets, carrots—would be stored in the cellars, along with gourds, artichokes, licorice-root, bins of onions, and baskets of leeks. Every kitchen in the castle and in the cottages was greenly pungent with herbs, picked fresh, bound, then hung to dry from ceiling hooks. Up there, fading and brittling, were verbenas and lavenders from earlier in the summer, now taken down to be sugared and preserved as delicacies, though the rose-hips had been carefully culled and stored by Alyce, who prescribed them as a preventive medicine to ward off winter colds and influenzas. Other blossoms—heliotrope, dandelion, and crocuses with their treasured saffron stamens—had long been gathered and dried or distilled, along with raspberries and blueberries, to be used as fabric dyes.

All this time—more than two months—the Bishop had been silent. Indeed, he had hardly been seen, except when celebrating Mass in the Cathedral once a week, and even then he had one of his priests deliver the sermon. His case was still pending in the courts, but rumour hummed that he would never come to trial, that he was making preparations to depart for France. People were beginning to assume that he had relinquished his Irish crusade. Life throughout the Ossary bishopric was back to normal, and the townsfolk in Kilkenny—occupied once more with daily cares, feuds, and gossip—had all but forgotten the crisis. Even the Wiccans began to relax their vigilance and, with the harvest labor at last beginning to ease, to turn their attention to the next Sabbat, the Samhain Sabbat.

This, the most solemn of all Wiccan holy-days, mourned the death of the Old Year and welcomed the birth of the New Year. It honoured the Dance of Shadows, the one night when a gleam of eternity penetrates time, when the membranes of reality shimmer at their thinnest between all the worlds—worlds known and unknown; worlds past, present, and yet-to-be. Unable to break the people's faithful observance of Samhain, the Church had adopted this night as its own, renaming it All Hallows' Eve. For the heathen, though, this Sabbat also served a practical purpose. It imposed a natural harvest deadline, since any produce remaining in the fields after sunset on the last night of the month of Deireadh Fómhair was forbidden for consumption. That food belonged to the spirits of nature.

But Alyce Kyteler and her people knew they would have the harvest gathered in and would be ready for Samhain—which was to be memorable this year for still another reason. Samhain Eve was not only the night that opened portals to the Otherworlds. It was also the Time of Reckoning—the moment to discard unwanted habits and influences while adopting desirable new ones. So it was at this Sabbat that Petronilla de Meath, as a Seeker who had completed her Neophyte studies for the requisite year and a day, was to be initiated into The Craft.

This made her even more apprehensive than usual. Alyce tried repeatedly to address Petronilla's misgivings, reminding her that she was fully prepared for the tests, had the basics of herbery memorized, was suitably versed in lore and legend, and was sufficiently knowledgeable about the public ritual Mysteries—as opposed to the secret Mysteries that required decades of study—so as to have no real worries at all.

"But what if I dinna pass?" Petronilla anguished, as they sat carding wools, "What if I be too scared at the last minute even to speak? What shall everyone be thinking of me then? What if I fail you? What if I fail and canna ever rise to the next level? Oh Jesu, Mary, and all the Saints!"

"My child," Alyce sighed, tactfully ignoring Petronilla's choice of words for an oath, "you *will* pass. Listen to me. Even if you do not pass, there is always the next sabbat, and the next, with easy space and time between them to practice what you know until you *are* initiated. Everyone would understand. Besides, who cares *what* anyone thinks! For that matter, Pet, let me say this again: please, *please* remember that you do not have to do this at all. We never force The Old Ways on people, you know that. We have no missionaries. You can remain a Christian, and we will all go on loving you the same as we do now. Or you can be part of both spiritual paths. Never forget: you are free to follow any road you choose—" Alyce paused, contrary words from her last quarrel with Will echoing through her mind "—and you will still be welcome at feasts and celebrations whenever you wish to come. We love you not because you came to us and stayed and eventually shared our beliefs, but because you came to us and stayed even when you did *not* share them. I cannot remind you of this too often."

"Nae nae, but I be *wanting* to join. I feel a part of it already. T'is my real longing to . . . ye all—ye be the family I never had."

"Then what is there to fear? I promise you, you will not get too scared. You are braver than you think, Petronilla. Believe me. Believe *yourself*."

"And if I canna remember the Password? Oh Jesu!"

"Well, scribble it on a scrap of parchment and hide it in your sleeve to peek at. You read and write now. You never credit yourself with being as smart as you are!"

"Ye could fill the sky above with all I dinna understand. And what if on the night I canna find the parchment and canna remember the Password, eh? What then?"

"Petronilla. You *know* that you know the Password."

"*Perfect love and perfect trust,*" Petronilla whispered.

"Exactly," said Alyce, striving for patience in this conversation, which was all but identical to one they'd had two days earlier. "And you know precisely what to expect, do you not? You know your Measure will be taken—"

"—with the Cord that gauges my height and by a pinprick of my finger to draw a single drop of blood—"

"—and you know that these are symbolic acts about defining who you truly are, your essence. . . "

"Like the snipped locks of hair and nail clippings in a love spell. . . "

"Just so, yes," Alyce smiled with tutorial approval. "In that case, those are metaphors for the essence of the beloved. Even the Goddess and Green Man are merely faces of. . . the Unnamable Chaos. It is all metaphor, really. The power of the word. The power of the gesture. That is, unless someday someone discovers a person's essence lurking in nail clippings and hair strands—though we know *that* will never happen. But don't you fret about any of this. You will enter the next stage, and then you can train toward what arts of The Craft you wish to make your own. Have you decided yet? Not that you need to. There is still plenty of time. . . ."

"I—I have thought about it. Many hours. I know t'is too stupid I am to be a Lore and Legend Keeper, and—"

"Nonsense."

"—nae, but I canna. . . and I think I be too shy to become one of the *seannachai*, a Tale Spinner. Then when I look at Alyce Faber's muscles I know I canna ever be strong enough to work metals or be a lapidary. But helping people not to feel pain—aye, t'would be a fine thing to do. So then I was thinking—you know—mayhap, a Healer? Or a show-the-way Hedgewitch, a teacher, a counselor? But ach, I am not so good with people, and I know I canna ever be wise, so t'is not likely I could—"

"*Petronilla*—" Alyce began, trying not quite successfully to contain her annoyance at this young woman's overly developed self-critical faculty.

"Nae, hear me. I be telling you my truth," Petronilla continued, unusually persistent, "I have thought hard on this. I pondered on trying to become an Animal Woman, a lady of the beasts, as animals dinna frighten me the way people mostly do. But I dinna think I've the knack for it—you know, for *hearing* the creatures and *understanding* 'em? So t'is this I've come to. I think mayhap—*if* I can pass Initiation, that is, and *if* I can commence studies on the next level—that I be liking to try for. . . becoming a Greenwitch?"

"A Greenwitch," Alyce repeated softly.

"Aye. T'is a feeling more natural for me to wander alone through the orchards and amongst the flowers and herbs— learning 'em, learning what they need to grow, learning how to use 'em. Like you. Oh, well, I mean, not like *you*, because you do so many other things—tale spinning, and you be knowing lore and legend, too. Everything. I only mean—"

"I think you will make a fine Greenwitch, Pet," Alyce smiled, "There is something in you—a strength, a force— something I cannot grasp or name. But I can recognize it, even though you yourself do not yet see it. You shall surprise us both, I think—as a Greenwitch or whatever you choose. Besides, you would be amazed at how knowing herbs leads to being a Healer—of people *and* animals. And then leads to teaching others how, like a Hedgewitch. And then to learning lore, and then to passing *that* on. Any single path truly taken leads to all the others. What matters is choosing a starting place—where to stand and begin spinning outward. Even then, you will find that outward and inward become the same direction. The center of the wheel is everywhere."

"T'is like—t'is all of one piece, is it then?"

"That is an excellent way to think of it, yes. Though it is not easy to *keep* that in mind. Everyday living can be such a distraction from seeing it all—life, death, everything—as of one piece. I mean, it is such a temptation to break it up into fragments, as if that might make things easier. Actually, I think that is what makes the transitions—the shifts from one bit to another?—so difficult. You see?"

"Oh aye. Aye, t'is. . . nae. Dinna see."

"Small wonder. I am not being very clear. Well, for example, look at the really big fragments. Life. Death."

Petronilla listened intently, fascinated. No one ever talked with her the way this woman did.

"Life feels natural and real for us," Alyce went on, thinking aloud as she spoke. "We feel alive, *simply*. Breathing, for instance. Without any conscious effort. Natural. And death is certainly natural. Also unarguably real. I imagine that being dead is simple and effortless, too—once you *are* dead. It is the transitions—*being* born, *dying*, becoming dead— that are hard."

There was a pause. Then Petronilla spoke, her voice hardly audible.

"Lady Alyce?"

"Yes, my dear?"

"Do ye believe. . . do ye think that. . ."

"What is it? Go ahead, you can ask me anything."

"Be there life after dying?" the younger woman blurted out. "The Church tells us the soul goes. . . but now I dinna know. Be there eternal life? Or something?"

Alyce put down the wool she was carding and looked into the clear, light blue of Petronilla's questioning eyes.

"What do *you* think, Petronilla?"

"Dinna matter what *I* think, M'am, because I dinna *know*. But *you* know. You know so many things. And the Church says. . . eternal life and such. But only for Christians. That Wiccans and all other souls—that *you*—be burning in Hell for all time. Yet Jesus went down to Hell and saved. . . but see, now I know the priests lie about things, so I dinna. . . so *you* tell me. What do Wiccans say?"

Alyce stared into space for a moment, then turned back to her companion.

"Well. For the Celts—and for Wiccans—there has never been a hell, or the idea that any afterlife could be a punishment. But different Wiccans say different things about what else it might be. Some still see it as the Celts did—an Otherworld, a place of spirits—called Lough-Derg or Tir na Noc, where the shades of those who have died exist not so differently from the way they did when they lived. That is why the Celts buried their dead with coins and cookpots and ornaments, even weapons. Then some think the afterlife is a sort of paradise or heaven that is like an orchard miraculously in leaf and bloom and fruit, all at once. Others believe there is no afterlife, nothing but the freedom and peace of forever sleep."

"You. What about you? T'is that what you believe? The orchard?"

Alyce looked down at her lap, fingering a gossamer curl of angora fleece lustrous as new cream.

"Me? No. I believe there is no orchard, Petronilla. I believe there is nothing at all, in fact—which is why life, every moment, is so holy. To feel, to *be*, the *heat* that we are. In *form*—bone, muscle, pulse—*right now*. How splendid. But I also think..."

"Aye?" Petronilla asked eagerly, hunched forward on her stool.

"I *like* to think that nothing ever really gets completely...wasted. So sometimes I like to think that whatever is left of us, all of us—tissue of flesh and tissue of fleece—goes back into creating something else, under the earth or through the fire or in the air or on the water. You know, the way compost enriches the soil? And then...why then I can let myself wander off nicely daft and begin to think that the rest of what was our living selves—that heat, that spark of us— somehow gets used, too. In—oh, invisible currents. Winds. Or humours we cannot see. Off up...toward the moon, mayhap? Or the heart of the sun?"

"Souls?"

"Mmm, no. More like . . . motes of wheat chaff. Or dandelion puffs. Or mayflies."

"D'ye think we recognize each other there? Me and Sara, like? Or you and me?"

Alyce laughed softly.

"No. I think if there was a 'there' at all, it would be so different a place that it would exist beyond even the one inhabited by our poor imaginings of The Sidhe or the faerie folk—imaginings based on who we are ourselves. But since no one has gone scouting there and returned with a report, there is no way to know, now, is there? "

"So then even *you* dinna. . ."

"Oh very much me: I do not know. Anyone who claims certainty is trying to convince others of something *no* one can know. I do not doubt there are honest Christians and other believers who are sure they will live eternally *and* be conscious while doing it—an exercise I personally find tiring. In truth, that certainty too often turns into promises of porridge tomorrow to keep folk starving submissively today. If the soul existed, I should think it would not be for harvesting by others. No. In my heart, Petronilla, I think there is nothing after we die. Nothing but what small good we may have done whilst alive."

"And children. Those of us who have 'em."

"And children," Alyce repeated, a shadow crossing her face. "Aye. Those we loved, who loved us and will remember us, for a little while."

Petronilla sat still, her brow furrowed in concentration, taking all these thoughts in.

But Alyce sighed and picked up her wools. Then, deliberately, she changed the subject back to Samhain. Striving for a merrier mood, she was soon jauntily listing the three worst habits she intended to strip from herself with the death of the Old Year.

"First, my weakness for overeating candied ginger.... Hmmm. Second, being a scold to William." Her expression darkened. Then she thrust up her chin, brightening again. "Last—*most* serious of all—" this with a straight face "—dressing up as a lady."

And laughter descended on their work.

XIII

THE DYING OF THE YEAR

SO THE DAYS PASSED, in conversation and silence, dreaming and action, external and internal harvests. Meanwhile, light leaked from the afternoons and darkness arrived earlier and lingered later, tarnishing the cold pewter dawns.

Early in October, Alyce had been brought word that the Church had intensified its campaign against heretics on the Continent. Harsh winters, drought, and failed crops had stirred the need to blame someone or something fearsome for bad fortune—and priests fed the people's panic rather than their stomachs. Townsfolk in Germany and France had begun slaughtering cats as the agents of evil. With entire villages bereft of felines, the rat population quickly quadrupled, spreading filth and disease, furthering the panic. This the priests blamed on Jews, Moors, and especially witches, claiming that Wiccan spells had brought plague in revenge for the killing of their animal Familiars. Since any person who accused another of witchcraft was usually rewarded by a full purse or fell heir to the property of the accused, denunciations grew in frequency and popularity, as did indictments. Executions by burning at the stake were now weekly—in some villages daily—public entertainments.

Lady Alyce had for years built a correspondence with the members of certain covens in France, Germany, and Italy—covens sometimes flourishing quietly on landed estates like her own, or in convents presided over by sympathetic or even participating abbesses. From parchments sent surreptitiously to her by these sources, Alyce learned that members of The Craft in Europe were fleeing from one place to another. Some had gone into hiding; others had attempted to disguise themselves and pass for Christians. The poor could rarely manage such escapes, so they fell victim with the greatest frequency.

Alyce Kyteler kept such information to herself, thinking that to share it would needlessly grieve and terrify her people, and believing that the Celtic spirit, recently deployed with such ferocity against the Bishop, would continue to protect them at home in Ireland. Yet since de Ledrede had not acted on his rumoured departure, she maintained an air of vigilance.

His exit was taking too long. She suspected that if he did not leave, he would again eventually move against her and The Craft. She further assumed that if he did so, he would not repeat his tactical error of relying on Irish hierarchy or absent English landowners near Kilkenny, but would circumvent both local and national powers, soliciting help from abroad.

She reasoned that if this came to pass, she might expect some Irish support but not enough, and would need to devote all her strength to fighting him. This meant that she should send those Wiccans who were identified with and dependent on her—certainly William, and her immediate Coven and their relatives—safely out of the country, perhaps to Wales. But uprooting her people from the land was an idea almost too painful to contemplate.

Such were her midnight thoughts of dread as she tossed and turned, to Prickeare's aggravation, through sweat-long hours of waiting for the first light.

In the daytime, however, she kept up her façade. She oversaw work on the last of the harvest, laughed with her women, prescribed a salve of hot peppers for John Galrussyn's painful joints, taught the children their letters and numbers, began tutoring Petronilla in herbery, and planned the nearing Samhain Sabbat. And waited.

Quietly, she had one of the large salting tubs lugged into a separate cellar chamber, and then kept that chamber locked. Down there, alone, she spent hours every week, soaking linen shirts and jerkins in wine and salt, then hanging them to dry inside the chamber. Thus cured and stiffened, such garments could stop an arrow. She was making crude armor. She couldn't have said precisely to what end, but the making and storing of it felt reassuring.

The blow fell late in October. A weary herald who had ridden hard all the way from Dublin stumbled in one morning with a message for Lady Alyce. The scroll was from the Lord Justice, Roger Outlawe.

It confirmed her deepest fears.

He wrote that the Bishop had appealed over the heads of the national authorities, by writing directly to his master, the Pope. Outlawe was now notifying her that Papal Orders had just arrived from Avignon, forcing the Irish leaders—secular as well as religious—to allow de Ledrede to mount heresy trials. He had not yet formally granted such permission to the Bishop, but shortly he would have no choice. Clearly, the Lord Justice wrote with some bitterness, the Church managed to trump the State on spiritual matters, even when such matters had nothing to do with the spirit but were, as he put it, about grinding Irish sovereignty into the dust. He warned Alyce that he had heard the Bishop was planning to bring men-at-arms to her Samhain Sabbat and arrest all participants. As kinsman to her son, he advised her to empty her treasury, pack as many chests with gold and jewels as the horses could carry, and flee with young Will at once. Surprisingly, he cited England as the preferable destination, for three reasons. First, despite the English being obviously detestable, they faithfully observed amnesty for nobles, and he grudgingly allowed that they tended to keep their word. Second, although Bishop de Ledrede was

English, he was apparently in ill repute at home—due to an old, still-notorious, financial scandal—which might favor a compassionate reception for two fugitives from his persecutions. Last, Edward, the English Crown Prince, was rumoured to be sympathetic to The Craft, possibly even—in private—a Seeker. The Lord Justice recommended against Alyce fleeing to Wales, adding dryly that despite being generally loyal to The Craft, Wales was a wild place filled, regrettably, with the Welsh, "who think themselves more Celtic than we, and resent us accordingly." In a postscript, he made it clear that, after this warning, Alyce could expect no further help from him. He directed her to burn his letter and cease all contact. If she failed to do so, he wrote, he too would be placed in danger.

He need not have worried. As she watched Roger Outlawe's letter blacken, flare, and curl to ash in the flames, Dame Alyce was already making plans.

*　　*　　*

The following morning, she summoned her people to assemble in the great cellar of Kyteler Castle after dark that night.

They trooped in, solemn as mourners in a funeral cortege. With an intuition bred through generations of suffering, the serfs sensed at the bone what their mistress would tell them.

Huddling together, they squatted and knelt in the light of sputtering candles and torches—fragile beings yearning to loom above their helplessness as hugely as did their shadows, which gestured with menace from the damp stone walls.

Lady Alyce was selective in telling them items of news from the reports on the Continent plus some information from the Lord Justice's letter, though she left its author unnamed. Telling them not to fear, and assuring them that she would as always care for their welfare, she announced her plans.

Regretfully, there would be no Samhain Sabbat two days hence. Instead, in the morning, William would be sent to study in England. Members of her immediate Coven and their families would shortly be resettled on one of the le Poer estates up north. She had already sent word to Lady Megan and had been assured in return that her people would be looked after. She herself would remain at Kyteler Castle, where she would oversee the digging of entrenchments, fortifications against siege, and preparations for battle—physical, spiritual, and legal—with the Bishop. Over the next days, each peasant would receive specific orders regarding resettlement. She then asked if there were any questions.

To her distress, Will, perched beside Robert de Bristol on the stone cellar stairs, was the first.

"Why do I alone go to England? Why does everyone else—"

"William!" his mother snapped, "Not here. We have discussed this! We can talk about it again later. *Not now.*"

Sullenly, he sat down again, muttering about mothers.

Annota Lange came next.

"Your Ladyship," the widow began, heaving herself to her feet, "If we dinna hold our Samhain, then why be we sent away? I canna grasp it."

"Because, Annota, this Bishop will hold trials with false evidence, trials that could bring about your death. Simply for being a member of The Craft, whether we celebrate a Sabbat or no. Your *death*. Do you not understand?"

"Aye, I understand well enough, not being simple in the head, M'am. But will he not seek *your* death, too, m'Lady?"

"My death is not your concern. But yours is mine."

"Ach, I have died before," Annota said with a wave of her hand, "when my man Seamus went from the ague. And again when my fair girl Grainne perished in childbirth. M'am, t'is not my place to question your plan. But—" she turned to the assembly," ye all know me for an old woman who says what she thinks." There were fleeting grins of acknowledgment, and the widow proceeded.

"I must be saying the truth, Your Ladyship. T'is not a good plan. The peasants at the le Poer estates will not welcome us willing-like, to share their wee bits of land. Also, we be marked—known as your people. The Bishop will pursue us wherever we be in Eire. And if t'is not safe here for the Coven, then t'is not safe here for our Priestess. T'is a brave plan, oh aye. But not a wise one. Forgive me, m'Lady. But I must say my truth."

"And so you have, Annota," her mistress replied, a bit brusquely, "Your care for my safety touches me. Yet my plan must be followed."

"But *why*, Your Ladyship? Canna ye give us some better reason?"

"Because.... It is my plan. That is all you need to know."

"*No*." All heads turned. It was John Galrussyn, struggling to stand, with the aid of his son Sysok. "Your Ladyship, I fear we need know more." The oldest of the elders present, his raised voice commanded respectful attention. He spoke with deference to his mistress, but in words that rang with his own authority. "Ye been teaching us to ask questions for many summers, M'am—so why not now? Ye be needing our understanding this one time... Your Grace."

Alyce sighed. "John," she said, "It is simple. Someone must stand up to this... invasion. I have decided that someone is me. The Bishop thinks to terrify Ireland into the narrowest of Christian paths. He knows that if he can best me, many will follow. But in me he chose the wrong victim. I have the power to fight back. I must honor that power. And so I shall. Yet any who might be more vulnerable to his trials and his tortures must be sent clear out of the way of this battle, safe—so as to preserve The Craft. Craft knowledge must not be lost. Preservation of The Old Ways is the most important task— more than any material concern—and I place this charge in the hands of all of you, my Coven. Though perhaps you are right about the le Poers. Perhaps I should send you to Wales, after all. There you will find support for The Craft, and you—"

"And our Priestess? She should not be sent clear and safe away?"

"From my own ancestral lands? I refuse to be driven off my own lands by a foreign, upstart, tradesman monk! Centuries of Kyteler bones are interred here. Be hounded from my home? *Never!*"

Old John was not cowed by his Lady's ferocity.

"Be it about the survival of The Craft, then? Or—pardon me, Your Ladyship—be it pride and stubbornness about your lands? Which is at stake? For all here know that there be more knowledge of The Craft—ritual and herbery, lore and legend, cure and spell and Mystery—in your head than in every one of ours all together, and in most of the books ye might teach us to read."

Alyce was growing impatient.

"What is it you are saying, John? Out with it."

The old man looked around the room. He knew what beat unsaid in the hearts of his neighbors—and knew it fell to him to do the voicing of it.

"My Lady. Ye be a peaceable woman. Your men-at-arms are few. So I ask ye, with all respect, where will ye get an army? I mean, where will outside aid come from?"

"I shall. . .I have assurances that the Lord Justice stands ready to help." She faltered for only a breath before regaining her firmness. "Again, you need not seek out such worries."

"Aye M'am, but the worries seek us out. Before, ye had the powers of Eire on our side—the Lord Justice and Archbishop and Seneschal and such fine folk. But now people be getting afeared. And this time we be dealing with foreigners, mayhap. The Bishop might call for English troops. Even *French*." An indignant murmur hummed round the room. "T'would do no good to set needfires to signal for help, if that happened. We be thinking that Kyteler Castle canna be defended for long. And sure not without a grand army. Even then, not all of great Finn's legions could protect this castle if the Pope sends his men against ye. I think—pardon, m'Lady, but . . . I think we *all* must flee. You too, Your Ladyship. With us under your protection. You especially. I do. I think it." He leaned against Sysok, panting slightly, weary from his outburst.

There was a sudden clamor of agreement. It stunned Alyce. She had expected the anxious, exchanged glances that followed her announcement. But she had never anticipated this response. The heath-folk were rebelling. Furthermore, they were immediate, unanimous, and firm in their rebellion. They did not want to remain in Ireland while the Bishop held sway. Nor would they permit their High Priestess to fight the Bishop while they fled.

Old lessons of blood privilege rose up in Alyce, and she addressed the assembly in words sharpened by her lineage.

"You forget to whom you speak!" she declared. "I know what is best, for all of us. You will do as I command! That is the end of it."

The ensuing silence lay heavy with hurt. Poised for the first time openly as opponents, Alyce and her people glared at each other.

It was Will Payn, the harpist, who broke the impasse, speaking gently from his half-kneeling position near her feet.

"Your Ladyship," he said, his eyes sadder than his smile, "This be a testing time for all of us. Even—oh forgive me for saying, m'Lady—even for yourself. You sought to create a change here, a different way. Not the distant Lady ruling her serfs, but something new. Something that taught us and healed us and. . . you changed us, M'am. We, all of us, *together*—we now be *feeling* that change, *living* it. Nor has it been swift, nor easy, this change, nor—begging your pardon—nor ever so solid we might rest on it for a given. Yet t'is this we have *done*. Changed we now *are*. What troubles we be forced to face in days to come, this night—here, *now*—mayhap t'is the hardest test of all. Will ye not hear us out? Please, M'am?"

Alyce stood rigid, staring over their heads.

"Speak, then," she said curtly. *Let them finish,* she thought, *Let them spew it all out. It matters not. I decide.*

Eva de Brounstoun spoke up then, her husky voice cracking with emotion.

"Oh Madam. T'is only in such a dire time I dare ask it. But ask it I must. Was it all a dream of faerie lore then? A sweet tale only, fit for children to believe? And us—your serfs—being those children? Fancying ourselves Her Ladyship's special people, fancying we be sharing our lives outside the ranks of great noble and base peasant? Because we all kept The Craft together? See, we *believed*. T'was it daft we were, then?"

Next, Alyce Faber the smith rose heavily to her feet and stood level with Alyce Kyteler, adding, "Or is it we stand on the same sweet soil—Smithy Alyce Faber to Dame Alyce Kyteler? Can we here—" she looked around the cellar "—have a voice in our own fate? Be we our own people, sistren and brethren in The Craft, deciding our lives, right or wrong? Or be we in the end forced to obey your will, brooking no dissent? Like—like serfs anywhere, m'Lady?"

Finally, Petronilla de Meath stood, speaking so quietly the others had to strain to hear her. At first she stammered with the effort. Yet as she spoke, she began to radiate a strange composure no one had seen in her before.

"T'is because she knows now all her fears proved right, I wager," Helena whispered to Sysok.

"T'would m-mayhap be said, Your Gr— t'would mayhap be said, Your *Ladyship*," Petronilla began, "that being what I am—what we are—serfs and peasants I mean. . . t'would mayhap be said that though all of us know nothing much. . . still,

some of us know better . . . what and who we be fighting here
than do you, M'am. Please, I mean no disrespect, m'Lady. But
mayhap ye canna see. We—I—we dinna know *how* to be grand
and make stands and fight and . . . be brave heroes and all. Still,
when t'is knowing *who to fear*, or *when to flee*, some of us know
better what that is, mayhap, than do you, M'am. We had our
lives to learn it, to learn how to . . . *gauge* that fear, gauge the
measure of that fear. T'is *our* measure what's been gauged in that
knowledge—if you take my meaning? While *your* measure be
lifelong as . . . but leave that be. Yet, if you could learn *this*,
m'Lady? What *we* be knowing? Care what *we* be thinking? Aye.
Join in it? If you could—if you could *trust* . . . "

Her voice died away. No one spoke.

Still disconcerted at having been challenged, Alyce
nevertheless could not deny being moved by Petronilla's
passion. *If I take her meaning,* she wondered to herself. Looking
round the cellar, she studied the massed faces. *They speak with
such certainty. How did they learn that?* Familiar faces. *They are
skilled in some wisdom I know not. Fear? Aye, they are skilled in
fear! It has kept them alive.* Sharp-eyed sunburnt faces, weather-
creased, labor-coarsened. *What did she say? If I could learn it,
join in it?* Something else shadowed the expressions on these
faces, something expectant, inviting, demanding. *My own
measure is being taken. If I take her meaning.* Suddenly
the Bishop's words floated through her mind: "the ideal

mistress—until you get bored or until the peasants you have indulged begin to take themselves seriously." She would prove him wrong. She would learn whatever it was they knew that she did not. *They are the adepts here, I am the neophyte,* she thought again. And with the word "neophyte" other words crystallized in her mind—clear as the peals of a bell at evening: *Perfect love and perfect trust.*

Her eyes stung—but whether with tears of embarrassment or gratitude, shame or pride, she could not tell. Barely able to speak, she whispered.

"Speak what is in your hearts, then. I shall listen. If it is wise, I shall—perhaps agree."

No one thanked her.

But from that moment, the meeting drew together in mutual planning—a council. And Alyce Kyteler read the character of her people as if for the first time. Watching them think through each contingency, hearing them briskly debate different strategic approaches, she was giddy with a confusion of emotions. Initially, she felt a profound relief, as at the setting down of a heavy burden. Then she found herself off balance, missing the burden, as though carrying its weight had defined her. Finally, she felt stabbed by regret—for all the hours she had focused on teaching these people, certain they had nothing to teach her; hours when she might also have been learning from them. . . .

But this was no time for regret. Fixing her concentration on the matter at hand, she stayed intent on keeping up with the rapidity and shrewdness with which her peasants were making plans. To her surprise, the various plans suggested were quite sophisticated. Finally, almost tentatively, she joined in the discussion. Gradually, the decision took shape.

Whatever they did, they would do together. Again to her astonishment, despite the depth of their lifelong roots in this land, and despite the fact that they had never in their lives ventured further than Kilkenny Town or possibly Wexford, the people chose exile and uncertainty. Yet even after hours of argument, Alyce still resisted flight for herself.

Finally, Old John, noticing his mistress's increasing adamancy as she cast about for reasons to stay when there were none, made a suggestion. Noting that he had seen many things come and go in his time, he pointed out that the Irish would surely outlast the Bishop, and that Lady Alyce would after all be leaving her lands merely as a temporary tactic, with imminent return fairly certain. That he did not believe for a moment this was true mattered less to him than that she might. And so she did. She changed her plans. If she could return, why then she would depart at the same time as her people, who would join her to live under her protection in England until they could all come safely home to Kyteler Castle.

Two days were left before Samhain. Together the group resolved *not* to leave the next night—when a group of traveling mummers was to perform in Kilkenny Town and the absence of everyone from the Kyteler estates would look suspicious—but the night after that: Samhain Eve itself. No one was eager to be out journeying on the Great Night of the Dead, but there was no help for it; the immediate, practical peril outweighed any dangers from Otherworlds. The fugitives would avoid suspicion by making their escapes at staggered times and in small groups, departing under cover of darkness, beginning at dusk and continuing until midnight. Taking separate routes, they would not ride the northern roads to the coast via Dublin; that would be a safer point of departure, but was too far. They would aim instead for the nearest harbor, at Wexford, thence to sail across St. George's Channel and Cardigan Bay. They would make landfall at Cardigan or, if weather there rose against them, at Fishguard, further south down the Welsh coast.

It was agreed that Lady Alyce should at once send a rider to the Wexford shipyards, to engage three small masted cutters to sail at different tides beginning with Samhain Eve on through the following day, as different bands of fugitives arrived at Wexford. It was further agreed that they would all meet up, once safely in Wales. If for some reason they should miss one another, they would seek each other out in England, now the destination for everyone, not only William—a change of plan that had the young man beaming with relief.

There was one last matter of contention.

The parents of the youngest children were insistent that their babes travel with Lady Alyce. William was to ride separately, as were the other young people, and the older children would go with their own families—but the heath-folk wanted the youngest in their mistress's keeping. In vain she argued that if she were taken by the Bishop's men, the children would be with the most wanted fugitive of all and would therefore be most endangered. Sysok replied that the children were in danger no matter whom they accompanied, since if caught they would be taken by the Church and whipped into conversion or face the same death as their parents. Helena added that sending the children with Lady Alyce ensured their best chance to begin a new life, with or without their parents. Back and forth the debate went. No one acknowledged that the real reason for this strategy was the assumption that Dame Alyce, despite being the Bishop's primary target, would be able to buy herself and their children greater safety.

At last she surrendered, agreeing to take responsibility for the youngest ones. It was settled that she and the seven littlest girls and boys would ride to the coast and set sail together, and that Petronilla de Meath would accompany them to help care for so many children on such an arduous journey. There was further debate about whether one or two of the men should ride with them, but Alyce argued successfully that two women with a brood of children would appear less threatening. Since nine people would constitute the largest party of travelers— and, as John Galrussyn pointed out, the one bearing the most precious cargo, their future—it was decided that this party would depart first.

Plans, times, and differing routes were restated and rehearsed over and over, until everyone claimed to know them by rote. At last, facing a multitude of tasks ahead in the next two days, the Wiccans rose and turned to take their leave.

But Alyce raised her hand. The assembly paused.

"There is something more," she said, and Petronilla noticed that her mistress's hand was trembling—how unthinkable!— as she drew a parchment scroll from her sleeve. "As you know, there will be no feast this Samhain. No roasting of apples, no quaffing mulled wine. No burning of wormwood to honour the lives of our ancestors, no leaving open the burial mounds so that we may speak with the Past. No Sabbat, no Ritual. We stand here with no Tools of Art. So must we be our own Tools. Air billows our lungs. Fire heats our blood. Water flows through our tears and spittle. Our flesh is earth. We are a living Covenstead. Wherever we stand is sacred space."

In silence, the people formed a ragged circle around her.

Turning rapidly to the east, the south, the west, and the north, she cried out, "*Spirits of Air, Spirits of Fire, Spirits of Water, Spirits of Earth, we welcome thee! The Circle is closed.*"

She addressed the assembly as she unrolled the parchment.

"These words of counsel come from our own kind across the sea. How these words came to me, and from whom, is a knowledge with which you need not be burdened. But know that these words come from those who follow, as do we, The Old Ways, and who have continued to follow them through times of horror and despair. These are words of survival. They should be known to you. It is your. . . right." Her voice was unsteady as she began to read, but she willed herself to continue.

> *We have come to the end of an age. We have come to a pause in the moonlit feasts, the bonfires, dancing, laughter, the open Pagan joy. A pause—because one day it shall return, for it breathes in the spirit, no matter how smothered.*
>
> *But not now, not for us. For us there is a new age, of suffering, secrecy, flight from enemies who are themselves trammeled in fear and ignorance.*
>
> *We have named this age 'The Burning Time.'*
>
> *Certain things must be done that our people may survive, and that the wisdom of The Craft may endure, even if it must be hidden for centuries to come.*

We have learned these lessons through affliction.
We offer them to others in The Craft who may yet be
forced to find them useful.

Keep a book in your own hand of write. Let sisters
and brothers copy what they will, but never let this
book out of your hand—for if it be found, you will
be taken and tortured. Never keep the writings of
another—for if it be found in their hand of write, they
will be taken and tortured.

Think to yourself: I know nothing, I remember
nothing. Chant this as poem, spell, prayer, meditation.
Will yourself to believe it.

Let the Working Tools be as ordinary things anyone
may have in their homes—a cracked bowl, the stump
of a candle, a kitchen knife. Let the Pentacles be
made of wax that they may be melted or broken at
once. Have no names on anything.

If you are taken, tortured, and confess, deny it
afterwards. Say that you babbled under the torture.
Drive this into your mind. If the torture be too great
to bear, then say: "I will confess. I cannot bear this
torment. What do you wish me to say? Tell me and I
will say it." Hearken well: There is no blame in striving
to survive. There is no heroism in embracing pain.
If they force you to confess impossibilities—flying

*through air, consorting with devils, sacrificing children,
eating human flesh—say simply: "I had evil dreams,
I was not myself, I was maddened."*

But herein lies the heart of the lesson: Name
no others.

*If you betray others, there is no hope for you, not
in this life or in any Mystery that yet may be to come.*

*If you be condemned, fear not, for The Craft has
its ways.*

If you are steadfast, you may be helped to escape.

*If you are sentenced to the pyre and yet remain
steadfast, potions will reach you so that you will feel
naught. Instead, you will pass through death and slip
like the babe from the womb into what lies beyond,
the Abyss into which all things fade and from which
all things arise.*

Alyce's voice broke. She paused, to regain her control.
Then she touched the parchment to a candle, watched it
crackle and flame, and dropped it to the cellar floor, grinding
the ashes underfoot. Only now could she look up at the surrounding faces, only now see that each face was as filled with
hope as with fear. So it had been worth telling them the truth.

"The Burning Time is come upon us in Ireland," she said.
"So I cannot bid you Merry Part until we meet again. But this

can I say: may we Merry Meet soon in a safe land, my people. Until such time, Blessed Be. And remember: *The blood of The Old Ones courses our veins. The Forms pass. The Circle remains.*"

She flung her arms wide, her torch-cast shadow spreading like a massive brood hen, wings extended, across the cellar walls.

"*Earth! Water! Fire! Air!*" she cried, "*Recognize thy children and protect them!*"

Slowly, the shadow folded its wings.

"*The Circle is opened,*" she said.

As the people filed silently up the cellar steps, no one looked back. No one saw her shoulders sag and her head droop, as if life had drained from her.

No one heard her whisper, the words evaporating into the dank air.

"The Circle is broken."

XIV

LEAVETAKINGS

THAT NIGHT WAS SLEEPLESS for most of the people of the Kyteler estate—especially Lady Alyce.

At dawn the next morning, she flung open her treasury and distributed gold coin and plate among her people—to keep them on their journey, in case they needed to offer bribes, and as insurance should they miss the arranged first meeting in Wales or, later, in England. Her own ancestral jewels—unworn for years but for the few items she'd donned in her recent masquerade in Kilkenny Town—she placed in a casket; these would buy security and lodging for herself, the children, and their parents, once safely across the sea. The only other possessions she packed were her writing materials and her Working Tools, placed in a second casket along with her Grimoire and a few other books—although choosing from her considerable library brought her to tears. Decades of study and practice were already packed in her brain, and she could reassemble her medicinal closet anywhere herbs and flowers grew. The brown woolen shirt and trousers with a man's leather jerkin she would wear should be sufficient wardrobe against the late autumn chill, along with her black cape of boiled wool so tightly woven it resisted rain.

That night, most of the peasants trooped dutifully into Kilkenny Town for the mummers' performance, striving to act relaxed and entertained while their hearts were cramped with fear. They could not help noticing more men-at-arms than usual patrolling the streets, yeomen now wearing tunics emblazoned with the coat of arms and stylized crucifix that denoted the Bishopric of Ossary.

The following day seemed to pass with frightening speed as well as drag with agonizing slowness. The castle's pantries were raided to assemble parcels of meat, cheese, bread, and onions, plus a flagon of wine and one of water for each traveler—each of whom also received one of the soaked, dried, stiffened shirts Alyce had made. The stables were opened so that anyone who lacked a swift horse or solid cart could choose what was needed. Some of the peasants made personal pilgrimages far out onto the heath, where generations of forebears had been buried, for one last visit to a particular grave. Others busied themselves trying to cram their worldly belongings into small wagons. Young lovers clung to one another, weeping, pledging devotion. Elders shook their heads at having lived to witness such a day descend on the Tuatha de Danaan.

From Alyce's perspective, however, the heath-folk were handling their leave-taking with an aplomb that again surprised her; she had assumed that being wrenched from the land would devastate her peasants utterly. But she had little time to mull this or anything else. Scheduled to depart first, she was a blur of movement—ensuring that everyone had gold coin, food, warm clothing, and means of transport.

By late afternoon, the youngest children began arriving in the castle courtyard, brought by parents doing their best not to weep and alarm the little ones. Fortunately, all the youngsters felt at home with Petronilla and even with Lady Alyce, since both women had tended or sat with them when they were sick. Still, the tangle of seven children under the age of six, gathered for a trip, was impressive.

Alyce had already bidden private farewells to the adults one by one, double-checking as she did so that each was properly equipped for the journey. She had pressed on each traveler a pottle of grapeseed paste for skin wounds, and a pouch of cloves, ginger, peppermint leaves, and pennyroyal, for seasickness. She had reminded Helena to bring a distillation of sage to dry up her breastmilk temporarily, since Dana would be traveling separately and having to make do with watered goat's milk sipped from a flask until they reached the Welsh coast and she could rejoin her mother. Having to abandon larders abrim with the harvest enraged Alyce, who continued to think of more items everyone should pack. Having to abandon the animals pained her even more, and she kept trying to think of ways to ensure the creatures would not be maltreated by those who might try to seize her holdings. The cattle and sheep were impassive creatures of habit. But she let the goats loose to wreak their natural mischief throughout the countryside—first saying a personal farewell to Greedigut, who gazed at her through white-lashed amber eyes, tolerated her embrace, and accepted a basket of dried rosebuds as a farewell dinner.

Prickeare's fate bore its own small tragedy. An elderly cat could hardly travel with seven children and two adults in a covered cart and then aboardship. Nor could he be left behind, since he was sure to be tortured to death by those who knew him to be Alyce Kyteler's cherished Familiar. There was only one thing to be done. The night before departure he had slept against her heart, purring on the beat of it and in rhythm with her breathing. Then, the following afternoon, unable to stop the tears running down her face, she had fed him the nightshade distillation that would cause no pain. She knew that he sensed what was happening. He walked about a little, but soon began to drag his hind legs. Then he could lift his head and front body only with difficulty, yet his jade eyes followed her everywhere. She picked him up and cradled him against her breast. He curled in her arms, gazing into her eyes, purring, understanding and forgiving everything. Then he drifted into a doze, and while she clasped his deepening sleep against her—the featherlight triangle of his head resting cupped in her palm—she could feel his ancient, loving heart slow, and then stop. She sat holding him this way as long as she dared. Then she carried his little body outside and planted him in the kitchen garden—in a particular spot where he had loved to lie sunning himself, nibbling the herbs and savoring the additional thrill of being able to flatten the lettuces at the same time.

It was there that Will found his mother, kneeling, slumped back on her heels, hands lying helplessly in her lap, weeping. The sight of her so defenseless thawed his last residue of resentment, and he knelt, too, flinging his arms around her.

"Oh Mum," he cried.

She reached for him and held him tight.

"Will. My dearest Will," she murmured. Then she leaned back, the better to perceive the soft young manhood in his face. Slowly, she examined the familiar features as if to imprint them indelibly on her sight, not knowing when her gaze would next trace the smooth slope of that cheek, the curve of that delicate nostril, the fine browngold hair of that eyebrow.

"Do you remember," she said, sniffling and trying to clear her throat, "when you were little?"

"Yes," he answered, clasping her more tightly.

"You were always there for me, through all the husbands—you, my joy, the one constant object of my love. You never really knew your father, of course . . . well, that was both loss and blessing. Then Adam complained that you were such a beautiful child—your green eyes, and your locks were red-gold then—too beautiful to be a boy, he claimed. He envied you, in truth—though beautiful you were. But for me, it was your glad spirit that was such a gift. You were my young knight, remember?"

Will nodded, working to hold back tears.

"One day, when you were only about six or seven, out riding with a tutor, you came across a fawn Richard had killed in his latest hunt—remember?—and you stormed home and bravely gave him such a tongue-lashing! 'Mum,' you proclaimed, 'I shall now protect you from Richard. From everyone. I shall be your knight.' And so you were. You protected me from John, too, in your way. And somehow you managed to endure all those stepbrothers and stepsisters passing through, leaving a spoor of quarrels and sour memories."

He shook his head and swallowed hard.

"Mum, I am so sorry for . . . for everything lately that—"

She placed a finger against his lips.

"Hush, my love. No need. I too have my regrets. I kept you young—younger than your years, I think. So that I might have one person to love steadily. . . . Perhaps I wronged you by not granting you more authority."

"No, t'is also true that I was not—"

"Never mind, none of that matters now. What matters is that we know we love one another."

"Mum…why do they—hate us so? What have we done to—"

"We have done *nothing*, my dearest, to them. Nothing to warrant such hatred. Except, perhaps, being different from them. Not seeing life as they do. But many people—perhaps most—fear what they do not know."

"Yet there will always be things unknown, things to learn, surely? And, too, why don't they simply get to know us? Why don't—"

"Because the fear is comfortable, familiar. It takes courage—and time—to learn . . . well, anything. Letters, numbers, people, ideas. Nor does it seem the Bishop will permit us that time. Perhaps he and his pope fear that knowing who we truly are might change *them*." Alyce sighed. "But that too matters not, not now. What matters is that we do whatever must be done to survive this—catastrophe; do you understand? What matters is that we flee to safety; that we return someday soon so that you become steward of your own ancestral lands. The land alone lasts, my dear; from it, everything else comes. *We must do whatever must be done to survive—and to protect the land.* And I believe you can do this, and that you *will* manage the estates someday, with skill and wisdom and compassion. I do trust you, you see."

They clung to each other. Then Alyce wiped the tears from her face and tried to smile.

"Now. Will, I want you not to be there when I depart in a few hours. I know you ride out an hour after me, and I know you have packing to do and. . . and your own farewells to say. Hard as it will be for me to tear myself from Kyteler Castle, it will be harder if you stand in the courtyard watching me depart. Can you understand?"

"Yes, Mum. I can understand."

"Good. Then go now, quickly. Wait, no, not yet—not before I bless you with a Three-fold Kiss." Taking his sweet young face between her hands, she softly kissed each eyelid and above, in the middle of his forehead. Then, holding back more tears, she tried to tease him lightly. "Remember, follow Robert de Bristol's sense of direction, not your own!"

He offered a faint smile, his own eyes wet.

"Go now, my son, my tender knight. Blessed Be. May you always walk in Her sight. Quickly. Go."

The young heir got to his feet, squared his shoulders, then strode off. At the edge of the garden he turned for one look back. His mother saw the last late afternoon sunlight slanting across his face, veining his hair reddish gold. Then he smiled, waved once, turned, and disappeared out of sight.

* * *

When it began blueing toward twilight, Alyce was finally forced to abandon the remainder of her last-minute tasks.

She did so reluctantly, with a sense of failure. But she permitted her women to bustle her out of her tower chamber with no backward look, and to hurry her to the castle courtyard.

There it stood: the large wagon boarded on three sides, roofed with planks covered by sheepskins and stained muslin so as to look like a peasant cart. The two fastest horses, Tissy and Makeshift, were being hitched up to draw it. The children had already been taken leave of by their parents and tucked inside with Petronilla, who was fussing over them lovingly, despite Sara's obvious displeasure at having to share her mother's attention with six other small beings.

There were curtsies, bows, embraces. Helena and Sysok kept peeking into the cart at Dana. Old John tried to kneel and kiss his Lady's hand. But she stopped him, bending to kiss his gnarled claw instead. Annota Lange was stoic as ever. Alyce and Henry were rechecking the horses' hooves to make doubly sure they were well shod. Eva de Brounstoun could not stop crying, but she strove to be cheerful through her soundless, soft, steady tears. Will Payne was there with his daughter Maeve, who was craning her neck in hopes of a glimpse of young William, while she herself was being hovered over by Robert de Bristol. They and all the others had assembled for this formal farewell to their mistress.

Then it was time.

By previous agreement, the Wiccans drifted off, alone, or in twos and threes, scattering to finish preparations for their own imminent departures. Their Lady had wanted this moment to herself.

Standing alone in the courtyard, Alyce looked up at the towers of Kyteler Castle, her family seat for more generations than she could number. Kytelers had come and gone, but these walls had endured—and the land even longer. Now, for the first time, she sensed in her soul that she might well be leaving forever. If so, what would become of the land? She knew the husbands' children would try to claim it—fight over it, carve up their former stepmother's lands, retainers, livestock, and possessions amongst themselves, not forgetting to share their confiscated spoil with the Bishop who had made such largesse possible. She bent and scooped up a handful of earth, pouring it into a tiny pouch and tucking that into the pocket of her jerkin.

Then she gazed out through the courtyard arch across the moat to the heath—heart-wrenchingly beautiful as it glimmered violet in the dusk—peering for one last look at the Covenstead. It was deserted. No Samhain Sabbat there this night. But tears blurred her eyes and made prisms in the failing light, and for a moment she saw a rainbow of Wiccans assembling there, Wiccans from out of time, from the Otherworlds, ancestral wraiths approaching from all directions, gathering at the Cromlech, chanting soundlessly, swaying, raising a Cone of Power. . . .

Then she blinked. And there was only the dolmen towering agelessly up out of the earth, the circle like the outline of a grass-fringed stone eye staring sentinel at the moon. Her chest constricted as if her heart were fracturing, while grief flaked through her in a thousand tiny crackled lines.

Crazing, the potters call that, she thought absently, calm, as if watching herself from outside herself. *I was so certain this rupture from the land would be unbearable for the people,* she thought, *but I am the one who finds it unbearable.* She bit her lip. *Because the land is mine. Not theirs. Because I own them—but the land owns me.* She thought of Eva's voice at the cellar meeting: *Was it a dream of faerie lore, then, after all, our community?*

"M'Lady?" called Petronilla from inside the cart.

No time for hesitation; no time for anything, anymore. Except flight.

"Yes. One moment, Petronilla."

She stood between the yoked horses, who were pawing the ground in a contagion of excitement from the anxiety they smelled on the humans. She stroked their forelocks, whispering into their pricked-up ears.

"Now love, now Tissy! Whoa there, Makeshift! Concentrate that spirit, *concentrate* it, dear ones. Together we must *fly.* To Wexford! To the seacoast!"

Then she sprang to the outside bench of the coach, seized the reins, and cried out:

"In the name of Magog, Mother of Sacred Horses! *Now!*"

The clatter of hoofbeats and thunder of cart wheels pounded over the drawbridge.

Echoes rippled across the heath, then died away.

There remained only silence, and what would outlast this assault as it had all others: a circle of stones.

X V

VISIONS

ALONE IN HIS CATHEDRAL study, Richard de Ledrede paced the floor in excitement. All day he had yearned for darkness with an anticipation he hadn't felt for years—not since that long ago evening when, as a young priest, he had waited so eagerly to celebrate his first Christmas Midnight Mass. Tonight, though, would celebrate not a birth but an ending—of heretical defiance. Tonight would witness his personal triumph over Dame Alyce Kyteler. But the waiting was agony. Darkness had long since fallen. It was past nine on the candle mark, but still no word. Why couldn't these heretics at least have the common sense not to gather in the dead of night?

When the servant knocked, the Bishop flung open the door.

"Yes? Are the pagans assembling on the heath yet? Have the look-outs seen anything?"

"No, my lord, no word yet. Perhaps t'is still too early. But this—" the servant proffered a sealed scroll "—just arrived by courier from Dublin."

He grabbed the scroll, hurriedly broke the seal, and unrolled the parchment. Growling "Go, go, go," in dismissal to his servant, he began to read. Then he broke into a rare smile of relief.

The letter was from the Lord Justice of Ireland. It was terse. It informed His Eminence the Bishop of Ossary that His Excellency the Lord Justice had received direct orders from His Holiness the Pope demanding heresy trials in Ireland, and that therefore secular permission could no longer be denied. Consequently, the Lord Justice was hereby formally granting to the Bishop, acting as Papal Emissary, permission to mount such trials.

De Ledrede laughed aloud with delight at both the contents and the brevity of the letter. How it must have galled the Lord Justice to be forced to write it! This was going to be a very good night indeed. He refilled his wine goblet and raised it in a toast to his vanquished adversary.

"To you, Lady Alyce. You led me a merry chase, and for that I thank you. Once I had engaged your enmity, Ireland no longer bored me. But tonight you lose. Not all your wealth, your ingenious plotting, your powerful family connections—"

He froze, goblet in mid-air, his own last words resonating through his mind, leaving a chill in their wake.

The Lord Justice was her relative. He had stood by her once before. He might have written to her now, warning her.

The Bishop had been certain all along that Alyce Kyteler would never relinquish her lands, the richest in Ireland. But if specifically warned... might she flee? She might. She might be preparing to flee at this very hour.

The Bishop slammed down his goblet and rushed through the door, bellowing, "Up! Saddle the horses now! We will not wait for midnight! To the courtyard! We ride to Kyteler Castle *now*!"

* * *

Through the darkness the cartful of children jostled on, stopping only for the two women to change places, taking turns at the reins or riding with the children inside. By midnight, the wagon and its occupants had reached the east coast. The children, at first mouse-still with confusion, had become noisy with adventure, then cranky with confinement, and were now all but yowling with dissatisfaction. They had eaten well enough; indeed, the cart floor was carpeted with crumbs. But their space was very cramped, and none except the youngest ones, including Dana the baby, had been able to sleep much in the jolting wagon. It would be a relief to rest before what was sure to be a choppy channel crossing.

Alyce reined in the horses at the edge of a pine forest high on a hill above Wexford harbor. Here they could remain safe until dawn and keep watch for any pursuers. Good enough, since by early light the first boat for which she had paid should be ready to sail.

Petronilla parted the muslin flaps and stuck out her head.

"Why be we stopping?" she called, "D'ye want me to take another turn at the reins?" Then she glanced out down the hill. "Oh! T'is Wexford!" she gasped, recognizing the place so familiar from years of unhappiness. "Then canna we—canna we go down and get on the boat? Canna we sail right away?"

Alyce shook her head.

"No, Pet. We are pausing here to rest a few hours until dawn. The captain sent word to me before we left home that t'is best for the first boat to sail with the morning tide, and he wishes us to board just before weighing anchor—so as not to arouse suspicion, I imagine. But we are here too early. I warned you that you were driving Tissy and Makeshift too severely when you had the reins."

"Oh but we *canna* stop, we *must* press on, we—"

"*No.* We must *not*," Alyce replied, her weariness taking on an edge of anger. "We have come a long way, and more swiftly than I had planned. The other thing I did not plan is *that*," she said, pointing to the north. "It looks to be a storm lowering an hour or so away. I do not relish the babes being in the open during a storm—but we dare not put up at the inn in town. And I know of no trustworthy Wiccan house hereabout to shelter us.

Wexford has become such a Christian stronghold." She leapt down from the cart. "Well, never mind. We will build a shelter of pine boughs and blankets, and hope the storm blows to the west or holds off till morning. The children are desperate for a bit of stretch. And you and I could each use a few moments of sleep. One can rest while the other stands guard."

Petronilla clambered hastily out of the cart, gesticulating wildly.

"*No!* Oh no, no, *no*, we dinna dare—"

"*Petronilla!* Stop it! What has *happened* to you? For months you were growing more confident, and night before last, at the meeting in the cellar, you were so—eloquent. But now you are again a timid, panicked *waif*. We need to be even-tempered, not—*convulsive*. So stop acting like one of the children! I have seven of them to deal with as it is." Alyce paused for breath. "Now. We will remain here for a few hours to rest and wait for dawn. No more hand-wringing. I *know* what I am *about*."

The younger woman glared at her, eyes wide, nostrils flaring like those of a cornered animal, lips curled in scorn. It was a sullen, vindictive face Alyce had never seen Petronilla wear.

"Oh aye, ye always be knowing everything, do ye not? Naught ever scares *herself* or worries *herself*!"

"That's not *true*, Pet, I—"

"I be *not* your *pet!* Even though ye be the great Lady Alyce. Aye, t'is the *perfect* Lady Alyce, the *generous* and *saintly* Lady

Alyce, the *wise* Lady Alyce who knows all what's to know! Pity the poor rest of us! We be mere mortals! We canna *ever* please Her Ladyship because we canna ever be wise and perfect as *she* is!" She spat the last word out as a hiss.

Alyce stood still, contemplating her maidservant. Slowly, she walked over and embraced her, feeling the young woman's body stiffen. But Petronilla pushed her off and backed away, her face contorted with rage and fear, her eyes wild as if seeing some vision only she could perceive, her voice pitched high and thin with fright.

"Ye dinna understand, ye *never* . . . t'is all for *naught*. Ye canna see what I see. T'is the waking dream. I *see* it. I see the Circle. But t'is a circle of skulls. Flesh cold as stone washed in moonlight. Dew aglitter on bones—*wee* bones, ach God, the bones of *babes*! Little, little bones. They be sticking out from all the corpses' bloody tangled curls—pretty and pearly baby bones like combs in Her Grace's long red hair. Oh God I see it! Death and life and the space between you tell about! But the space between *not* be empty! It be *full*! It be *crowded*, oh God—with burning souls! The skulls be cracked, broke open, the nightmare spilling out! I see horror! Oh God I *see*—"

Alyce slapped Petronilla, hard, across the face.

The two glared at one another.

Then Petronilla's chest began to heave as her sobs rose. Quickly, Alyce put her arms around the younger woman and held her, rocking her, humming softly in her ear as she would to one of the children. They stood swaying that way until gradually the storm inside the little maid subsided. But Alyce, staring over Petronilla's shoulder at the sky, saw that the other storm was blowing in their direction.

"You see?" she said to Petronilla, holding her at arm's length, "Is this not proof that we both need some rest? You are out of temper, and *me*—look what a harridan I am becoming, to have scolded you so. Come. I will unhitch the horses to have a graze and a drink—I think I heard a brook over that way, a little into the woods. If so, they can be tethered to one of the saplings there—but loosely, so they can reach the water. Meanwhile, you bring the children out of the wagon so they can toddle around a bit before we put them down. Is that not a good plan?"

Spent by her weeping, Petronilla wiped her eyes, nodding. Then both she and Alyce set to work. In a short while, as the older tots were groggily shuffling through the pine needles, the women had brought sheepskins from the wagon and made an outdoor bed for them to lie on. Then, while Alyce was lashing a quilt between two tree branches as a canopy above the improvised bed, Petronilla wandered off, staring out over the valley and seaport town below them.

"Look," she called to her mistress in a strained voice, "That church there? T'is my old parish chapel, where I'd be going for shelter—first from Cook, then from my husband. T'is there I'd be sitting—oh, not often, and sure not long— when I dinna have to be up and doing, fetching, dodging... t'was lovely. So *quiet*. A body be hearing the heartbeat inside herself. I be lighting a candle, praying for mercy. Hearing the plainsong and chants, breathing the incense—sweet, so sweet. And the bells! I be *loving* the bells, the Angelus most. I be loving all of it, really. And Mass! T'was so beautiful, so comforting.... Aye, but that was before I left my husband and the evil Father Donnan said... he be still there, you know! He might— "

"Oh, I should not worry about him, Pet—*ronilla*," Alyce replied, busy creating the rain canopy. "De Ledrede would be sending his own men-at-arms after us—and they cannot even know we have fled yet. Or if they do know, then by now they have probably been distracted by looting my castle and pilfering our harvest," she muttered bitterly. "But even the Bishop is not able to alert every parish priest in Ireland to the threat of our banshee presence. Though just the same, for caution's sake, we probably should not build a fire, pleasant as that would be."

Petronilla didn't answer. She stood gazing at the little stone church, twisting her pale braids. At last, Alyce, struggling against exasperation, called her to please come help tuck in the children.

Dana had long since dozed off in her swaddling, cushioned by pine needles. The women hustled Sara and the other toddlers to the blanket bed where, despite their elation at being let out of the cart and their glee at this adventure of sleeping outdoors in a forest, they dropped off immediately, too exhausted even to protest being put down.

Embarrassed by her outburst, Petronilla offered to take the first watch. But she still seemed agitated, so Alyce decided to sit with her for a few minutes. She uncorked a flask of wine and took a swallow, then passed it to Petronilla, urging it on her for warmth and hoping it might relax her a little.

The two women sat together on a large rock in the pine forest, saying nothing, each alone with her thoughts.

*　　*　　*

"May the most wrathful God of Abraham punish such stupidity!" the Bishop shouted at his manservants, who had just helped him dismount into a puddle.

"May Christ Himself have mercy and rescue me from such incompetents! *Why* am I never told anything until it is too late? Is all Ireland one conspiracy, serfs through nobles? *Is this sabotage or idiocy?* Does it matter? *No*, the result is the *same!*"

In full roar, Richard de Ledrede stormed through the hall and back into his study, slamming his door in the faces of the apologetic gaggle of priests trailing after him. He did not care to hear any more excuses from people so thick-headed that they assigned look-outs to one place only, the Covenstead, ignoring the Castle itself.

He flung off his cloak and sank into a chair. Now that he finally had won permission to hold his heresy trials, he had lost his chief heretic.

He reached for a beaker of brandywine and poured himself a cup, draining it in two gulps. Then he sat back and closed his eyes, shuddering to recall how he had ridden triumphantly across the drawbridge to Kyteler Castle, there to sit astride his horse, circling the empty, echoing courtyard lit only by his men's torches, forced to acknowledge the truth—Alyce Kyteler was gone. She had abandoned her beloved ancestral lands. So The Craft meant that much to her. He had underestimated her again. He could not afford one more miscalculation.

What was to have been the best night of his life was rapidly becoming the worst—certainly the most humiliating since that dinner last Christmas honouring Bernard Gui, Inquisitor of Toulouse, when Cardinal de Blanc had so cruelly jested that he...

What an absurd position the Church had placed him in, really. He was a linguist, an administrator, a diplomat—what right had they to thrust him into the position of military tactician? Yet even at that, God knows, he had done his best.

He had sent pursuit after Kyteler and her retinue, splitting his men-at-arms up in all four directions to follow every road out of Kilkenny. Delegating nothing this time, he had personally instructed their commanders to break down doors and do whatever convincing was necessary to solicit information about any passing travelers. He had sent yet another complement of yeomen to seek out those serfs known to be special pets of Dame Alyce, on the chance that she was hiding out with one of them. He had covered all escape routes. Unless the cursed witches really could fly.

He groaned and rubbed his eyes. Then he filled another cup with brandywine, trying to savor how its topaz colour glinted in the candlelight as he poured. But it gave him no pleasure. All capacity for enjoyment felt suspended until he had that vile bawd of Satan safe in his dungeons. Even the wine tasted of fear, fear that she was gone for good, fear. . .

Christ! If he failed, what remained for him? In order to elicit the Pope's personal missive to the Lord Justice, he had needed to convince Avignon that the arrest, trial, and condemnation of Kyteler were central to gaining Church hegemony in Ireland. He had succeeded in this by writing numerous letters of appeal to the Papal Court over the past months, even exaggerating Kyteler's importance to convince them. If she eluded him now, how could he explain his failure? And if he failed, the Church in France would not have him back.

He knew that. Without the Pope's support he could not carry on in Ireland, either. Furthermore, he still faced those revived fraud charges in Kilkenny. England had long been sealed against him. Where could he go? Not only would a cardinal's hat be forever out of reach, but he would *fall* instead of rising. He would end up as a parish priest in some dusty Italian village, begging his superiors for pence to fix the roof and baptizing litters of squalling peasant brats.

He began to pace the room like a celled prisoner. He *needed* this triumph, needed the spectacle of Alyce Kyteler repentant in chains or aflame at the stake. He needed this more than he had ever needed anything in his life.

He glanced at the hourglass. Each grain of falling sand meant increasing likelihood of her escape. Charging to the door, he opened it and peered out. But other than the sentry dozing at the end of the hall, no one was there. No breathless messenger running toward him with news of her apprehension, no word. He yelled once to startle the sentry, then banged the door shut again. He had not felt so totally helpless since his boyhood.

Pouring another cup, he drank it down, feeling its anodyne begin to blunt the edge of his fear with a growing sense of pity at the injustice being done him. This Irish assignment was equivalent to Sisyphus's boulder. They *expected* him to fail. Back in Avignon they were laughing, laying wagers only as to *when*. Here he was, fighting for the Church, *his* vision of the Church—the centuries of individual sacrifices, the millions of prayers, the last thoughts of myriad suffering martyrs; the countless lives fed, housed, educated, *saved* by the Church—*that* was what he was defending. Not that Avignon would notice. . . . But *God* certainly should notice. He stared accusingly at the gilded crucifix across the room. Tears rose in his throat. He deserved better treatment than this. Stumbling to the prie-dieu, he fell heavily to his knees and crossed himself, bowing his head above interlaced fingers, his lips grazing the bishop's ring as he prayed.

"Holy Saint Francis, help me. . . . I know I have fallen away from my youthful reverence. But I have given all in a greater service, to the Church. I have been obedient. I have bargained with Hell to preserve the idea of Heaven. Are not my labours worth *something*? I denounce false gods every day!. . . Blessed Francis, have I—have I fallen into idolatry? Have I sinned against God by loving the Church too much? *Mea culpa, mea maxima*—but *how* can I be idolatrous? The Church and God are one! I am God's scholar, God's voice in different tongues, God's steward! Why then do I go unnoticed, as if I were God's serf? Intercede for me, Blessed Francis, that I may be *noticed*—and. . . and awarded this small payment for my loyal service: victory tonight, victory over this woman!

"And you, Blessed Saint Patrick. You see how I have fought infidels and apostates to sustain your mission here? *Grant me, Holy Patrick, the body of this foul witch!* Give her into my hands! *Ad majorem Dei gloriam!. . . In nomine. . .*

Mumbling the last words and crossing himself, he struggled to his feet, wove a few steps, shuffled back to his chair, and half fell into it. He desperately longed to go to bed. But rest was out of the question.

He would wait—though in the dizzy haze of righteousness and brandy he was no longer sure for what. Ah yes, for word about the pursuit of his prize, the witch. But something else . . . recognition. Yes, of his *merit*, yes! He refused to be ignored. Even if the Church abandoned him, he would not go quietly. At least *God* would not be ungrateful, *God* would notice . . . .

But that would mean—no, cannot be—*No*. Oh then how—no. Cannot. . . . *But that would mean that the Church and God were not the same thing after all. . .*

He closed his eyes to shut out the pain in his head.

It didn't matter.

He would wait.

For what he had paid for dearly.

For what was owed him.

If he was God's serf, he would wait, for as long as it took, to be noticed.

* * *

"What *is* it, my dear?" Alyce finally asked gently, "Petronilla? Cannot you tell me? Is it simply that you are afraid?

I mean, not *normally* afraid the way everyone else is now, but afraid the way you used to be when you first came to us— *consumed* by it?" There was no answer, so Alyce went on. "We are all afraid, you know. Certainly *I* am. All I am doing is holding on—being afraid for just a few moments longer, then a few moments after that, moment by moment—which others mistake for courage. In times like these, anyone who is *not* afraid is demented. But my child, we cannot let fear churn us up so that it immobilizes us. That is where the *will* comes in, the concentrated will. You remember: '*Chant the Word and let it free. As my Will, so mote it be...*' "

Petronilla sat holding the flask, not drinking. Finally, she spoke.

"...'*An it harm none.*' Aye. T'is that I mean. The harm. What if I *want* some of 'em harmed? Like Donnan? Or the Bishop? What then? Ah, t'is such a stew in my mind, m'Lady," nodding her head toward the distant silhouette of the Wexford church, "All my days I be wanting to please 'em— that was *all* I be knowing. Such a knowing—t'is not what a body can forget. Might be no one can ever unlearn it, sure not in a year and a day. And oh, I *do* fear 'em—ye canna know how much. T'is many mysteries ye know, Your Ladyship, but this I be knowing in some way you canna: them and their power. T'is a knowing I wear tucked inside my skin. Just to think of 'em, I can feel myself quaking—and shamed by the quaking. But I be feeling more than myself. I be knowing what they leave behind when they pass through lives like mine in their grand processions on the way to their cathedrals and their noble courts. Not just the cruel ones or the ones who judge us or the greedy ones with ice shards cold as diamonds hanging from their hearts. But the ones who just...dinna *care*. Aye, they just dinna care. The ones who be believing folks like me are naught. The ones who be not noticing who gets crushed under the hooves of their sleek horses. . . ." Her voice dropped to whisper. "Sometimes, in my dreams, or even awake—I think I be actually *seeing* all who have perished. Those you told us of, too—folk accused on other shores. Ach, such suffering I see! Those who be tortured, those who canna speak or who be forced to lie, who be beaten, chained, dying. *I see 'em*. I see 'em hunger and sicken and freeze. I see 'em thirst and despair."

"Perhaps you have the Sight, Petronilla," Alyce murmured, regarding her student with new respect. "Like the seers. Like some of the bards and poets. Perhaps that is your strength. You must give it your attention, whatever it is. T'is a great lesson."

"Ach, another lesson, is it," Petronilla said dully.

"I know,"Alyce laughed softly, "Wearying, eh? But everything can teach us something. The only question is whether we are open to learning what—"

"—so when I see it, all this suffering. . ." Petronilla's voice deepened and her pale face flushed and darkened, "then I be—changing. Then I be wanting to *slaughter* the men who do this. Then I be longing to see other sights, to see *them* suffer, to see their surprise that a body so low as me could make 'em suffer, to see my own hands gloved with their blood—feel it sticky and red and warm, smell it, even taste—"

"Hush, oh *hush*, child. Do not say it. Do not *think* it. Remember: "*Do what thou wilt, an it harm none. For the Law of Three will return to you what you send against another thricefold.*" Alyce made a wide flinging gesture with both hands, as if casting away the thought. "I deflect these thoughts that haunt you! I cancel them, cancel them, *cancel* them!"

But Petronilla was not finished.

"Ye may think me truly daft, I know. But there be something even worse than the fear and the hatred I feel for them. For I also. . . I be *part* of them, *part* of their world—and they be part of me. I can *feel* them waiting for me. Mayhap I be not meant for Initiation into The Craft. Mayhap I be meant to stay with what I grew up on, what I always trusted would save me. Christian mercy, Christian forgiveness."

"But Petronilla, you have done nothing, *nothing*, to *require* forgiveness! Quite the opposite! You have—"

"Ye canna see it, m'Lady, but I have such—*hate* in me! Rich, thick hate. I *need* that mercy, I crave it. Ye be talking about power and about will. But there be no power in *me*. T'is—all *outside* me, power belonging to God or Christ or the

Blessed Virgin. Or The Great Mother. Or the Green Man. To some body or spirit other'n me. But me... there be *naught* in me. I be empty. And I be so tired of trying to—what you say, be myself—when I got no self to be."

The older woman reached for Petronilla's hand, gripping it tightly.

"My daughter," she said hoarsely, "that is a lifetime's task, learning to be oneself. Petronilla, hear me. If you want to return to Christian ways, you should do so. All I ask is that you not feel yourself *driven* to a decision, especially now, at this time of crisis. Please, please, trust *yourself*. Trust what you have known all your life, yes. But also trust what you have learned this past year, too. To conceive power in the spirit of The Goddess is for a woman to discover that spirit also in herself, you see? So acknowledge your fear— yet *keep faith with your own power*. And believe me when I tell you that your strength springs not from hatred. It comes from love, Petronilla. I see it in your every act. Not a passive love, either: a *fierce* love. 'By *naught but love may She be known*.' Remember? So hearken to your own desire. Then you will come to understand what it is you most long to do, were born to do, *must* do. And you will find you have the courage to do it. This is my sole wisdom, my sole mystery, the secret that guides me when you assume, wrongly, that I am not afraid."

Petronilla looked down at their entwined hands, barely listening. *Clenched together this way,* she thought, *two women's hands are still only the size of one man's fist. How innocent Her Grace is really,* she mused, and felt for the first time as if she were the elder of the two. But she did not say that.

"I will try to trust myself. Ye be teaching me much," she said instead, "Ye be like an *amchara* to me. I canna say..." She could not continue. The women huddled close, hands clasped, with no need to speak.

"So now. Ye go and rest awhile, m'Lady." Petronilla managed a wan smile.

"Very well. But wrap yourself warmly while you sit sentinel," Alyce replied. Then the maidservant watched her mistress enfold herself in a quilt, curl up beside the sleeping children, and fall instantly into a deep slumber. *Like Sara,* Petronilla thought again, *like a wee innocent child.*

A wind sprang up, rustling the pine boughs, releasing the scent of resin in the cold air. But once it passed, the forest seemed to hush itself, densifying its darkness around the visitors.

Petronilla de Meath, alone in her wakefulness, walked to the hill's crest and sat on a rocky promontory, hunching against the chill, drawing her cloak tightly around her. She scanned the night sky, trying to draw down strength from a moon obscured by storm clouds, its glowing face hidden from her sight as if veiled in mourning for the dying year.

There was a sudden scream. Startled, she spun around to see a rush of black wings as a raven erupted in flight from a nearby juniper branch, screeching as it flew. *The Badb, the Macha,* she thought with a chill at the spine, naming the crow shapes of The Morrigan, *the Battle Crow who flies at Samhain to pick the bones of warriors soon to die.* Then she remembered. There was no Sabbat Ritual, and no Initiation, but it was still Samhain Eve, when the membranes between this world and the Otherworlds tremble at their sheerest and most permeable. It was the night of death and birth.

Here was no birth.

Here was only cold, silence, emptiness. The dark.

"Great Mother of All," she began, "and Holy Mary, Mother of God," lowering her eyes in shame at the double address. *Ye be trying to have it both ways,* she thought, harshly condemning herself. *Coward. Ye still be trying to please everybody.*

"Mother of—" she began again.

Then she stopped.

There it was.

She felt it even as she saw it.

A lifetime of tension shattered inside her, beginning in a trickle and swiftly flooding outward as if freed by the bursting of a dam. This was the certainty for which she had been waiting all these years. Unsurprised, she stared in recognition.

It was real. It was vivid as each nightmare, every waking vision, each foreboding, every dread.

There, well below the hill's crest, crawled a caterpillar of torches borne by at least fifty men-at-arms, their tunics in the fireglow clearly bearing the crest of the Bishopric of Ossary.

Petronilla blinked twice to make sure it was not another vision like all the others that had flickered through her over the past days.

But these men were real.

They were inching closer.

The column was winding its way up the road directly to where the fugitives had made camp.

XVI

THE BREAKING OF THE STORM

IN THE ETERNITY of a few seconds that followed, Petronilla sat utterly still, numb. She opened her mouth, but could make no sound. She tried to stand, but her body wouldn't move. She had once seen a hare rapt with terror, paralyzed, its eyes huge, watching its death advance in the shape of a nobleman's hound.

Then, suddenly, involuntarily, her body did move. It began to shake uncontrollably.

She glanced back to where Alyce and the children lay sleeping, then swung her gaze again to the marching column of armed men—but in the blur between, one image lodged on her sight: the little stone church, bleared with moonlight diffused by the scudding clouds.

Slowly, an expression of comprehension blossomed across her face.

"If I trust myself," she breathed, so low she could barely hear her own whisper among the shushings of the pines, "really trust *myself*—then what I choose to do...I be not caring how it looks. Not caring what anyone thinks. *Anyone*. If I really..."

She staggered to her feet and hastened, stepping lightly so as not to crack twigs underfoot, to the sheepskin bed. All was motionless, everyone sound asleep.

Still, even with so many others near, she could recognize her own child's breathing, distinct from the rest. She followed its soft, even cadences to where Sara lay. Unable to see her in the dark but unwilling to risk waking anyone by groping for the little form, Petronilla crouched at the edge of the makeshift bed. There, helpless, unable to touch her daughter, she knelt on a cushion of pine needles, drinking in the rhythm of this sweet childish breathing—steady, delicate, fragrant as music.

Sara, Sara, she mouthed wordlessly, *most dear loved child, forgive me for what I canna help but do. I canna stay, I canna be brave and fight that way. You be growing up strong and wise, I pray it. You be growing free from your mother's cowardice. T'will be for you what never could be for me. T'is why I canna take you with me. Ah, what a fresh grief, this! The worst of all my griefs, to leave you. And shall you be hating me, then, not knowing how much you be loved? Shall you ever forgive me for what I canna help? Oh little heart, like once I carried you inside my body, I carry you still, wherever I be going, I carry you wrapped inside this rag that be left of my soul. T'would have been grand, watching you grow to the fullness of womanhood. But t'was not meant, not for me. Too much fear in me, too much pain. Oh God, I canna bear it! Sara, Sara, my only child, the one perfect thing I made. . . .*

The words made no whisper, the cries no noise. Only the pines sighed and swayed in the wind with the woman as she rocked herself, keening soundlessly, beside the shape of the child who slept on, untroubled by such suffering, innocent of its proximity, its depth. Silently, the mother pounded her face with her fists. *I canna leave her—but I canna help it—oh Blessed Mary please Holy Brigid sweet Jesus somebody give me the strength....*

At last she rose. She hesitated, a stunned woman seeking her bearings. Then she moved swiftly toward the wagon, tiptoeing past the sleepers. From deep in the woods, where the horses had been tethered for grazing, Tissy sensed human movement and snorted softly. Petronilla paused, peering back at her companions. No one stirred.

She reached the cart, fumbled for the muslin flaps, and slipped inside. Quietly, she groped for what she needed. Locating the tinder box, she struck a flame and lit a small candle, closing the flaps after her to ensure no light would be visible from the outside. Hurriedly, behind the food bundles, she felt for the casket she sought. She found her mistress's Book of Shadows, a quill, and a tiny vial of ink.

How mystical, how holy, these writing tools had seemed to her once, back when Lady Alyce had begun teaching her to read and write! How long ago that seemed now—back when each morning had opened with the gift of every day. Back when she had gulped her sudden unimaginable freedom like deep draughts of water after a lifetime of thirst, back when she could not believe her good fortune, when she thought she had escaped forever from this dull, familiar universe of threat and pain and punishment.

She remembered the day she'd arrived at Kyteler Castle, one stray among what she would later learn were many who drifted there, wounded, in search of healing. She remembered how she had been terrified by encountering the famous Lady Alyce as a ghost—chalky white from head to toe, eyebrows to ankles—until the playful wraith who greeted her apologized for coming straight from a flour fight with her son in the bakehouse. She remembered the day she danced—*her*, Petronilla!—for the first time in her life. She remembered the day she heard Sara's laughter for the first time in either of their lives, that laugh like a hundred tiny gold bells chiming at once, a laugh that compelled you to join in for the sheer bubbling bliss of laughing. She remembered the day she'd begun learning her letters, while Lady Alyce had winked at her, "You know, Pet, learning to spell and learning to Spell are not unconnected. . . ."

Guiltily, Petronilla tugged a leaf of parchment from the book and dipped the quill into the ink vial. For her, the act of writing still exercised mystical powers, even now. But there was no time to draw her letters properly. She blinked away that shame, trying to concentrate on the message she needed to write.

The note, scribbled in a shaky hand, took only a few moments. She folded it and placed it between the leaves of the book, with one edge protruding. Respectfully, she restoppered the ink vial, wiped and put away the quill, blew out the candle. Letting herself out of the wagon and stepping with care, she carried the book to where Alyce lay, tucking it gently into the folds of the sleeping woman's quilt where it could not be missed.

Then Petronilla ran once more to the hill's edge to check the column of torch-bearing armed men.

Nearer, nearer.

She inhaled deeply, filling her lungs as if with her last breath. Then, with no glance backward, she gathered up her things and slipped off deeper into the woods to where the horses were tethered, disappearing into the dark.

*　　*　　*

The first crash of thunder woke Alyce from her sleep. If there had been none, still she would have wakened, startled more by something she could not name than by the noise.

She struggled with the quilt's folds, trying to rise—and her hand grazed instead the familiar, heavy shape of her own Book of Shadows. Certain now that something was wrong, she lurched upright and stumbled to the hillcrest, softly calling

Petronilla's name. There was no answer. Behind her, one of the children whimpered with a bad dream.

Rolling fog now totally obscured the valley and the road below. It was as if the hilltop and forest were adrift in a Samhain mist, an Otherworld terrain suspended outside its own space, like the Day Outside the Year. She could see nothing beyond her own hand held directly in front of her face. Clutching the Grimoire, she groped her way toward the wagon, tripping and falling over a dead branch in the darkness, muffling her cry and scrambling to her feet as noiselessly as possible. Finally she could make out a solid black shape looming against the more intangible blackness. It was the outline of the cart.

Once inside, she reenacted the same ceremony with tinder box and candle that Petronilla had performed earlier.

Then, in the dim light, she saw the parchment's edge, a small white flag protruding from the Grimoire.

Her teeth began to chatter. She closed her eyes and told herself it was merely the cold. Then she forced herself to open her eyes. Unfolding the note, she began to read.

> *Alyce, amchara, I dare be calling you by these names now, for the first time and the last. Please be not hating me for a coward. I go to seek sanctuary at my Church. Tomorrow I will confess all my sins. If I be truly penitent, I know I be forgiven. You shall have sailed*

by then. Do not stay, for the babes' sakes, and because the People said you must go. I pray you all get free and safe.

Take my Sara as your own. When she is older, name her Basilia in The Craft. Help her. But let me go. I be what I am. Inside me is a room so filled with fear there be no space for fearing one thing more. I be at home in this room, I be safe from hope. Try to forgive your friend and student—who is grateful to you and who did trust herself and who did find her own way at last. Petronilla de Meath.

Stupefied, Alyce tried to grasp her thoughts as they raced through shock after shock.

She must follow Petronilla. She must find her.

She must not let her be driven back to the very sources of her fear.

She must keep her from Donnan's vengeance.

She must *rescue* her, she must—

Alyce burst from the wagon, to be met by a wash of lightning that drenched the sleeping children with a harsh blue brightness. *The children!* They could not be left. How could she seek out Petronilla and leave seven young children alone?

A deafening bellow of thunder opened the storm itself, downsweeping in torrents—needles of rain, chunks of hail.

Like a madwoman, Alyce reeled in the wind to where the small ones were waking, wailing. Already, the hail was bringing down the canopy above their heads.

A child under each arm, Alyce dashed back and forth, trip after trip, between forest-bed and wagon, bundling them back into the covered cart. Meanwhile, thoughts kept shuddering through her in spasms, like the lightning.

She dared not risk taking the children to the church to retrieve Petronilla. But there was no place safe to leave them—not even a goatshed or pigsty in sight, as glare after glare of lightning made punishingly clear.

She ground her teeth in fury. Trapped. She was trapped into forsaking Petronilla, trapped into abandoning her to an old slavery from which she had all but broken free. Trapped into defeat at the hands of these malicious foreign churchmen who had come to wreak ruin on her Ireland. Trapped. Humiliated. Powerless.

Numb with sorrow, she staggered out of the wagon, now sour-smelling from so many wet children packed whining, half-asleep, into its confines. She slipped in the mud and fell, then slid again trying to stand, and finally pulled herself up to lean against a wheel, raving into the wind.

"Oh Petronilla, how could you abandon Sara? How *could* you? *Damn* you Petronilla, *damn* you to all your Christian hells!"

The hail started to lessen, though lightning still rinsed the air between thunderclaps, and the rain swept on in a steady, thrumming downpour. But Alyce's tempest was not spent. Soaked to the bone, she turned her wrath on herself.

"*How* could I not have seen? *Why* did I not take the first watch, *why* did I not take her terrors more seriously?" She lifted her face to the elements, sobbing her rage at the moonless sky.

"And *You*, Morrigan, Great Queen! Where are You while your people are driven from our homes, our lands, our lives? Where are You this Samhain Eve, this Night Between the Worlds, this time of descent when the Sidhe mounds gape and the past wakens and walks visible? Why are Your eyes fixed inward, indifferent to us, pitiless? Why do You show us only The Crone, The Hag, thrilling to bloody justice and hidden purpose? Show us Your face again as Maiden, generator, possibility—or as Mother, nurturer, preserver! *Appear to us, Morrigan*, as You did to the Ancient Ones! Aid us! Aid thy daughter Petronilla in her dread! Give me the power to save her, give me the power to protect these children!"

A fresh shaft of lightning flared, and she addressed it directly, shouting into the storm's howl.

"*Evo Kore!* Hide Your countenance from me no longer— even if it be The Cailleach! Even if it be the Unnameable, the Ancient Chaos! *Show me Your face, though it be the Face of Nemesis!* Aye, *even if it be forbidden*, still I summon You! *Badb*,

I summon you! *Macha*, I summon you! *Nemain—I summon you!* Appear to us, Key Holder! *Whatever the cost*, fill me with Your Frenzy! Even if it *destroy* me, grant me Your Power! Old One! *Appear to us now!*"

* * *

Less than an hour later, the rain-sodden, grumbling men assigned to the Bishop's search for Dame Alyce Kyteler heard distant hooves pounding toward them. Then they spied the outline of a lone horse galloping through the fog, down the hill road toward their column.

The commander ordered a halt as the animal's shape drew nearer and pulled up on an outcropping of rock above them. Their spitting torches glowed yellow through the fog, reflecting on the men's spear-points and drawn swords. But as they peered upward, the flares began forming strange fogged aureoles of light, through which floated a spectral form.

It sat astride the horse with an air of unchallengeable authority. A heavy black cape denoting rank and wealth billowed from the rider's shoulders. The figure's face was veiled by a curtain of rain, its hair drenched by the storm to the colour of shadow.

But with the next stab of lightning, the men started in terror, many of them dropping their weapons, falling to their knees, and crossing themselves.

For the flash had imprinted on their gaze a sight they would never forget. The lightning had carved out the reflection of a shining crown the rider wore. It bore the shape of a full moon cradled in the arc of a crescent moon, its two points upreaching, shaped as a pair of bright horns.

Motionless, the apparition shimmered at them, waiting.

The commander knew he must address this creature. He opened his lips and worked his jaw, but no words came. His voice shriveled into a knot of panic in his throat.

Then all his questions were answered at once.

It spoke.

It called out to them with a ringing voice, in a tone of absolute command.

Phrases clipped with contempt came riding over the storm's roar with the majesty of lightning itself.

"Merry Meet, this Samhain Sabbat. You need search for Me no longer. You have met the One you seek."

XVII

A MIDNIGHT CALLER

DAME ALYCE KYTELER, fugitive, exile, former Lady of Kyteler Castle and numerous Kilkenny lands and estates, pinched out her bedside candle flame between calloused fingertips and slumped back against her pillow.

She was tired. She was often tired these days, and her bones ached from ten years of enduring the damp English climate. She remembered with something akin to awe how energetic her former self had been, always up and doing, confident of her judgment, acting decisively.... She offered a snort of sarcasm to the room's darkness. These days, although she functioned well enough, she did so at a slower pace, finding herself grateful for gradual progress, simple daily accomplishments, small victories. She'd assumed it was a sign of age. Knowing herself stubborn, she had always found transitions difficult, but this particular transition—from the Mother cycle of life to that of the Crone—seemed especially trying. Certainly she *felt* ancient. Too ancient, some might sniff, to be raising seven children and overseeing a modest but productive manor that provided for its own and managed to send surplus wool and fresh produce to market at fair prices.

She stretched warily, feeling joints creak and muscles twinge as she turned over in bed. Grimalken, a scrap of dove-grey velvet barely out of kittenhood, woke from her nest in the quilt's folds. All eyes, ears, and tail, she came alert in an instant, decided the movement signaled playtime, and pounced on Alyce's toes with the full ferocity of her tiny body.

"Alright—Owww!" Alyce called out, "I said *alright*! You caught the toe and bravely killed it, alright?" She feinted a little kick in self-defense and Grimalken, now in full night-hunter mode, leapt off the bed with a low growl to go in search of other prey.

"Yes, please do," Alyce called after her, "Go sit watch at the hole where you once spied a mouse back in 1066. But keep that watch, now! One never knows. . . ."

She eased herself back onto her side, curled her legs up into a position that relaxed the ache in her spine a bit, and with a wince of a smile wondered why she could not success-fully treat herself as a patient. She had long ago reconstructed her medicinal shelves. She had brought the children through croups and teethings, fevers, broken bones, influenzas—and now, with the older ones, adolescent skin rashes, first blood, stomach-ache, and the heart-ache of unrequited love. She had a healer's reputation again, for miles around. But she could not heal herself—not from the black, cold sickness deep inside her.

She knew she hid it well. None of the children suspected. Except perhaps Sara...

At the thought of the children, her heart lifted a little. If Sara's curiosity continued to drink in knowledge as it did, she would grow into one of the most skilled Lore and Legend Keepers in all the Isles—and the child only twelve summers old. So self-assured, too; when she spun tales for the other children, even the older ones sat spellbound. She had a way with language, sensing naturally how well-spun words could ensorcell. And how enchanting she looked, with those blonde ringlets, not as pale as her mother's white-gold hair but with the same fine texture.

Her mother. . .

Feeling suddenly chilled, Alyce pulled the quilt up tighter under her chin, her thoughts turning obsessively to the past, as they had for so many nights over so many years. This was an interval she had come to loathe: the drowsy time when her brain rang, helpless, under the same hammering questions before sleep lent her a brief, merciful unconsciousness; it was the space where she knew her thoughts were spinning but going nowhere, like cart wheels mired in mud.

Will, sweet young Will. . . a man now. All her letters unanswered. Surely there would have been some way, some secret manner in which. . . beloved Will, whose heart was always greater than his judgment. Again and again, her brain dredged the lake of memory, trying to find an acceptable answer to the puzzle; over and over, as one might pick through poppy seeds to estimate the safe amount for a soothing balm of forgetfulness.

And why had she never heard from any of the others? Surely most of the fugitives had made it to England, or at least Wales. Even if—she tensed at the thought—even if some had been apprehended, why no word from the rest? All of the scouts she had employed to search for them, both in England and Wales, to no result. . . . Perhaps they had not *wanted* to be found? Perhaps they wanted to resettle on their own, free from all attachment to their mistress? Certainly she had seen to it that each of her people had been given more gold coin than they had ever seen before. Nor had she forgotten those faces, fervent with their own purposes, defying her in the torchlight of the castle cellar. Yet surely the parents of the young ones she had been raising, they would have tried to find their children! Night after night, year after year, these questions. But there were no answers, and no forgetting. Only the same riddles, the same sick wave of despair at never, ever, being able to solve them. . . .

A banging at the door brought her fully awake again.

It was not her bedroom door. It was the great door downstairs.

She sat up, listening cautiously. No one wished her harm here in England, but she was on guard all the same from years of habit. The pounding came again, louder. Then she remembered that she had sent her doorkeeper—Edgar, the tottery old man she had taken in as a stray last year—to bed with a poultice for his ague. So she heaved herself out of bed, grunting with soreness and effort, and drew a cloak around her nightdress against the Eanáir cold. "*January*," she muttered, as she thrust her feet into slippers and reached for the added warmth of a heavy wool shawl, "January, not Eanáir. I *must* remember to name the months in English, not Erse. You would think after all this time...I am a slow learner, t'is the wretched truth..." She struck tinder for a flame, then hastened down the stairway, clutching her candle.

"Who goes there?" she cried, scuttling through the lower hall toward the door.

The reply came as if from a far distance, as if from out of time.

"Helena. Helena Galrussyn. From Kilkenny."

"*Helena!*" she gasped. Fingers fumbling in eagerness, she hurriedly unbolted the door.

But when she swung it open and peered out, no one was there.

Then she looked *down*—but scarcely recognized the creature hunched on the snow before her. It was a woman half as tall as Helena had been, a woman stooped and twisted, leaning heavily on a gnarled staff. Only the face squinting up at her was vaguely familiar.

"Helena!" she cried again, trying not to show her dismay. She engulfed the woman in an embrace and hurried her inside.

"Where— when—" Alyce began in a frantic voice. But seeing how haggard her guest looked, she drew her quickly through the hall to the kitchen, where she stirred alive the last embers glowing in the fireplace, adding some kindling and a log. Her visitor slouched down onto a stool, wordless, staring at the hearth as flames began to lick and crackle, feeding on the fresh wood.

"Well," Alyce said nervously, "I—I shall not ask, hear, or answer anything until you are warmed and fed, so. . . so you rest there."

Swiftly, she cleared the table of its pile of books, a spindle, and a skein-winder in mid-yarn, and brought bread and cheese. With shaking hands, she poured brandywine into a goblet and pressed it on Helena, who took a gulp and collapsed in a fit of coughing.

"No, no, sip it *slowly*," Alyce said, "Oh. Water. You are thirsty. Of course." She poured some from a jug and placed the cup before Helena, who grabbed it and gulped it down. "Good, good. Drink, my dear. Here, more water. Then sip some brandywine, but slowly. It will warm you. Warmth, yes. Here." She stripped off her heavy shawl and wrapped it around Helena.

"Soup. You need soup." She ran to the larder, took down a kettle, and filled it with soup from a large crock, then rushed back to the kitchen—Grimalken having reappeared to weave between her ankles in hope of getting fed. Swinging the spit to one side, Alyce hung the kettle on its hook over the fire. There she hovered, stirring it with a wooden spoon, hardly able to keep from gawking at her visitor's haggard face.

Helena drew her stool closer to the stone-topped table and fell on the bread like a starving beast. While she ate, she watched her host through wide, frightened eyes, as if seeing a phantom. Alyce ladled the now steaming leek-and-mushroom soup into a bowl and placed it in front of her. Helena ate and drank rapidly, furtively, glancing over her shoulder, as if the food might be taken away at any moment.

Finally she slowed her pace, breaking her silence with one word:

"*Dana?*"

"Safe. Thriving. A bonny, bright, loving child. Almost ten and a half. I have told her many stories about her parents and her grandfather and how much you all loved her. Do you want to see her now? I can wake her—" Alyce was moving toward the door, but Helena stopped her.

"No. Later. Not while I be like—this. I only needed to know if she—if she be—" Helena broke down, able only to sit clutching a chunk of bread, tears raining down her face. Alyce ran to her side, knelt, and held her. The half-sentences that followed were fractured by sobs.

"—to know if she be . . . *alive*. Safe. Fed. Ten summers old already and I never even . . . my nursing babe, my Dana. Sysok's daughter. John's grandchild. Came so early and so hard. You remember . . ."

"Yes, Helena. I remember the night she was born. She is safe and healthy and fine," Alyce soothed.

Gradually the outburst subsided, and Helena was able to speak without gasping.

"I canna remember when last I wept. Years, mayhap. I dinna think I ever could weep again. . . . Ach, what have they done? What have they done to us?"

Alyce drew up a stool and sat beside her. Fire-lit, the women's shadows were cast high on the walls, two giant house-spirits outlined against the stone of an old English dwelling. A lame wren fluttered down from a shelf, hopping about the table with a slight limp to peck at Helena's crumbs. One wing was bandaged while its fragile bones, reset by Alyce, were knitting.

"Tell me." Alyce placed her hands perfectly still in her lap by an act of will, readying herself for the news she had hungered for yet dreaded over ten years. "Tell me, Helena. Please."

"What do ye know? Have any of the others—"

"I know almost nothing. I have made inquiries, countless times. All my inquiries, formal or private, have gone unanswered. It is as if a wall rose between me and Ireland. Finally, last year, I gave up sending scouts. I continue to write to my son, but he. . . I know one thing only. I know that Will was captured and imprisoned for two months, but then released. He himself has never written. I am certain he dare not, even after all this time. Or perhaps my letters have never reached him. It was Roger Outlawe, his kinsman, who sent me word, years ago. But he too has not written since, no matter how often I have sent to him. . . . He wrote that Will had been fined—sentenced to pay for the cost of re-roofing St. Canice's Cathedral all in lead—and also ordered to attend mass thrice a day."

"Aye," Helena said, "t'is true."

"Apparently Roger did much to help Will, paying his fine and bringing family influence to bear. The sentence seemed fairly light—thanks be to The Mother—so I assumed that others, too, if they had been apprehended, also had...that is, I hoped."

Helena closed her eyes at the realization of how little this woman knew. She felt unspeakably weary, and her breathing came hard.

But she opened her eyes, looked at Alyce, and began, as gently as she could.

"T'is true the Lord Justice and your son's other relatives on his father's side came to his aid. With great pots of money. But they did so only for him. T'is also true that in further penance, your Will was sent on a pilgrimage to Saint Thomas's Shrine at Canterbury. Ye were not told about that?"

Alyce shook her head.

"At Canterbury... Your Grace, at Canterbury... he recanted. He renounced The Craft. He forswore everything he had ever done as a Wiccan."

"Oh... well. That is to be expected. A public recantation hardly means—"

"Then your William was wed, M'am. To the Seneschal's niece. The Bishop celebrated their nuptial mass at the Cathedral. They were permitted to take up residence at Kyteler Castle, but Lord William was allowed to preside only over the castle keep and nearest outlands. All other lands are confiscate."

"All other... well, at least Will is alive. And at home, on his own ancestral land, even if there is less of it now.... I promised him that one day he would manage the estate, and be good at it, too. I am certain he secretly welcomes Wiccans and quietly holds Sabbats. I am certain he—"

"He holds no Sabbats, Lady Alyce. Him and his Lady be active in the Church, giving alms and observing saints' feast days and proving they be devoted Christians. I heard tell the Covenstead is grown over in tall grasses and briars. Your son be lost to The Craft, my Lady. He *renounced* it. He renounced *you*. By name. Publicly. As apostate, heretic, and *damned*. T'is sure the real reason he has not written."

A tiny muscle jerked in Alyce's temple.

"He—was ever a dear lad, though... sometimes a bit clumsy. You remember? He must have had no choice. You know, he was really so impressionable. . . I remember how he scampered after Robert de Bristol like a puppy, wanting to imitate whatever Robert did. He was too young to face this. And I myself told him . . . I told him we all must do *whatever* was necessary to survive this catastrophe, whatever was necessary to keep the land. So it is not his fault, you see, really, he merely—" She knew she was babbling, and she could not avoid seeing the pity in Helena's eyes. Tears smarted, but she controlled them. "So. It would seem that the precious land *was* saved—well, a bit of it. If the precious son was lost, that was a too-costly exchange. . . . Still, the land may yet work its own magick on him, so that someday he will remember, he *will* realize—perhaps when he himself has children. . . do you know if—?"

"Sorry, M'am, I dinna know," Helena shrugged.

"By now, probably he—he surely must. . . " Alyce's words were withering in her throat. She knew that she must put this subject away for now. She knew that later, when alone, was the time to unfold it, in what would be many private midnight grievings, for the rest of her life. She swallowed hard.

"May my son Will carry himself honourably. May he act like the gentle knight he is. May he walk always in Her sight, whether—whether he knows it or not." She paused, bracing herself. "Please. Go on."

"The Cailleach be demanding Her justice, though. T'was less than a year after the Cathedral was repaired—all that costly lead roofing being too heavy—that the roof caved in.

Aye. Brought down the choir, the side chapels, all the bells. No one can claim She be lacking a sense of humour," Helena murmured, the wince of a smile flickering across her face.

"But Helena, the others. . . you. How did your back—"

"Me. I. . . be in prison these seven years. On bread and water. Chained to the floor."

"Oh Helena," Alyce whispered.

"T'is part of why my back got twisted—though also I did heavy labor, later on. . . . The sole reason I be set free was the Bishop made himself too many important enemies, himself wanting ever more power than he already had. At last, the Archbishop of Dublin brought a charge of heresy against him—aye, he did. So the Bishop was forced to scamper back to France, to hide beneath the Pope's skirts. . . . Otherwise t'is in prison I should be still—caged, chained, for the rest of my days. In a foul, stinking cell acrawl with vermin."

"Helena, my dear—" Alyce reached out to her.

"Dinna touch me. If ye do, I likely canna finish. The Bishop, he be gone. But naught will ever be the same. People be practicing The Craft only in secret now. Can ye believe it? In Eire!"

"But—then the people themselves are still. . . ? Where is Sysok?"

"Dead," Helena replied in a flat voice. "We be captured that very night, right outside Clonroche. He struggled with the yeomen. They killed him. One sword thrust, just like that. He looked so surprised. Only later did I come to grasp he had good fortune. To go so quick, I mean. His father perished on the way back to Kilkenny. Soaked, frozen. The yeomen took the warm clothing ye gave us. And the horses. And the cart. And sure the gold. They marched us that whole night through with no stopping, in the harshest storm in memory. John was old, you know. He tried hard to keep up, but he fell again and again and they..."

Alyce stared into the fire, thinking of Sysok in the prime of his manhood, Sysok of the quick temper and quick intelligence. And Old John, whose gnarled, skilled cooper's hands she had never seen idle, Old John who voiced what others dare not speak.

But Helena had lived so long with her dead that she continued her narrative in a level tone.

"Henry and Alyce, they be taken in the forge before they even had a chance to leave. The Bishop must have suspected we be fleeing. Henry and Alyce were both slain on the spot. They fought, though. They took four of the Bishop's men with them to their deaths.

"Eva de Brounstoun—we be in prison together. Not at the beginning, but later on. A bitter first winter it was there, and them permitting no aid for any sicknesses. Her lungs, you know . . . she be coughing red spit and she be daft with fever at the end, ranting on about how it was time for lambing and kidding and that she was needed out in the fields . . . . She died in my arms."

Alyce moaned softly. But Helena continued in her calm, listless voice.

"Annota Lange, somehow she be getting separated from her traveling companions. Once at Wexford, she must have gone about trying to find the others. But twenty of the Bishop's men found her first. Twenty soldiers against one widow. By the time they brought her body back, she had abandoned it."

Alyce covered her face with her hands.

"Robert de Bristol was in prison, too. But I dinna know what became of him. I heard he was pardoned at last and planned to take holy orders as a friar, but I dinna know for certain. Will Payn and his family. . . they were sentenced to be whipped through the streets to the marketplace with the rest of us—Eva and me, too, before we were shut in prison—but Will Payne, somehow he kept singing through it, to keep our spirits up. So they took him and they. . . they burned a cross into what was left of the flesh on his back.

"Others mayhap got away, for some were sentenced, 'in absentia' they call it, to banishment and excommunication. I be thinking that likely means they had already escaped the Bishop's reach . . . . Still, whilst I worked my way here these past three years—in contract serfdom to pay my passage—along the way I be asking everyone did they know anything. But people be fearful about saying things now. One man who worked the boats at Wexford said he thought he had once shipped across with some people who sounded like ones I be describing. But he said t'was a long time ago, and then he said his memory was faulty. Nobody at the Cardigan port in Wales be remembering a thing. I went to the Fishguard port, too, in case . . . . But if you heard naught about 'em or from 'em, if they never tried to find you, as I did, t'is not likely . . . " Her voice trailed off. "So now I finally know, too," she added dully, "I be the first. And t'is all but certain I be the last. Likely the rest never even got so far as Wales."

She sat motionless, empty from her recital, drained of all her deaths.

Alyce was weeping silently, tears cascading down her face. Helena lifted her head and stared at her, as if surprised to see her old mistress sitting nearby, in a kitchen, by a fire, crying.

"There, there, Lady Alyce. T'is all long ago. They all be gone. They be gone a long, long time."

"Not for me. For me they die tonight. For me they die backwards from tonight. They only now . . . "

Alyce looked up at Helena through brimming, red-rimmed eyes. Even in her grief, she missed the name not spoken. She opened her mouth to ask a question, but Helena spoke first.

"And what of ye and the children, Your Grace?"

"I . . . we . . . "

She had no names for safety, plenty, or peace after Helena's news. She gazed into the fire. Then she settled for a recitation of plain facts she thought she could enumerate without breaking down. That much she owed Helena. She wiped her eyes with the sleeve of her nightdress.

"We have—fared tolerably. Certainly compared with what you. . . we did find sanctuary here, though not quite what I would call welcome. After some time, it became clear that we were not. . . not soon to return home. So I bought land and— tomorrow I shall take you round and show you everything. We live quietly here in England. King Edward ascended the throne six years ago. The rumours beginning back when he was Crown Prince were true. He *is* drawn to The Craft, though he must keep his Seeking private to himself and a few trustworthy friends. He would have liked me to be one of them—but court life was not for me, and that displeased him. It matters little, though, since he usually is off fighting France and massacring the Scots. But the man is no fool. I myself have heard him vow to curb Church power. He wants to abolish Peter's Pence, a tax every household in England is being forced to pay the papacy. And Helena! Five years ago, Edward seized the revenues of Richard de Ledrede. He swears if the Bishop is ever fool enough to return to England, the Crown will ensure he is ostracized."

Helena drained her soup bowl and set it down, turning eyes dim with fatigue on Alyce, who realized that her guest hadn't comprehended most of what had just been said.

"More talk can wait until morning, Helena, after you have rested. Come now and—"

Then Helena, speaking absently from inside her own thoughts, interrupted.

"T'was the first thing I noticed when you opened the door. Your hair. Your fiery red Celtic hair. You be old enough for some greying, mayhap, Lady Alyce. Yet your hair be paler than Petronilla's. Why be your hair stark white?"

XVIII

A GIFT OF SHADOWS

ALYCE SPOKE SLOWLY searching for the words she needed, finding them one at a time, losing them again, seeking a way to say what she had never yet spoken aloud and feared to name now.

"The night. . . the night after we left home, the eve of Samhain, we stopped in the high woods near Wexford. We were waiting for dawn, when we could board the boat. Something. . . happened there. During the storm. I cannot describe it. I—I fell. Into a—a *somewhere*. I became. . . snared, sucked into this place. It is a perilous place, from which there is no way back, no way forward. No way out. . . I gazed directly at Her—at The Morrigan. I saw Her true Face. Death Bringer. Mother of Despair. The Tomb of Every Hope. Finally I saw Her truths. They were—unspeakable. Indifferent to our puny truths, unaffected by our pathetic faith. Hideous.

"Her truth—the real truth—was that The Burning Time was neither rumour nor myth, not something hideous happening somewhere else to other people. The truth was that the Inquisition had arrived where *we* were. It was happening *now*, to *us*. The truth was that I had been a fool to think us safe from the world on our little island, a fool to be sure I could do what was necessary to defend us, a fool to feel secure under Her protection. . . and something else. The cruelest truth. I realized that I knew nothing, understood no one. I, always so certain I could read people well—I was ignorant, witless. And cold inside, *cold*. Colder than I had ever. . .

"Then I saw—I saw the skin of the universe peel back. Festering there under the surface—alive, squirming, heaving, crawling up through the rip in the skin—were *lies*. They glowed a greenish white iridescence. It was a cosmic nest. . . of maggots. Huge, fat, flagrant lies; tiny, winged, subtle lies. Lies about the existence—even the possibility—of health, friendship, trust. Sly, side-glancing, hypocritical, grinning, giggling lies. And everywhere, *everywhere*, betrayal.

"Simply, I saw life. Bare, sour, brutish, unadorned by illusion. Nowhere a gleam of honesty or sweetness. No way to lend purpose to meaninglessness, not even in passing, not even as a gesture. Only contempt for others—their stupidities, vulgarities, self-important scurryings busy as insects. Only disgust with myself—my conceits, willfulness, ignorance, spite. . . .

"I died that night. Like the banshee, I became a host for the dead. I welcomed it, welcomed death into my heart. It lent me an armor against feeling anything—pain, joy, curiosity, love. It brought a strange solace—a hard, icy power. It settled the nausea of boredom, because it assured eventual release. I could *believe* in death, because death alone has proven its existence. That night I lost my faith in everything else I had been foolish enough to build my life on. The sole order I could recognize was disorder. The sole promise I could trust was death."

A brief, bitter smile curled her lips.

"But the children... the children were still there, still needed me, still had to be carried to safety. I *hated* them for that. Aye. I hated the burden of them, hated the pledge I had made to care for them, hated all you serfs for having extracted that pledge from me at the moment I humbled myself to what I thought were our shared beliefs. So had I been neatly trapped between all of you on the one side, and the Bishop on the other. So did I hate you both. It was then I discovered the *energy* of hate—a formidable energy. Hate drove me, by dawn, somehow to get seven screaming children—in a mud-mired, rain-soaked wagon hauled by one wheezing, drenched horse—down to the wharf and aboard the boat. At daybreak we weighed anchor. By the time the storm lifted and the sun burned through the fog, we were into clear water. It was in that sunshine I first saw it, after—still fueled by hate—I had fed the children, bedded them down in their cabins, and sung to them until they slept, warm and dry. Then I climbed back abovedeck to see if I could spy any receding outline of Ireland through the haze. I could. Just barely.

"It shrank as I watched it fade. One final sight, to last me the rest of my life. Eire. Erin. Home. The land I knew, the hillocks and paddocks; the rushing sound the river made in spring. The stones I knew, the echo of footsteps in familiar chambers where dust would fur my silent loom now; the stars seen from my turret window. The people. My son—child, man, heir; the rebel nuns who raised me; my parents' graves. The dull gold summer evening light, the expressions on certain animals' faces; the rich brown smell of onions stewing in wine near suppertime in winter. The child and girl and woman I had been, the only self I knew. . .

"I stood in that sunshine, watching it all go. The wind freshened and began billowing the sails and whipping my hair about. I reached to brush some strands from my eyes. It was then I saw that my hair had turned pure white during a single midnight storm."

Helena looked at her with the glint of an all but forgotten pride.

"We were right, you see," she said, "You saved our children. And our children saved you."

"I saved your children, aye. But I was not saved. I have never spoken these dark things aloud. I have paced through these ten years an imposter of myself—for your children's sake. Oh aye, I can pretend through the daylight hours. I have learned to practice lying as an art. I can act as if I believe

The Craft was worth such loss, as if I believe The Craft is more than yet another myth. How can I blame my Will for recanting when I myself pretend to believe The Old Ways still have power or meaning? Oh, I can celebrate a Sabbat convincingly for the children's sake; children need the illusion of hope. But I have lost the voice of a High Priestess. My spells ring as rote, like those Christian parishioners I once pitied for mumbling their rosaries without conviction or even attention. I can *act* as if I remember how to feel joy. . . . Yet in the nights, alone, I know who I am—and who I am not. Then the bleakness tightens around me and swallows up the air. Then I cannot breathe. . . and then I know I am a charlatan among the living, an imposter, a dead woman. Not even properly dead, merely in a lifelong transition, dying down all my hours. Until someday I am let go, finally. Safe from living."

"Why, then?" demanded Helena, "Why did ye not abandon our children? Or leave 'em in some home, with payment for their keep? Why, unless ye felt obliged to us somehow? Unless we were people ye cared about, people ye—"

"You made me give you my word."

"People break their word all the time."

"Not a Kyteler. I was bound."

"So ye kept faith with our babes only because ye gave the word of a noblewoman?" Helena narrowed her eyes and peered at Alyce. "I dinna believe it," she announced. Then she shook her head sadly. "But I dinna know about such a dark place as you tell about, m'Lady. I dinna know what to say, or how to help ye."

"There is no help for me, Helena," Alyce said. "Nor might I recognize it if it appeared." She smiled, that caustic smile again. "But my state is not important. I told you because you asked, and because you have earned the right to an honest answer. My troubles should not even be mentioned, given the—torment you all. . . "

In the long pause that followed, Alyce realized she was wrestling with the one question she most needed to ask but could not frame. She could manage it only as statement, as presumed fact. She began to speak rapidly.

"Is— Petronilla de Meath is safe, of course. They would not harm her. I mean, not since she returned to the Church, repentant. You did not mention her fate—and I can understand that, in the circumstances, given what happened to the rest of you. But still, I should like to know—"

Alyce stopped as she watched Helena's expression change from confusion to dread.

"I dinna mention her because I thought you knew."

"What. Why would you think—? What would I know? *What?*"

"I thought the night she left you, she told you what she planned to do. I thought you had tried to stop her but failed. I thought she. . . "

Alyce Kyteler's hands found each other and formed a knot in her lap.

"She did tell me. She told me she was horribly afraid. And I thought, well, she is usually afraid, and now we are all afraid with reason, so I . . . we quarreled. I was patronizing and cross. I struck her . . . but then we made our peace. Or so I thought. She took the first watch. Then, while I was asleep, she vanished. She left me a letter. She wrote that she yearned to return to the Church. Yet she also asked me to raise Sara—and in The Old Ways. I was stunned, hurt, distraught. I was desperate to go after her. But how could I leave the babes alone? And in a tempest?

"Then I discovered that Petronilla had taken one of our horses, and that she had even stol—*taken*—other things with her, things I have never understood. Why should she steal from me? I would have given her whatever she asked for. She was like a daughter to me. . . . But it was not merely the horse or the objects she took. You remember the legend that one must sleep warily on Samhain Eve for fear one's spirit may be stolen? T'was like that. Her leaving and taking what she . . . something broke inside me. I was sleeping, and when I woke, my essence—what made me *me*—was gone.

"I have never told Sara the whole story, of course. She knows only that her mother longed to return to the Church— yet wanted a different way for her daughter, whom she loved above all else. I have been unable to answer her questions—

other than telling her that adults can become set in our ways yet still may wish different choices for our children. Which is what Petronilla wrote to me, after all, even if it did not make much sense. That is what she *did*, too. Did she not? Helena? *Helena. Did she not?*"

Helena stared into the middle distance, possessed by a knowledge too painful to be uttered. Yet she knew it must speak through her.

"Not far down the road from the forest where ye and the children were sleeping, the Bishop's men-at-arms were closing in. Ye all would have been captured within an hour. Petronilla de Meath intercepted them. She claimed to be Alyce Kyteler. She was wearing the cloak and the silver Moon Helmet of a Wiccan High Priestess, so they believed her. Triumphant, expecting a fat reward, they sent a runner ahead to Kilkenny, saying they were bringing her back as their prisoner. I heard tell the Bishop went to the sacristy to prepare a mass of thanksgiving. Then, when he saw who it was they had captured, he fell into a fury. He dispatched more troops after ye. By then it was too late. Your boat had sailed.

"Never have I seen such rage as his. Rage he spent on Petronilla de Meath. Interrogation, trial, sentence—his vengeance took less than three days. Yet those three days were endless. She begged him not to torture her. She said she be greatly fearing pain and willing to confess to whatever he wished. So he had her confess. Holy Erin, what he had her confess to! Sorcery. Murdering infants. Making pacts with Satan. Consorting with a horned incubus, concocting potions from the brains of unbaptized infants—everything his sick madness could imagine. She confessed and confessed. Then he demanded she name her brothers and sisters in Satan. She knew from his ravings that ye had escaped his clutches. So she named Dame Alyce Kyteler. She confessed she be acting as go-between, arranging trysts for ye with the Devil. She be naming ye the most skilled sorceress in the world, swearing Lady Alyce had done whatever the Bishop told her to say ye had done. Then he be wanting *more* names. But she be naming no one *except* you. T'is why I be alive at all. Else, those of us sentenced to prison would have been burned.

"But when she would not name any others, de Ledrede had her publicly flogged in the marketplace. The whole county be summoned and forced to watch, including us prisoners. We be brought from jail in irons. That body of hers, so frail. . . . But ach, her spirit! I dinna believe this was the child-woman I had known. After the flogging, when offered forgiveness and the sacraments of the Church if she would name others, she *laughed*. In the Bishop's face. In the marketplace. With the crowds watching. 'Fie,' she sings out, '*Fie, fie, fie, amen!*' T'was so cold the vapor from her breath was like smoke, I remember. As if she be breathing fire.

"Next morning he had her flogged again. Five times that day. Every two hours. They be having to work in shifts so the torturers could rest, for even the men doing the flogging be too tired to continue. In between, they left her raw body bound to the whipping post, exposed to the freezing rain. There were rumblings of outrage in the crowd but no one moved for fear of the men-at-arms. We prisoners were kept standing in our chains. The Bishop, he sat to one side, wrapped in his furs, fingering the rubies in that big gold cross of his. He kept drinking heated wine and calling for more flagons. Every minute he watched us, as if feeding his empty eyes with the sight of us. He spoke to the crowd only once— a strange speech, like he was pleading with us. He said we be having to understand he was a good man, he was only doing his duty, he was saddened but forced by righteousness to carry out divine punishment, he was forced to be an instrument of God's wrath. He said God be no base merchant haggling for souls that were his by right. He said heavenly light needed human darkness so as to show itself clear, so what ill he be forced to do, it be for her salvation and ours. Then he pulled his cowl down, so his eyes be hidden.

"Five floggings. All day long. After the third lashing she dinna scream anymore. After the fourth, the man plying the whip flung it down in disgust and walked off. But the Bishop ordered a yeoman to pick it up and go on. . . . Then, when it was finished, de Ledrede pronounced sentence: Petronilla de Meath would be burned alive at the stake in the marketplace on the following day.

"We be dragged back to prison. I knew they put her in a cell near mine, so I kept calling to her softly. No answer. Then I hear a key turn in the lock of my cell grate, and who should walk in but Father Brendan Canice. Do ye remember who he—? Aye? Well, he told me the moment he had heard what was happening, he had ridden hard from Kells at Ceanannus Mór to Dublin, where he got himself an audience with the Archbishop, then had ridden on without stopping all the way to Kilkenny. The Archbishop had granted Father Brendan special permission to visit Petronilla and to offer her repentance, the sacraments of the Church, and delivery from the stake if she recanted her defiance—even *without* naming any others. From her cell, he had heard me calling to her. Always a fair man, he was. He bribed a guard to let me join him in Petronilla's cell."

Helena paused, passing a hand over her forehead and eyes as if to wipe out a sight sealed there past any forgetting.

"I canna describe what she—how she—I tried to talk to her. Then I tried to chant at her, teach her some of the meditations on pain. Such a young Seeker, a Neophyte. She never had time to learn more than the basic rituals. . . I canna be sure she even heard me. But I lay down next to her in the filthy straw. I cradled her head in my arms. Her hair looked almost as red as yours once did; t'was matted with blood, stiff with it. I dinna know what to do, so I said the spells to her over and over, trying to squeeze years of Craft study into hours, trying to fill her brain with the disciplines that would lift her outside her body. I dinna believe they would work. They dinna always work; they dinna work for me in childbirth, remember? Aye. But I dinna know what else to do.

"Brendan kept talking to her, too. Pleading with her to recant, saying her death was a waste, a selfish waste, since now t'would change nothing, save no one. He beseeched her to let him make the pact with the Bishop for her life—prison instead of the fire. He begged her to choose to live, for his sake, for the sake of true Christianity, for the sake of humanity. I remember him telling her that grace belongs to all humanity—not just each of us, not just her, not just one miserable sinner. T'was odd. Through that whole night she opened her eyes and spoke only three times. The first was after he said that. She tried to—stutter through those cracked lips. We leaned in closer. T'was like straining to hear someone underwater, drowning. 'One miserable sinner,' she gasped, '*is* all humanity.'

Then Brendan wept, and he be saying curses on the Bishop and be begging her to let him tell de Ledrede she had recanted, even if she dinna mean it. 'Let me lie,' he pleaded, 'let me bear the sin instead of you. *Pretend* to go through with it, what does it *matter*, t'is only *words*. In Christ's name, I beg you, let me carry the lie, let me save you!' She looked up at him—a look so mellow with tenderness! But when she tried to smile, blood bubbles be frothing from her mouth. Then she spoke the second time. 'I own my courage now,' she chided him mildly, 'Why would you be taking it from me?' After that, he ceased his pleading. Poor man, he be sobbing, muttering things like 'Not my church, not my Christ, not this, oh Jesus not this.'

"So then I told him what to do. 'Sean Fergus,' says I, 'If you truly want to help her, here is what you must be doing.' I told him to hurry out to the Kyteler estate, to Sysok's and my cottage, to my pantry. I told him what to be looking for and where to find it and how to mix it. But he stared at me in such horror before he wheeled and rushed out, t'was clear he would never be able do it. I knew he would not be coming back. A consecrated Christian priest, after all. . . .

"But I dinna have time to be angry. I went back to trying to concentrate her, trying to teach her how to block the pain. Through the night, as the hours passed, I be saying over and over how she be not really there, not in prison; how the cell be not real; how she be lying in a green apple orchard in full Mayday bloom, just before the Beltane Sabbat. I told her how the blossoms be trembling on the warm spring wind, the air heady with the wine-scent of fruit to come and abuzz with the sleepy drone of nectar-drunk bees, how the creamy petals be tumbling like snowflakes down to the soft emerald grass where she lay, under a bowl of sky so clear and blue it arched on forever. . . . That was the third time she opened her eyes. 'Apples,' she says, 'I like apples.' Like a child. Or a madwoman. But she be speaking so calmly I felt mayhap I reached her after all.

"Then, like a sign from Brigid the Healer, there was the turnkey again. And in walks Sean Fergus. The man looked blasted. He had brought what I asked for, though, mixed as an ointment. Properly mixed, too—all the correct proportions. He puts it in my hands. Then he crosses himself."

Rapt, Alyce leaned forward.

"Aconite," she whispered.

"Aye. And cinquefoil. And foxglove. In beeswax and almond oil. Though fairly little of it. Still, Biddy Róisín would have been proud of her boy. I told him that, I said it. Poor Sean Fergus. He be like a man sleepwalking, a wraith. 'What do I do now?' he mumbles. I could give him no answer. 'I know not what to *do*,' he kept saying. 'My Church is killing Christ again,' he says, 'What can I study now that I bear this knowledge'—but flat like, not like a question anymore—'How do I live the rest of my life.' I dinna know how to answer him. When I began to rub the ointment on her I be looking up at him—that he should step out, for her modesty's sake. Then he be backing away out of the cell, crying all soft, still asking those questions that not be questions, still staring at us. . . I dinna know what became of him. I never saw him again.

"Then I sat with her, holding her, waiting for her to die. T'was not enough ointment he brought to pass her over, but sure I knew she would not last the night anyway, and at least it eased the pain. A long night, that.

"Then t'was morning. We all were dragged in chains to watch the execution. The Bishop be in his big chair, in his furs, with his cowl covering his eyes again. I think he be sweating, because the lower part of his face be wet. He be so drunk they had to help him into his seat. They carried her out, too, but when they bound her to the stake, she be so limp they had to lash her tight with ropes, to hold her upright. I thought—I hoped—mayhap she be already dead. She seemed not conscious, and I be thankful for that.

"But then, as the smoke swirled closer to her body and the rags of her skirt caught fire, she opened her eyes again. She looked straight in front of her. I canna ever forget it. That small face... it be hugely swollen now, a purple, scarred, bloated pulp between those blood-caked braids once the colour of the snow-heavy sky. I could smell her flesh beginning to sear. I tried to not breathe her, not to *breathe* her *in*. I tried to look away. But the guards wrenched my face back again and with their filthy fingers forced my eyes open and held my eyelids up. Snowflakes were starting to swirl. Her feet were blistering, charring black in front of me. I started to vomit.

"But then. . . then. . . what was left of that face. . . started smiling. Those swollen slits of eyes fluttered open, and she started smiling. She called out. *'Look!'* she cried, *'The petals! In leaf and bloom and fruit, all at once! Look!'*

"Then, in a clear voice strong above the crackle and roar of the blaze, she began singing,

> *No other law but love She knows,*
> *By naught but love may She be known,*
> *And all that liveth is Her own,*
> *From Her they come, to Her they go.*

"The flames started wreathing her body. Her hair caught fire. She be changing into a living torch in front of my eyes. Still, she repeats the last line. But this time she sings

> *'From Her I come, to Her I go'*

—and dies. Simple. Like a child dropping off to sleep."

Helena sat up on her stool as straight as her twisted back would permit, her head held high.

"That is what became of Petronilla de Meath."

Only the *tac tac tac* of the little wren's pecking for crumbs broke the silence. But Helena sat as if refreshed, her face radiant with the reflected serenity of that other, long-ago-lost face.

She sat that way until a sound she had never heard before shattered her reverie.

It was an unearthly sound. Small as a far-off echo at first, it was rising, growing nearer.

It was an inhuman sound.

It was coming from Alyce Kyteler.

XIX

THE MIDWINTER SUN

THE SOUND WAS ALIVE. It was struggling to be born.

Harsh, guttural, it was roiling inside the belly of Alyce Kyteler—deep in the belly of what a moment ago had been Alyce Kyteler, in the belly of what now was a creature crumpling from its stool to the floor. The creature hunched there. Then she dropped to all fours. She writhed, trying to crawl. She crouched, squatting, her fists pawing and beating the stone floor. Her head swung from side to side, the face swiveling slowly to stare at Helena. The mouth grimaced, spasming from an O to a grin to an O again, tongue lolling.

The sound was clawing up from the creature's belly. It was rattling from her breast, her throat, her mouth.

"Ngeh," she said. "Gegghhk. Gahgh."

The sound was ripping its way through her, rupturing tissue, scraping vocal chords, talons forking blood tracks in its wake.

The sound clotted and chunked, and the creature grunted and gagged. The sound whined and whistled through her, and she groaned and hissed with it. It became a watery crooning, and she wept and drooled. She gibbered as it heaved and ebbed, to rise and heave again. Blood vessels bulged on the creature's throat with the effort to spew it. She gibbered as it chattered through her teeth, drizzled from her nostrils, leaked from her eyes, slobbered from her mouth. She felt it pop and gush from her womb, her bladder, her bowels. It oozed across her tongue, her spittle tasted brassy. It hummed and droned along her limbs, twitching and shuddering her to its rhythms. The scream possessed the creature. The creature became the scream.

Then, crouching on all fours, the creature threw back her head, her jaws stretched wide—and the long curling breath-riding arc of it slimed free of her and crashed into the air. A newborn raptor in first flight, it keened a wild glad grief as it soared. Swooping, it bashed against the walls, howled at the ceiling, shrieked along the floor, shrilled its echoes at the hearth, moaning up the chimney to peal its death-knell dirge into the night. Trapped, the scream mourned at the door and wheeled, circling the room, a raven cawing, keening, beating its huge wings in claps like struck gongs of bronze. The creature was sliding toward darkness. Her head hit the stone floor yet still she could hear far off the scream circling, keening, clanging its wings until, dizzy with no air to ride now, the scream swooped, descending, dwindling, wheeling down one last high long wail of loss. The creature reached out her hand, but slid into darkness before touch could restrain her. Whimpering soft then, the scream drifted down trembling to light on her outstretched wrist where, breath short in feathery gasps, it folded its great wings and bowed its fierce head, and knew itself, finally, as love.

*　　*　　*

An outline shimmering in the firelight was the first thing she saw when she opened her eyes. It had a shape like a face. It was human. It was bending above her.

A familiar face, coming into focus. Helena! Helena Galrussyn. Helena Galrussyn was bending over her, glittering tears falling from her grey eyes, falling and falling. Helena was holding her hand. Helena was stroking her head, murmuring something.

Slowly, the wood-beamed ceiling above Helena's face returned, flickering in the light from the hearth. Then the walls, dancing with shadows thrown upward. Then the cold stone floor beneath.

Slowly the room came back.

Helena half-pushed and half-dragged Alyce closer to the hearth's warmth and slumped there on the floor beside her, holding Alyce propped against her breast, partly in her lap, as she might hold a child.

The two stayed this way, in silence, their faces turned toward the flames.

After a long time, Alyce wet her lips, swallowed, tried to speak. Her voice was hoarse from the scream, low, croaking.

"All these years," she rasped. "All these years I betrayed her. By believing she had betrayed me. All these years."

"You dinna betray her. You dinna betray anybody. You dinna *know*."

"I *should* have known."

"Petronilla dinna *want* you to know."

"I should have thought it through. She sacrificed herself for me, Helena. She suffered the tortures meant for me. She died the death meant for me."

Helena shifted her position. She propped Alyce up, half sitting, against the rungs of a stool. Then she leaned back and regarded her with a tinge of disappointment.

"We each of us be having our own suffering, m'Lady," she said mildly. "We each be dying our own death. She dinna sacrifice herself for you."

Absent-mindedly, Alyce realized that her lip was bleeding. She licked away the blood.

"She dinna do it for you," Helena repeated softly.

Alyce turned to Helena, her cheeks flushed from the fire.

"Sara. Of *course*. How could I have.... It was all for Sara. The lies in the letter, the taking of the Moon Crown and the

Lunula and my cloak and the horse—all for Sara. The refusal to name others, the defiance, the willingness to die—for Sara. For the legacy of a better kind of world she wanted to leave Sara."

"Nae." Helena frowned. "T'was all for Sara but the last three."

"What?"

"Not the last three. The ones you said."

"Which. . . I do not—"

"Once she knew Sara safe away with you, there be naught she could do for Sara. Not anymore. Not ever. She be making herself let Sara go, like she be making *you* let *her* go. Not naming any others—that she be doing for *us*. For me. For Eva. For Robert. Aye, for your son Will—and for whosoever of the others she thought be taken. She gave us our lives, aye, that she did. But she dinna die our deaths for us. We each be doing that for ourselves."

"I do not understand."

"I know." A keen look. "I know you dinna understand."

"Help me understand, Helena."

"I believe Sean Fergus—blessed be that man, wherever he's got to—could have saved her life. By a good lie or whatever—and I do think there be such a thing as a good lie. When truth-tellers lack all power to be heard, a good lie mayhap be the only thing to tell. I believe Sean knew he could save her life if she let him, and I believe he will always carry that knowing as his own cross. I believe Petronilla could have lived, in prison, as did I —if you call that living. And mayhap even get free years after, when I be freed. Mayhap have come with me and this night we two both be rapping at your door together."

"Then. . . why. . . I still do not—"

"I be saying that after six floggings even the Bishop dinna dare more torture to get her to name us. I be saying she knew Sara safe away and she knew the rest of us would not be burnt. I be saying she *knew* she could be saved from the stake. And *still* she dinna recant. Still she dinna want their sacraments. Still she defied 'em."

Alyce winced and leaned forward, trying to read Helena's face.

"Now that. . . t'was not for you, m'Lady. Not for us. Not even for Sara."

"*Why* then? Such a waste! For what?"

Helena frowned with surprise at Alyce.

"Why, for herself."

Then she sat back, wrapped in the satisfaction of her certainty. It was soft, warm, vast, merciless. It filled her with triumph. Her face was luminous with it.

"For herself alone," she repeated.

Alyce Kyteler's hands lay motionless in her lap—open, as if by an act of faith, as if the empty, upturned palms held a gift beyond claiming.

There was another long silence.

Then Helena spoke, gently.

"In a way, t'is harder for you, I think—all this. We *lived* this story—through days and weeks, months, even years. But you meet the whole tale in a single night's black hour."

Alyce, returning from her thoughts, lifted her head.

She began speaking, and her voice grew stronger with every word. She sat up straighter. Her eyes were wet, but they flashed with a glint of their old iridescence.

"Petronilla de Meath," she said, caressing each syllable.

She got to her knees. Then, with a hand out to ward off Helena's aid, she struggled to her feet.

"Petronilla de Meath," she said again. "She shall not be forgotten, this poor little—no. This magnificent woman. This—Initiate, this Wiccan. This *amchara*." She bowed her head in humility. "This. . . Priestess."

Alyce threw back her shoulders and stood, tall, fierce. Her gaze penetrated the walls of the house, seeing far out into the night. She was speaking to the past, to the mounds of the ancestors in distant Eire. She was speaking to the future. She was speaking to herself.

"The courage Petronilla de Meath struck on the forge of fear must not be forgotten. She may seem lost to us, as Eire may seem lost to us. But she is ever ours as Erin is—greenling isle of glens and mounds afloat in white sea-foam, there in the West where we can go no longer. . . not until we drift westward home with our own dying, as does the sun returning home from exile every dusk. Petronilla de Meath must live in our lore, in all our days' memories, in all our nights' dreams—as the land, the homes, the customs we were forced to leave still and always live in our days' memories and nights' dreams. The snow's crunch at the Brigid Sabbat in the wintry blue light of Imbolc. The bright vernal Equinox. Beltane's swollen buds and lovely riotous lust. The great Solstice of summer and the year's Longest Day. The first-harvest fires of Lugnasad. Autumn's crisp Equinox flaming the trees red and gold. The solemn dark frosts of Samhain and the Otherworlds. And the longest night of all, the Winter Solstice, the Black Sun, the Day Outside the Year."

Helena recognized the intensity before her. She strained to rise in its presence, the dazzle of a High Priestess. Alyce reached out to her. Helena grasped that strong hand and was pulled to her feet in one fluid motion.

"The Forms pass, the Circle remains. Petronilla de Meath is free now, and unafraid. She shall live," Alyce went on, pressing Helena's hands between her own, "in our breathing in and breathing out, as does the Eight-Spoked Wheel that Turns the Year. She shall flow through our lore as do the holy springs of Erin, the rivulets, rivers, and wells. And this I swear in the Name of She Who is Nameless: that wherever this story is told, silence shall be shattered, secret pain made visible, and terror thaw from hearts wintered with fear. This Magick has Petronilla de Meath given us."

In the glimmer of fading embers, the faces of both women glowed. No innocence there, only resolve. They embraced.

Then Alyce was no longer a High Priestess, merely a woman wearing a sad, crooked smile.

"We will talk again tomorrow, Helena. There will be time now—years—to talk. To heal. And to marvel at the strange clarity of Her ways. . . . But tonight you shall sleep in a soft warm bed with clean linen and a goosedown quilt. And every night thereafter, for all of your life. Come upstairs, rest now."

Limping, Helena followed her old mistress out of the kitchen.

"We will look in at Dana for a moment, quietly, so as not to wake her," Alyce said, a mother's insight in her whisper. "Then, in the morning, what a surprise she shall have, what bliss for you both! I have told her stories about you, and Sysok, and Old John. She has always said, 'My momma will come for me one day. I know it.'"

A sob broke from Helena. It bent her double, suddenly, like a blow to her breast.

"Hush, dear, hush," Alyce said. "Perhaps. . . we must take this joy of reunion morsel by morsel, like food after long starvation. Else it may crack our hearts and kill us outright. Come. Tonight you will see her sleeping, perfect as a faerie child. Then, tomorrow, you shall hold her and play with her as long as you like, hour after hour. And again, through the next day. And through the luxury of the next, and the next. And you shall rest and eat and sleep, and become well and strong again. Welcome. . . my friend. You are home now."

"I know I am. Blessed Be, Alyce Kyteler."

"Blessed Be, Helena Galrussyn. Merry. . ." She raised her head high, her voice breaking. "Merry Meet at last. Here," Alyce added, putting an arm around the other's waist, "I will help you, Helena."

Helena looked at her.

"We will help each other, I think. . . Alyce," she said.

Arms entwined, the women slowly mounted the steps one by one to where the children lay sleeping—children innocent as yet of what extremes the human heart could bridge, what atrocities it could devise, what transcendence it could conceive.

They were children still, their youthful dreams vivid in anticipation of the Brigid Sabbat approaching in the month of Feabhra. Brigid, they knew, was the Goddess of poetry, and healing, and fire. So there would be poems and lays chanted aloud, and flutes and tambours played, and woven briar garlands with tiny white candles blazing in them for everyone to wear at the dancing. Long tables would be set in the Great Hall, laden with the Sabbat feast. Ice on the wells would be broken and fresh water hauled up to be brewed for ale.

The Druids had called this festival Imbolc, and in England they called it Candlemas or Ladyday, but in any name the catkins and snowdrops would soon be in bud.

Whatever it was called, the children knew it for what it was: the Festival of Returning Light, the celebration of finding at the center of darkness an invincible radiance, the holy-day at which people of The Old Ways call forth the rising of the midwinter sun.

EPILOGUE

THESE MANY YEARS have I been blessed to breathe the air and quaff the water, to tread the earth, to warm myself beside the fire.

These many years have I been blessed to learn the great legends and pass them on to those who will come after. Folk arrive, young and old, from all points—the far reaches of Britannia, even from the Continent—to listen to the great Tale Spinner pour into their ears stories to sober or gladden their thoughts. Yet this is the first tale I have committed in writing to parchment. It belongs to us all, yet is such a personal story that until now I have lacked both will and skill to set it down. But I am old now, and have at last learned how to be myself without effort. It is time to entrust these words to writing, so that the tale may outlive the teller.

I wince when they call me Spellbinder, for I know the enormity of my failings too dismally well. I know I am merely an old woman who plays with words, an old woman with aches and creaks galore—though able to kick up a small

Morris Dance nicely enough when no one can see to chide me that I should rest. So I marvel that they marvel—visitors, pilgrims—at what they call my wisdom, my perception, the store of my knowledge.

I laugh to myself, aware that mere age accounts for most of it. Almost eighty turns of the Year's Great Wheel have I seen spun now—even the change to a new century two years ago. What others mistake for wisdom is the simple accumulation of experience: repeated lessons that even the stubborn ones, like myself, eventually manage to learn—but not easily, never easily. Why should any lesson of worth be easy? If it were, would we value it?

That accumulation of experience is all any of us truly knows. Although in my case there was also the manner in which I was raised—growing up under the wing of one who taught me everything she knew and was still learning lifelong: Alyce Kyteler, my adoptive mother. From the first, she had confidence in me. She swore I would surpass her in learning, and because I believed what she said—she did not lie to me— I came to believe that, too. When I was yet a Maiden, she named me her heir in every way, ensuring I would inherit all that was hers—her books, lands, fortunes, skills, memories, friends. And responsibilities.

I have beloved memories of Alyce, who was called by many "The White Haired Witch." I have memories of her

love and her gentleness—despite the shadow of sorrow, like a
sheer ribbon of darkness streaming from her, that pervaded
my childhood. And I have memories of how she changed after
Aunt Helena arrived and stayed to live with us. Alyce told me
once that when she had been young, she had cared greatly
how she was regarded by others, though she admitted she
would never have acknowledged it at the time. But now, as an
old woman, she had become more interested in being the
observer, and less and less willing to be observed at all. Old
now myself, I understand what she meant. But I still like to
recall watching her transformation after Aunt Helena's
arrival. The sadness shadowing her eyes never quite vanished,
but now she blazed such warmth and energy, such mirth. A
great Crone she became, embracing her many summers with
both arms, seizing age with both fists. How her green eyes
would flame with anger at injustice. Yet how tranquil her
voice could sound, when I would ask her to sing me to sleep
as she had done when I was but a little girl. . . .

I am glad she lived so long—long enough to witness the
return to England of her old adversary, the former Bishop of
Ossary, Richard de Ledrede, who was sent home from France
in disgrace. I am glad she lived to witness the ostracism King
Edward III pronounced on the Bishop, tantamount to solitary
confinement under house arrest, since his land had been confiscated and no one in England would have dealings with him.

He lived long though, alone and poor, and his death was the subject of much talk. It was said that he ended his own life, that there were self-inflicted wounds, which to their way of belief would mean he had deliberately damned himself beyond any hope of mercy, for eternity. The priest who attended him in the final hour would say naught of the wounds. But in his distress he did tell others that the Bishop had sent him away, refusing the last rites of their faith. He said the old man spat out the communion wafer, laughing wildly that he had lost his appetite at last. Then, the priest said, he began ranting that he was tired of waiting, that as the second Saint Patrick he had earned the right to go somewhere beyond bargaining. He raved on, boasting that he had drowned Saint Francis in a fountain in broad sunlight while the larks chanted their approval. The priest said he was quite mad. Mad or sane, that was his wretched end. Still, I believe it required considerable restraint—plus respect for the Law of Threefold Return—for Alyce Kyteler personally not to arrange an even more dramatic fate for Richard de Ledrede.

She died, in the fullness of her seventy-two summers, almost the same month he did. But such a different death! She slid from this consciousness smooth as a spoon through fresh curds, with a look, a smile, and a sigh. I was at her side—together with my sister, Dana Galrussyn, who was the Healer tending her in those last days, and Dana's mother, Aunt Helena.

Alyce was surrounded by her other adopted children, too, and her Familiars, and her strays—human and animal both—and the many in these parts who had come to love her. Whatever else we Irish may say about Britain, the English respect eccentricity.

Alyce was always insistent that the human heart and mind were slowly maturing, that we ourselves were sacred, that *we* were the Goddess and the God, if we would only recognize that. She always said things would improve—though she usually added cynically that things would also relapse before they improved further. Such faith she had in cycles and in spirals!

I wish she had lived to see the changes in the world. True, some it is as well she never knew. Such as the Inquisition's increasing power on the Continent. Such as King Edward's passing. Such as a second Richard coming to reign here, eager to revive the war against the Irish. Happily, he has now gone. Though it is still too early to tell about this fourth Henry. And Alyce would have grieved over news of the Black Death in Europe, and would have raged that the fools who had killed cats and let rodents breed unchecked should be held responsible for their savage ignorance.

But she would have delighted in other news. She would have celebrated the peasant uprisings across the Continent. She would have been especially amused at the confounding of her old enemies, now that the Church seems to be turning on itself. How she would laugh at three popes reigning simultaneously, scrambling in contention for power from competing thrones in Rome, Avignon, and Pisa! How pleased she would be to read the reports my own couriers now send me from Europe—reports of new cosmologies and scientific theories, bravely being put forth even in the teeth of persecution!

Were I a younger woman, I might climb upon that broom they claim we ride and journey all the way to Italy, to partake of this feast for the intellect. But it is just as well that Alyce and Petronilla, my granddaughters, have gone in my stead, to learn what they can and carry it back here to the Isles—this despite the clucking father-hen worries of fussy Sean Fergus, my son. Still, I must be fair: Sean, himself a homebody Greenwitch, did find the courage to let them go, with his paternal blessing.

But all such little chronicles are postscripts to the story. They are like the afterbirth that trails a newborn babe from the womb. The story is the babe, and that have I now safely delivered.

So have I set down on these leafs the tale of my other mother, my mother in blood—birth-blood and death-blood—Petronilla de Meath, she who was also The White Haired Witch.

Often did Alyce and Aunt Helena speak to me of my mother. The Tale I have set down here is spun with their yarn. It is spun with something else, too, something eternally lost and endlessly familiar—the weave of memory. I have no memories of Erin, the land I long for, mourn for, and never shall visit, even though now I could. I treasure the wee pouch Alyce gave me when she died—filled with Kilkenny earth, still faintly fragrant after so many years. But my mother's blood has soaked that earth, and never shall I return there.

Of my mother, I have few memories. They are dimmed by time and worn by use, for I cherish every one.

Far, far back, the sound of her voice, higher and lighter than Alyce's, singing me to sleep.

Thin childish arms wrapped round me in a willed, fierce strength.

Church bells pealing.

A whiff of marzipan. A taste of gingerbread.

And a dream I had once, and almost still have sometimes— wherein she kneels in a dark wood and reaches for me, but does not touch me. She speaks to me, then, wordlessly on the wind, of how much she loves me. But that is not a proper memory, merely a dream.

Therefore have I set down here, that it may enter the Lore of the Tuatha de Danaan for all time, the true Tale of Petronilla de Meath—the first person to be condemned to death in Ireland for practicing The Old Ways, the mother who loved me more than her life, the shy warrior who found her defiance, the Neophyte who initiated herself into her own Powers at the last.

In her name and to her honour, to endure for so long as stories are remembered or the magick of ink on parchment remains, these words I set down in my own write, and mark with my Seal, time out of mind by Wiccan reckoning, in the year Christians number 1402.

Sara Basilia de Meath
High Priestess of the Craft of the Wise,
Tale Spinner of the Seannachai,
Lore and Legend Keeper,
Lady of Kyteler Manor, Midlands, England

The Burning Time is based on historical fact. The story of Alyce Kyteler and her circle comes to us from records of the time, demonstrating three elements always found in witch persecutions: the attempt by a conqueror's religion to colonize, demonize, and eradicate older, indigenous belief systems; economic motive (since the accuser profits by being awarded the accused's properties); and misogyny—fear and hatred of the female. (A more extensive Author's Note, a Glossary of names and terms, and a full Bibliography of works consulted for *The Burning Time* can be accessed at *www.mhpbooks.com*)

Christianity's arrival in Ireland in approximately the fourth century C.E. gave rise to a unique Celtic Christianity: a syncretic mix of Roman Catholicism with indigenous Pagan beliefs practiced by the majority of people calling themselves Christians. This was not uncommon throughout the British Isles; as late as the early fourteenth century, the Bishop of Coventry openly admitted to being an observer of the Old Religion, or The Craft. Consequently, it was considered shocking when, in 1324, Dame Alyce Kyteler (sometimes written as Kettler or Kettle) of County Kilkenny was charged with heretical sorcery—the first person in Ireland to be persecuted as an observer of The Craft. Formal charges were brought by Bishop Richard de Ledrede, an Englishman ordained as a Franciscan. He arrived in Ireland from the Papal Court—based in Avignon, France, from 1309 to 1378—with the blessings of Pope John XXII, who authored papal bulls commissioning inquisitional campaigns against sorcery, and declared St. Francis's doctrine of Christ's poverty to be heretical. Bishop de Ledrede's mission was to ferret out witchcraft in Ireland using Inquisition procedures—including torture to exact confessions and the naming of others—that was already in use in Europe.

The peasants were mostly helpless. Alyce Kyteler was not. She and the Bishop engaged in quite a personal war. Of those accused with her (see below), the fates of only two are known for certain.

William Oultawe, Alyce Kyteler's son by her first husband, was imprisoned for nine weeks and fined. He was then allowed to recant and receive Church sacraments, on condition that he make a pilgrimage to the Shrine of St. Thomas at Canterbury, and pay for the re-roofing in lead of St. Canice's—today St. Mary's—Cathedral in Kilkenny Town. (Modern Kilkenny residents still wink at the witchly irony that this penance caused the too-heavy roof to cave in, as described in Chapter XVII.)

The records also show that Petronilla de Meath, a member of the Kyteler household, was flogged six times. She confessed to sorcery and all charges of the Bishop's court. Once certain Kyteler had made a successful escape together with de Meath's daughter Sara (sometimes listed in the records as Sara Basilia), she named Kyteler—but only Kyteler—as an accomplice. Refusing to name any others, she scorned the sacraments of the Church, and was declared apostate, excommunicate, and damned. She was burned alive at the stake in the marketplace of Kilkenny Town on November 3, 1324—the first person ever to be executed for witchcraft in Ireland.

The Burning Time in continental Europe and the British Isles lasted approximately 600 years, peaking in the sixteenth and seventeenth centuries but persisting well into the eighteenth century and the "Enlightenment." In Ireland the last witch trial was held in 1711, in England in 1717. But in Germany the last person accused of witchcraft was executed in 1775, in Spain 1781, in Protestant Switzerland 1782. Catholic Poland burned alive its last witch as late as 1793 (the year George Washington held his first cabinet meeting). Ideological-political battles between the Reformation and Counter Reformation literally fed the flames, with newly minted Protestants competing with Catholics for the most fundamentalist interpretation of the Bible.

The result was widespread slaughter. A short sampling: in 1482, in Constance, France, 48 women were burned; in

1507, in Calahorra, Spain, 30 were burned; in 1515, in Geneva, Switzerland, 500 accused witches were executed in a single day; in 1524, in Como, Italy, 1,000 were killed; in 1622, in Würzburg, Germany, 900; in 1670, in Mohra, Sweden, 70 women and 15 children were executed and 136 other children between the ages of nine and 16 were sentenced to be whipped together at the church door every day for a year. In Germany, the sixteenth century saw witch burnings almost every day; complete villages were "cleansed" of women, girls, and cats. In 1586, only two women were reported left alive in an entire Rhineland district. Whole convents were indicted and sentenced for harboring "rebellious, learned women." The children of victims were especially suspect, suffering incredible cruelties: as late as 1754, Veronica Zerritsch of Germany was compelled to dance in the warm ashes of her executed mother, then was burned alive herself, at age thirteen. Some scholars, focusing on the continental persecutions between 1550 and 1650, conservatively estimate the number hanged or burned at 60,000. Others, charting the entire 600-year span of The Burning Time in Europe, estimate that between eight and nine million persons were massacred. It is impossible to know for certain. We do know, however, that although men were also accused, tortured, and killed, the vast majority of victims were women and girls.

A few more words on fact and fiction in this book.

The Song of Amorgin quoted in Chapter VI dates back to 1268 C.E.; this version is, according to Robert Graves, an English translation from the colloquial Irish, itself translated from the Old Goidelic. *The Song of The Running Seasons* in Chapter VII is a variant of a shape-shifting lay dating at least to the eleventh century, in turn based on a theme prevalent in classical Greek poetry; a modern English version survives as *The Ballad of The Coal Black Smith*.

The advice quoted in Chapter XII—Wiccan guidelines for secrecy, ways to survive interrogation and torture, even endure death by fire—is authentic. The text has been passed down for centuries, and is thought to have originated in a European country in the grip of witch persecutions. The guidelines are quoted in numerous works.

The various recipes and herbal medicines are accurate, drawn from the period, and based on Wiccan sources. Wiccans have always been sophisticated herbalists. In fact, the recipes are so effective that I have omitted proportions and, in some cases, ingredients, when a hallucinogenic or possibly dangerous mixture might result.

The two healer-women denounced by the Bishop in Chapter II—Jacqueline Felicie de Almania, and Belota—are named in French trial records of the day. Bernard Gui, mentioned in Chapter XIV, authored *The Conduct of the*

Inquisition of Heretical Depravity and from 1307 to 1324 was Chief Inquisitor of Toulouse, where he condemned a long list of accused heretics.

Dana Galrussyn, Sean Fergus/Father Brendan Canice, Maeve Payn, Father Donnan, and Lady Megan are all purely fictional creations of the author.

Not so the others.

In 1577, Hollinshed, in his germinal *Chronicles of England, Scotlande, and Ireland*—Shakespeare's historical source—wrote of the Kyteler trials. The trial record, as edited by Thomas Wright (London, The Camden Society, 1843) is, according to the medieval scholar Dr. Margaret Murray, the earliest source to give the full names of those accused:

Proceedings Against Dame Alyce Kyteler
County Kilkenny, Ireland, 1324

1. Dame Alyce Kyteler
2. Alyce, wife of Henry the Smith
3. Annota Lange
4. Eva de Brounstoun
5. Helena Galrussyn
6. Sysok Galrussyn
7. John Galrussyn
8. Robert de Bristol

9. William Outlawe
10. William Payn of Boly
11. Petronilla de Meath
12. Sara, daughter of Petronilla
13. Robin, son of Artis ("the Devil")

R.M.
New York City
December, 2005

1. Alyce Kyteler is a noblewoman, teacher, and healer. Why is it important that she is the sole owner of her estate? How would the story be different if her husband still lived with her?

2. Richard de Ledrede explains his beliefs to Alyce by saying: "I have faith in the *Church*. God . . . God is an argument." How does his perspective on religion compare to Alyce's belief in The Old Ways? At the end of the story, does de Ledrede still believe that God and the Church are separate entities? And what happens to Alyce's trust in The Old Ways?

3. Are Richard de Ledrede and Alyce Kyteler alike in some ways? How are they different? Do you think it would have been possible for them to compromise? If so, how?

4. How are the Sabbats of The Old Ways similar to holidays that are celebrated today such as Thanksgiving? In the description of the Sabbats, do you see any similarities to religious rituals practiced today?

5. How is Alyce's relationship with her son, Will, symbolic of the relationships throughout the novel?

6. Would you consider Father Brendan Canice (Sean Fergus) to be a main character in the story? What do you think ultimately happened to him?

7. Petronilla de Meath's religious struggle is a key point in the novel. Discuss the ways Petronilla feels bound to the Church as well as to Alyce and The Old Ways and how Petronilla's actions illuminate the themes of the novel.

8. Alyce says to Father Brendan: "This much I know: almost no one committing evil *believes* he is committing evil… at heart even the worst villain *wishes* to do good." Do you agree? How is "evil" defined by various characters in *The Burning Time*? Could you interpret that the "villains" of the story wish to do good?

9. Discuss the distinctions of class in the novel, from the serf to the nobleperson, and how each is portrayed. For example, why does de Ledrede think it is wrong for Alyce to teach her serfs to read? What is the significance of de Ledrede coming from a family of merchants? Why does Alyce tell her son

he must "wed someone of his station"? How does class contribute to the events that lead up to the inquisition depicted in the The Burning Time?

10. Teaching is a theme in the book, from de Ledrede's efforts to teach the peasants that the Church is the only valid religion to Alyce's teaching of the Old Ways to Petronilla. But in what ways do the teachers become the students? Who ends up learning the most important lessons?

11. Strong women are found throughout The Burning Time: Alyce Kyteler, Petronilla de Meath, Helena Galrussyn, Annota Lange, and Sara Basilia de Meath. Compare their actions and characteristics to those of the men in the story. Do you feel that women and men are both fully portrayed? Why or why not?

12. Toward the end of the novel, Helena describes to Alyce how the members of the Covenstead have fared since The Burning Time. Do these descriptions remind you of the fate of people in other historical times?

13. "That night I lost my faith in everything else I had been foolish enough to build my life on. The sole order I could recognize was disorder. The sole promise I could trust was death." Alyce tells Helena this about the night she fled Kilkenny and Kyteler Castle. Why is Alyce's experience important to the story?

14. Why does the novel end with Sara Basilia de Meath's perspective? How would the novel have been different had it been narrated by Alyce, or if the book's narrator had remained mysterious?

15. The Burning Time is based on real people and real incidents. Do you think that setting these happenings in a fictional narrative adds to the understanding of the historical events? What makes a novel like this different from one where an author is inspired by a real person, but doesn't use real events in the narrative?

A more in-depth Author's Note, a Glossary of names and terms used in the novel, and a full Bibliography of works consulted for The Burning Time *can be accessed online at www.mhpbooks.com.*